Pregnant! **"Are you**

Dr. Landry smiled and reassured them, "The blood test does not lie about this."

Talk about an unexpected turn of events! "But we were so careful!" she blurted out.

"No contraception is one hundred percent effective," the doctor said. "But I know you'll both need a few moments to absorb this. Everyone always does. If you'd like to hear the heartbeat today, we have a medical student interning in the ER right now who is eager to have more experience with the Doppler."

"Yes," Ellie and Joe said in unison. "We would."

Ellie turned to Joe, her heart suddenly pounding. She had always hated the unexpected, but this...this was something wonderful and thrilling.

"A baby," he whispered reverently.

A baby. Their baby.

"Yes," she whispered back, her heart filling with bliss in a way she had never even imagined. "We're having a baby, Joe!"

Dear Reader,

We all make deals with those we love. Ellie Fitzgerald
and Joe McCabe have made a deal that has
lasted well over a dozen years. After their botched
elopement, at age eighteen, they knew certain
things. They would always love each other. They
still wanted to be together whenever possible, as
intimately as possible. But for them, marriage was
not really necessary. Especially when they could have
all the benefits of a lasting relationship without all the
hassle of a legal union.

And then...a surprise happens. One that forces them
to consider the fact that their current arrangement
will no longer work. Neither wants to renege on
their long-lasting deal. They also know their life is
changing. And there are many more "Christmases"
ahead. Can they make a new pact with each other
that will be just as satisfying? Only time will tell.

I hope you have a very merry holiday season and
enjoy reading this book—the first of a brand-new
McCabe series.

Best wishes!

Cathy Gillen Thacker

PS: Visit me at cathygillenthacker.com or on
Facebook at my official author page.

A DOUBLE
CHRISTMAS SURPRISE

CATHY GILLEN THACKER

SPECIAL EDITION

 **Harlequin®**
SPECIAL EDITION™

Recycling programs for this product may not exist in your area.

ISBN-13: 978-1-335-40210-3

A Double Christmas Surprise

 Harlequin Enterprises ULC
22 Adelaide St. West, 41st Floor
Toronto, Ontario M5H 4E3, Canada
www.Harlequin.com

Printed in Lithuania

MIX
Paper | Supporting responsible forestry
FSC® C021394

Cathy Gillen Thacker is a married mother of three. She and her husband reside in North Carolina. Her stories have made numerous appearances on bestseller lists, but her best reward is knowing one of her books made someone's day a little brighter. A popular Harlequin author, she loves telling passionate stories with happy endings and thinks nothing beats a good romance and a hot cup of tea! Visit her at cathygillenthacker.com for information on her books, recipes and a list of her favorite things.

Books by Cathy Gillen Thacker

Harlequin Special Edition

Lockharts Lost & Found

His Plan for the Quadruplets
Four Christmas Matchmakers
The Twin Proposal
Their Texas Triplets
Their Texas Christmas Gift
The Triplets' Secret Wish
Their Texas Christmas Match
A Temporary Texas Arrangement

Visit the Author Profile page
at Harlequin.com for more titles.

Chapter One

"Have you heard from Joe?" Mitzy Martin McCabe asked.

Ellie Fitzgerald looked at the tall, lithe social worker who would have been her mother-in-law. Had she and Joe ever married.

"You mean besides the text he sent me this morning?" The one that had said his flight to Texas had mechanical problems and had been canceled.

Ellie and Mitzy were standing in the service alley behind historic Main Street in Laramie, Texas, the centuries-old red brick buildings bathed in late afternoon sunlight. A soothing July breeze wafted over them. It was the perfect time for a burst of summer love. The perfect day for Joe to come home to her. And his immediate family, of course. Ellie knew his three quadruplet brothers, only sister and parents were eager to see the Special Forces soldier, too. As was her beloved gran—Eleanor regarded Joe as the grandson she'd never had.

Ellie flashed a grateful smile as Joe's dad, Chase, carried boxes of cupcakes out of her family's bakery, Sugar Love. He had the same tall, buff physique and commanding air as his four sons. The same McCabe charisma and charm. It was impossible not to admire their ambition and competence in anything they tried. Like all native Texans, McCabes weren't afraid to dream big.

"Was he able to get on another flight? Do you know?" Mitzy asked with parental concern.

Warning herself not to absorb the other woman's worry, Ellie went back to securing the five-tier cake. Its box was fastened to the floor of her van and would keep the confection from being knocked around during transport. "I'm sure he'll be here for my gran's party," she said calmly.

Mitzy frowned in annoyance as she glanced down at her watch. "It starts in an hour."

Ellie was *well* aware. She, too, had been watching the minutes crawl by all day, the way she always did when she was awaiting the arrival of the love of her life. But since it wouldn't do any good to share her impatience, she kept it to herself.

"Either way," Chase said in his calm and authoritative CEO voice, "he should have kept you updated."

Except, Ellie thought, the two of them had a deal. Neither would micromanage the other's life. *Micro-worry*, either. And with Joe a Special Forces officer who specialized in counterterrorism and extraction—as well as navigating treacherous mountain terrain—there was often plenty to worry about. If she knew exactly where he was and what he was doing when he was deployed to hot spots around the world, that was. Which, luckily, she did not.

Joe's younger sister, Sadie, wheeled out yet another baker's rack of cupcakes for the party at the community center and slid them into the back of the Sugar Love van, one box at a time. She was the mirror image of her elegant mom, four years younger than her quadruplet thirty-year-old brothers and the closest thing Ellie had to a sibling.

Sadie's dark brown ponytail bounced against her slender neck and shoulders as she worked. "He should do more than that," she harrumphed. "He should put a ring on it. How long have the two of you been serious anyway? Ten years?"

"Twelve," Ellie said before she could think. If she didn't count the two years when they dated in high school. Then it would be fourteen years since she had been romantically entangled with anyone else. Which was, as it turned out, almost half her life, since she was now thirty years old... Same as Joe... Even more daunting was the fact she couldn't remember her life without Joe being a major force in it.

But it had only been twelve years since their botched elopement at age eighteen, which was when things had taken a serious turn.

No matter what, Joe was her man. She was his woman. And that was all they needed. All they had *ever* needed.

"And that is exactly my point, Ellie," Sadie said, continuing her rant. "The two of you have been together forever! And now here you are, twelve plus years in, and acting like an old married couple, barely communicating."

"Sadie," Mitzy cautioned.

Ignoring the warning to avoid an unnecessary family conflict, Sadie paused to throw up her hands in frustration. "Well, *somebody's* got to say it, Mom! Joe needs to step up and do the right thing by Ellie. And honor his relationship with her. With vows!"

Suspecting Sadie's angst had more to do with her own unrequited love for a military man—her best friend, Will—than what was going on with her and Joe, Ellie murmured, "I know you mean well, Sadie, but Joe and I have made all the promises we need to make to each other right now."

And maybe forever... After all, why change any of the parameters if everything was working so well?

"And then some," a low masculine voice agreed.

They all turned in unison. Just in time to see Joe Mc-

Cabe—the wildest and most fearless of Mitzy and Chase's four sons—walk around the corner of the building.

As always, Ellie's breath caught at the sight of him. In his camo utility uniform and combat boots, he was so big and strong and tough looking. His thick dark hair was cut to military regulation. His smoky blue eyes were happy and intent. Focused only on her.

The next thing she knew, he had dropped his olive green duffel and backpack to the ground. Swiftly and purposefully, he closed the distance between them, grabbed her around the waist, lifted her off her feet and swung her up against him. Her body melted against all that warm, hard muscle. The masculine scent of him was familiar and intoxicating. And brought forth a staggering wave of bliss. "Joe!" Tears of delight blurred her vision, and happiness flowed through her. Then his lips were on hers in a brief, hard, possessive kiss. A more intimate reunion would come later, she knew.

But for the moment, this meant oh so much.

Slowly and reluctantly, he ended the kiss. Still holding her tight, he whispered against the top of her head, "Hey, darlin'."

"Hello yourself," she whispered back, a lusty sigh catching in her throat.

Eyes glimmering ardently, he squeezed her hard, then reluctantly lowered her back to the ground and let her go. Turning, he greeted his parents and sister, who were suddenly all misty-eyed, too. Everyone was so glad when Joe made it home, safe and sound, Ellie noted gratefully. Which was something military families never ever took for granted.

The welcome-home hugs and greetings complete, Joe turned back to Ellie. "What can I do to help?" he asked in a gravelly voice. As always, ready to step in and give aid wherever and however it was needed. It was this generosity of spirit, mixed with his take-charge attitude and innate selflessness, that made him such a fine soldier and a beloved member of the rural west Texas county where he had grown up.

"We've got the delivery to the community center handled," his dad told him.

As they had previously agreed, Ellie handed Chase the keys to the pink-and-white van. "Gran and her friends should already be there setting up."

"We'll help get everything ready for the birthday celebration," Mitzy promised.

Ellie sent a grateful glance to her. "Thank you. We'll be over there to assist as soon as we get changed into our party clothes."

Sadie's eyes lit with a romantic glint. "Just don't get too sidetracked!" she teased before getting into the passenger seat of the van.

Mitzy climbed behind the wheel of their SUV while her husband took command of the bakery van, and they were off.

"Alone at last," Ellie murmured happily, taking Joe's hand in hers.

He brought her in close, inundating her with his masculine scent. "Our favorite place to be…"

Fortunately, they didn't have far to go to achieve even more privacy. All the historic buildings had interior back stairs next to their service entrances, which led to private apartments on the second floor. Ellie had been living in the one above the Fitzgerald family bakery since she had returned home after college and culinary school. Joe stayed with her whenever he was in Laramie, his clothes and other belongings already upstairs in her apartment.

"So what was going on when I arrived?" Joe asked as they headed up the stairs to her one-bedroom apartment above the bakery. A happy woof sounded on the other side of the door.

Deciding the last thing he needed was to feel the familial pressure she just had been put through, Ellie shrugged. "Nothing." She scooped up her white West Highland terrier and bussed the top of her head.

Instead of cuddling close the way she usually did, Scout wiggled and lurched for Joe. Chuckling, he caught the Westie in his strong arms and held her up so they were face-to-face. Scout let out another happy woof and licked Joe beneath the chin. Again, and then again.

"I guess I'm not the only one who missed you," Ellie said dryly.

Joe grinned and gave Scout another affectionate squeeze before gently lowering her to the floor. Then he grabbed Ellie around the waist and tugged her against him. "Glad to hear it," he murmured, his lips lowering to hers with intent, "because I missed you, too, darlin'. So much."

He covered her mouth with his own and delivered a sizzling kiss that turned her limp with longing. Her lips parted beneath the sure, steady pressure of his, and he dipped his tongue in, tangling it with hers. Heat roiled inside her, and her knees went weak. She wrapped her arms around his broad shoulders and held on tight, loving their fierce, elemental connection. The soaring passion the time away from each other always engendered.

She moaned as the kiss deepened. If they didn't have a party to attend… But they did.

Reminding herself this was a hugely important evening, and they'd have plenty of time to make love later, Ellie reluctantly broke off their damn-but-I'm-glad-we're-together-again kiss.

His low, tortured groan matched her own. Finally, he let her go. Stepped back and looked her over in a way that set her every nerve ending on fire. With a wicked smile that told he was already thinking about all the things they would do later—things that likely would keep them both up all night—he wrapped an arm around her shoulders, kissed her temple and purposefully headed for the closet. "You didn't answer my question. When I arrived a few minutes ago, it seemed like you were getting the business from my family."

She had been. Although it had been mostly Sadie voicing her frustration. His parents had just subtly evidenced their concern.

Ellie removed her dress for the party from its hanger and laid it across the bed. "They were just worried that I hadn't heard from you since this morning."

"I said I'd be here for your gran's big night."

She toed off her sneakers, unbuttoned the pink chef coat she wore to work and shimmied out of her jeans. "I know."

He frowned, the way he always did when he was forced to hold himself accountable to other's expectations.

She found herself defending his family anyway. "Your folks just wanted to know if you'd managed to get on another flight and pick up your rental car at the airport and all that. Or if you were going to be late…"

Joe went to find his electric razor. Flipping it on, he ran it over the stubble on his jaw. Returning to her side, he added with exaggerated patience, "I would have called you if I couldn't get here in time."

Their gazes clashed. He looked irritated. Which was, Ellie thought sympathetically, completely understandable. He was part of the Special Forces. Had been on missions all over the world and, against all odds, always managed to come out unscathed. "I know you would have," she said softly.

His broad shoulders tensed, but he threw her a grateful glance. "Thank heaven you don't try to control my life."

His parents' overprotectiveness was one of the things that

had driven him to enlist at eighteen and ask her to elope with him. Thanks in part to her own family's interference, the second hadn't worked out, but the first had. And now twelve years later, they had established a relationship that worked for them. She was taking over Sugar Love from her gran, and he had a thriving career in the military and plans to stay until it was time to retire.

Their future was set.

Unfortunately, their relatives just couldn't accept it as it was.

Joe tossed his razor aside. "Or worry the way our families do," he continued with a sexy smile, taking her into his arms and holding her close once again.

Except she *did* worry, Ellie thought as she laid her head against his warm, hard chest. Every time he was deployed. Or was in dangerous territory and went long periods with no access to phone or email. And when he came back, he could tell her absolutely nothing about what he had been doing or where he'd been. During all those long weeks and months and all those dark, lonely nights, she worried. And wondered, would she ever see him again? Would he come back to her, safe and sound? Every single time, she hoped and prayed he was okay.

She just couldn't let him know it. Because that wasn't part of their deal. Knowing that could distract him. And that could put him in danger. Which was something she wouldn't allow. So she did what she always did and kept her anxiety to herself. It was better that way. For all of them. Especially Joe.

Reluctantly, she eased away from him. "We better get a move on, soldier. If we don't want to be late!"

Four hours later, Ellie and Joe surveyed the community center. Glittering banners hanging across the ceiling read

Happy 70th and Well-deserved Retirement, Eleanor! A table set up with balloons held flowers and gifts that only added to the ones that had already been sent to Gran's home and the bakery over the past few days.

"Oh, Gran, I have to admit I never really thought the party would do you justice," Ellie murmured happily.

"Was there *anyone* in the community who didn't show up tonight to honor you?" Joe grinned.

In a beaded silver dress and heels that set off her silver-blond bouffant and delicate ivory skin, Eleanor turned to face them. Happy color highlighting her pretty features, she winked. "I think it was the incredible potluck and all the baked goods that brought them in," she joked.

The spread *had* been magnificent. Which was no surprise. Laramie County was full of wonderful cooks.

"And you." Ellie kissed the top of her petite grandmother's head. As the last of the guests collected their empty casserole dishes and filtered out, she noted the weary lines around Eleanor's eyes. "But we should really get you home."

"The cleanup..." her gran protested.

"Is being taken care of by the janitorial staff," Ellie said soothingly.

"But what about the gifts?" Eleanor continued.

"They can be left here overnight and picked up early tomorrow morning," Joe said with his usual take-charge attitude. When there was a task to be done, he was right on it. "Ellie and I can do that for you."

Ellie nodded.

Eleanor looked at them hopefully. "Do the two of you have time to come by for a bit and talk with me?" she asked.

Ellie worried about how long a day it had been for her grandmother. And it was closing in on midnight. "You sure you're not too tired?"

"This is important," Eleanor said firmly.

A little unsettled by the unexpectedly sober tone, Ellie drove her grandmother's car to her home, with Eleanor in the passenger seat beside her. Joe followed in Ellie's vehicle. They parked side by side in the driveway, then headed up the flagstone path to the three-bedroom cottage with the gingerbread trim.

Ellie had grown up here, with her mother and grandmother. More than anything, it signified home to her. The lights had been left on. Which was no surprise because Eleanor hated coming home to a dark house, especially late at night. What *was* unexpected, however, was the way the dining room table had been set. With her best tea service and stacks of what appeared to be documents at each place setting.

"I'll put the kettle on," Eleanor said.

Ellie blocked the path to the small, cozy kitchen. "Uh-uh. I'll heat the water. You find your slippers and get out of those heels. Your feet have to be killing you."

"My goodness, you're bossy tonight!" Eleanor teased.

Joe grinned. He put his hands on his hips, pushing aside his sports coat. During times like this, except for his regulation haircut, Ellie could almost forget he was in the military. Almost. "What can I do to help?" he asked.

Ellie shooed them both in the opposite direction. "Keep Gran company while I make the tea."

The two of them ambled into the formal dining room. Ellie could hear them chatting as Joe entertained her grandmother with stories about his hellacious travel day. He'd had to run to catch three different flights, then hitch a ride to the nearest car rental place to make it home in time.

"I never had any doubt you'd be here tonight," her grandmother said as Ellie rejoined them.

Ellie poured the tea into the mugs, then set out the lemon,

cream and sugar. She settled opposite Joe while her grand-mother reigned at the head of the table. The manila folders with their names on them, full of documents, were the elephant in the room.

Unable to contain her curiosity a moment longer, Ellie asked, "So what is this all about, Gran?"

It couldn't be about the transfer of ownership of the Fitzgerald family's bakery. That had been taken care of weeks ago, well in advance of Gran's retirement. Thanks to her grandmother's generosity, Ellie was now sole proprietress of what more and more seemed like a staggering responsibility.

Not that she dared admit that to anyone.

Eleanor sipped her tea. "I have something for you and Joe."

Joe quirked a brow at Ellie. She shrugged lightly, letting him know she had no clue, either.

"Open your folders," Eleanor continued.

Mouth dry, Ellie obeyed. The first page held what appeared to be a copy of the title for Eleanor's house. But instead of Eleanor's name, it listed Ellie and Joe as the legal owners.

"I'm gifting you and Joe my home, effective immediately. Well, actually, effective a few days ago. I'm just telling you now because I wanted to do it when the two of you were together."

So many emotions roiled through Ellie. Shock. Disbelief. Gratitude, that her grandmother could be so completely generous. Guilt, that maybe she didn't deserve it. But most of all, worry.

What could possibly be behind Eleanor's sudden distribution of all her property? She had lived her entire life in Laramie—was she planning to move somewhere else? Like Phoenix or Florida or some other retirement mecca? Was she planning to leave first the family business and now Ellie behind?

"Gran, you can't give up your house!" Ellie protested.

Eleanor sipped her tea. "I already have, darling."

Hot tears pricked the backs of Ellie's eyes. She hadn't felt this abandoned since her mother had unexpectedly died of an embolism, seven years before. She leaned across the table. "But *why*?" she asked urgently.

Eleanor handed over one last folder, filled with colorful brochures and a signed contract, for them to peruse. "Because I'm moving into a suite at the Laramie Gardens senior community."

Well, at least she was staying here in Laramie, Joe thought.

Although it seemed small comfort to Ellie. Her sage green eyes welled, and her delicate cheeks flushed a becoming pink. She drew a deep breath, the swell of her breasts rising beneath the shimmering gold party dress with the cap-sleeved bodice-hugging top and full knee-length skirt. She'd twisted her long, honey blond hair into an elegant knot at the nape of her neck. The sideswept bangs and wispy tendrils framing her feminine features only added to her allure.

Knowing just how badly she was in need of comfort, it was all he could do no t to get up and haul her into his arms.

He figured that could—and would—come later. He would see to it she got all the physical reassurance and cuddling she needed. Although Ellie hadn't come out and admitted it, Joe knew she was having a heck of a time handling her grandmother's retirement. The thought of no longer spending her days working side by side with her beloved gran was daunting to her.

It shouldn't have been. Ellie had lived independently from her family before, when she had gone to college and culinary school. Plus, she had worked at the bakery since she was old enough to hold a rolling pin. She'd also been second in command since her mother passed away. Whether she knew it or not, she was more than up for the job of running the generations-old family business.

Her hands clasped in front of her, Ellie leaned toward Eleanor, then asked gently, "Is this about you not wanting to live alone in this house anymore? Because I could give up the apartment and move in with you."

Eleanor shook her head. "Darling, you need your own space," she returned. "You and Joe both do. For whenever he *is* home."

Ellie's luscious lower lip trembled slightly. "But this is such a big change!"

And Ellie hated change, Joe knew. Especially ones not driven by her.

"And it's one I'm looking forward to. My two best friends, Francine and Wanda, are already living there. They love it! And Betty is selling her home and moving there next month."

"It is pretty nice," Joe felt compelled to put in. "The food is great, there are a lot of social activities and field trips, and there's medical care on-site if you need it."

Ellie glared at him. Reminding him what a passionate person she was beneath her easygoing exterior. "Whose side are you on?" she demanded.

Knowing he would kiss all that excess emotion away the first chance he got, Joe shrugged. He looked at both Ellie and Eleanor. "Um—everyone's."

"What did you think I was going to do when my retirement was official?" Eleanor asked lightly.

Ellie waved a hand. "What you already do. Come in to the bakery from time to time. Run errands. Cook. Take up some new hobbies, maybe."

Eleanor sipped her tea. "Well, I do plan to do that," she confided with an excited smile. "Laramie Gardens has all sorts of classes. Everything from yoga to decoupage. As for the rest, after fiftysome years of waiting on customers all day six days a week, I'm ready to have someone wait on *me*. In fact, darling, I'm really looking forward to it. Which is why I am wasting no time starting my golden years."

Ellie tensed all the more. She stared at her grandmother in trepidation. "What do you mean?"

"I'm moving the things I'll need immediately over to Laramie Gardens tomorrow. And I'd like the two of you to help me," Eleanor said.

Ellie nodded. "Of course we'll help you move," she said, near tears once again.

Unsurprisingly, Eleanor soon pleaded fatigue. Promising to talk more the next morning, she showed them to the door.

Ellie was silent during the short drive back to her apartment. Figuring she needed to process everything that had just happened, Joe quietly accompanied her upstairs, where Scout greeted them happily once again.

Still looking shell-shocked, Ellie reached for the Westie's leash. "I need to walk her..."

Joe stripped off his sports coat and loosened his tie. "I'll go with you."

Together, they headed out. Well after midnight now, historic downtown Laramie was bathed in the golden glow of the street lamps. A crescent moon and a blanket of stars twinkled in the velvety sky overhead. Ellie turned her head up as the warm nighttime breeze swept over them.

Acutely aware the last time he had seen her this dejected was the night their planned elopement had gone awry, Joe gazed down at her. He knew he had to say it. Even if she didn't appear ready to discuss any of it yet. "I'm sorry," he told her softly.

Her chin lifted. "For what?"

Joe drew a breath and held her gaze. "Your grandmother never should have gifted half her home to me."

Chapter Two

Ellie stared at Joe, wondering if this night could get any worse. First, her grandmother no longer wanted to be as close to her as they had been. How else was she supposed to interpret her wanting to move on to a new life at Laramie Gardens, with new activities with old friends and probably lots of new friends, too? And now Joe was telling her in his own way that he didn't want to be tied to her, either.

Unfortunately, she knew that co-owning a home together was only half of what Gran had planned for the two of them. Ellie turned to gaze at Joe's ruggedly handsome face. "Because it was clearly a matchmaking ploy?"

Blue eyes solemn, he shook his head. "Because Eleanor's home has been in the Fitzgerald family for generations. Her parents lived there, then she and her husband and your mother and you. It needs to stay within your family. Which means you should be the sole owner, instead of gifting half of it to a McCabe."

What he was saying made sense. And yet...

He caught her skeptical glance, as usual reading many of the things she was reluctant to say out loud. "Even if we were...married... I would still feel this way," he said gruffly.

Except they *weren't* married.

And both of them had decided years ago that they never would be. The relationship they had suited them just fine.

Seeing Scout had finished her business and was ready to go home, Ellie spun around and began walking in the other direction. The Westie pivoted with her and took the lead.

Ellie drew closer to Joe, loving the scent of him that enveloped her, just as it did when they made love. She turned her attention to the full moon overhead and drew a long, pensive breath. Appreciating his calm when her own emotions were so tumultuous, she turned her full attention back to him. "So what are we going to do?"

One broad shoulder lifted in a barely expressed shrug. Their eyes met and held. Casually, he returned, "Nothing now."

Another surprise. She had half expected him to want to gift his half of the property right back, rather than stay tied to her this way. It was sort of what she wanted. Otherwise, things felt too complex. She wanted them simple. Easy.

Oblivious to her urge to run from the confusing situation, Joe continued, "Eleanor is making a lot of decisions very quickly. The way I see it, she's driven by some pretty powerful emotions."

That was definitely true. Retirement was challenging for everyone. And Eleanor had worked at the bakery her entire adult life. Maybe walking away from everything she had known would not be as uncomplicated as Gran was thinking. Hope flaring within Ellie, she murmured, "You think she might change her mind about moving into senior living?" And not push for such drastic change. Especially all at once.

Joe wrapped a comforting arm about her shoulders, drawing her in close to his side. "No clue. But we ought to at least leave as many options as possible open for her." Together, they entered the building and climbed the steps to the second floor. "In the meantime," he rasped as they walked back into her apartment, "you and I have some catching up of our own to do." He pulled her in tight against him.

Their bodies aligned as if they were made for each other. Completely caught up in the moment, the way she always was when he held her in his arms, Ellie splayed her hands across his chest. "Is that right, soldier?" she teased.

With the pad of his thumb, he traced the lower curve of her lip and looked deep into her eyes. "Absolutely, darlin'."

She gazed up at him, recognizing just how much she loved having him here and how much she missed him when they were apart.

"And because we do..." he drawled.

A thrill soared through her as he stroked one hand down the nape of her neck, placing the other on the middle of her back. Her knees grew weak as he left a trail of light kisses across the top of her head, down her temple, across her cheekbone, to the sensitive place just behind her ear. She moaned as his tongue swept the inner shell of her ear. The hardness she felt pressing against the front of his trousers made her shiver even more.

"We've got no more time to waste."

Joe had meant the remark as a joke. A way to speed up their evening to what was always the best part of any homecoming: the very first time they made love again. It was always exhilarating. Passionate. Unbearably sweet and emotional, too. A way to forget the weeks and months apart and come together as if nothing had changed.

Except it always had. Just a little. There was always so much left unsaid, so much unknown. A gap of time to erase. The physical activity of learning anew each other's needs and wishes helped to bridge the residual loneliness.

Her green eyes glimmering with desire, she stepped out of his embrace. Turning her back to him, she gestured at her zipper. "Help me with this?"

"My pleasure, sweetheart." His pulse racing, he drew it down.

She shimmied out of the dress and turned to face him. He hadn't seen what lingerie she was wearing when they were getting ready for the party.

Now he knew.

It was sheer and tight fitting, a low-cut bustier that laced up the front and the tiniest bikini panties he had ever seen. Inhaling deeply, she locked eyes with him and began taking the pins out of her upswept honey-gold hair, until it tumbled down over her shoulders in loose waves.

Unable to hold back, he breathed. "Damn, Ellie, you are so amazingly beautiful."

She sashayed closer, tipping her face up to his. He started to reach for her, but she shook her head and inched back slightly. Indicating his clothes, she prodded lustily, "Your turn, soldier."

Aware he was already way too aroused to hold back for long, he warned, "Ellie, darlin'…"

She tilted her head tauntingly. "I like to look, too."

Fair enough.

He undid his tie and swept it aside, unfastened a couple of buttons, then tugged his shirt and T-shirt over his head. His pants were next. Instead of the white military-issue briefs he knew she was expecting, he had on the pair of sunset-print silk boxer briefs she had given him when they'd been in Hawaii in March.

Grinning, she let her gaze drift lower to the bulge pressing against the silk. There was no hiding his desire now.

Unable to wait a second longer to make her his and sensing she wasn't feeling all that patient, either, he pulled her closer. He ran his thumbs over the crests of her delectable breasts that were pushing against the sheer fabric.

Her arms came up to wrap around his neck, and she stepped all the way into his arms. "Oh, Joe," she whispered, pressing her body flush against his. She threaded her hands through his hair and fit her lips to his. "I've missed you so… so…much." All the tenderness he had ever wanted to see shimmered in her eyes.

"Same here, darlin'." He returned her soulful kiss with every ounce of pent-up passion that he had. He unlaced the front of her bustier, watching as the plump mounds of her breasts fell free. Loving the sight of her, he dispensed with the bustier, then her tiny bikini panties.

Her eyes darkened. "Planning to seduce me, soldier?" she purred.

"More like ravish…" He got busy shedding the rest of his clothes, too. Taking her by the hand, he drew her down onto the bed. Determined to give her all the pleasure she deserved, he rolled her onto her back. His lips and hands made a leisurely tour of her body.

Ellie offered a soft sigh of acquiescence, then trembled when he found the sensitive place between her thighs. The satin of her skin grew as hot as the fire burning inside him.

His body pulsed with need. He loved her like this. All soft and womanly, open to everything—and anything—he wanted, yet wanting to give back, too, smoothing her palms over his shoulders, down his spine. She cupped and molded his buttocks as he moved his mouth to her breasts, nibbling and suckling, making sure there was no pleasure point he missed.

He took her mouth again, determined not to let their first lovemaking go by too fast. Yet he could tell from the way she was surging against him that she needed more, too. Wedging his knee between her thighs, he spread them. Her breath caught as he stroked, finding the wet, silky heat of her center.

"Joe," she whispered against his mouth, urgent now. "I can't wait…"

He deepened the kiss as her hands found him, too. "Me, either." She stroked the length of him, making him moan, as she helped him roll on a condom.

One clever move, and he was inside her. He pushed to go even deeper. She pressed her mouth to his, kissing him deeply, erotically. Wantonly. Reminding him, even as they soared into ecstasy and beyond, that they had always been each other's soft place to fall.

Joe woke several hours later. It was still dark outside, but the bed beside him was empty. Curious, he got up and walked out into the living area.

The light above the stove illuminated the space with a soft, nocturnal glow. Ellie was sitting in the big club chair she used for reading and watching TV. She wore one of the striped cotton nightshirts she favored. Her knees were drawn up to her chest, and she had a half-empty tumbler of what appeared to be milk balanced on one knee.

He pulled up the ottoman that went with the chair and settled in front of her. Damn, but she looked pretty with her lips still swollen from their kisses, her hair all tousled. "Hey," he said, aware he wanted her all over again.

Her hand still gripping the tumbler, she flashed him a fragile smile. "Hey yourself."

Sensing her guard was up, he took her free hand and treaded carefully. "What are you doing up?"

She gazed down at her their hands. "Thinking."

He kissed her knuckles. "Come to bed."

"I can't."

Another surprise. He noted she was not looking him in the eye.

Ellie sighed. Turning her gaze back to him, she admitted with obvious reluctance, "I've got heartburn. I need to wait for the milk to kick in."

Heartburn! He surveyed the suddenly flushed features of her face. "When did this start?"

Another sigh. "I've always had it. Off and on. As far back as I can remember."

"You never mentioned it."

She shrugged.

He stood, wanting to do more to help. "Do you have any medicine for it?"

She lifted the tumbler to her lips and took another tiny sip. "No need." She waved off his concern. "A glass of milk always works." Tilting her head, she squinted at him thoughtfully. "You should probably go get some sleep, though."

He wondered what else she had neglected to tell him. Then again, maybe this was just the stress of her grandmother's news, and she just needed comforting. He was definitely up for that. He ran his hand over her hair, smoothing the tousled strands away from her face. Ignoring her implied entreaty to get lost and leave her to suffer alone, he promised, "We will sleep. Eventually."

She scowled at him, reminding him just how much she loathed being given orders. "Bossy!"

"In a situation like this, someone has to be." Standing, he lifted her into his arms, then sat in the chair, settling her in his lap. Loving the feminine weight and feel of her, he sighed in satisfaction. "That's better."

"True," she admitted, snuggling against him. Silence fell. Tenderness wafted between them. Figuring she would talk to him about her feelings when she was ready, he let her process the events of the evening as she quietly finished her milk. Finally she rested her head on his shoulder. "Sorry I woke you."

He hated it when anything made her unhappy. "I'm not," he told her gently, still stroking her hair. He lifted her knuckles to his lips and kissed them once again. "It gave me another chance to hold you some more."

Her body softened in contentment. "Can't say I mind that, either," she murmured.

The scent of her filling his senses, he stroked her silky hair, wishing they could always be together like this. Every night, every day. "You know what we need? Another week in Hawaii."

Tracing an idle pattern on his chest, she nodded in agreement. "Like the one we spent there in the spring."

Just three months prior. He pressed a kiss to the top of her head.

"Without all the events for Kali and Kane's destination wedding this time," she said wistfully.

"Yep. Just the two of us." Joe cuddled her even closer. "With a week to ourselves."

Ellie closed her eyes. Completely relaxed now. "Sounds good to me," she murmured sleepily. "Really good."

"I think that's it for the dresses," Eleanor said early the following afternoon, adding one last garment to the stack on her bed.

Ellie had to admit although it was quick, it was a good day for her gran to move into her new place, since the bakery was closed on Sundays. Plus, Joe was here to help with the heavy lifting.

Gran surveyed the three open suitcases that were already

filled. "And we've got the sleepwear and my favorite robe and slippers, workout clothes and all my jeans and sweaters."

She had already boxed up her books and crocheting materials. Joe was loading them and her TV in her car. The rest of the personal items would be placed in Ellie's SUV.

Ellie looked back at the closet. "What about shoes?"

Eleanor smacked her forehead. "I knew I was forgetting something. Would you mind bringing them all out so I can choose what I want to take?"

"Sure." Pushing her sadness aside, Ellie knelt on the floor of the walk-in closet. Her grandmother's footwear was mostly in a large bin with few pairs scattered around the perimeter. A lot of it was half-hidden by the clothes still in there.

"I'm missing a silver glitter sneaker," Gran said. "Do you see it?"

"I'll look." Ellie crouched down even farther, finally spying it in the far back corner. Pushing beneath a row of winter clothing hanging on the lower rack, she stretched her arm out to snatch it. She pulled it free and, still half-sprawled on the floor, tossed it over.

Eleanor caught it with one hand. "Thank you, darling!"

Ellie dove back in for a few other stray shoes. When she heard Joe coming back down the hall, whistling cheerfully, ready to carry another load of Gran's stuff, she started to sit upright.

Suddenly, the room spun like a Tilt-A-Whirl. She felt like she was about to pass out. Unfortunately, it wasn't the first time she'd had a sudden loss of equilibrium in the past few months. Knowing the best way to avoid fainting was to put her head between her knees, she bent forward and took a few long, slow breaths. The Tilt-A-Whirl eased.

"Ellie?"

The next thing she knew, Joe was hunkered down beside

her, all masculine intensity and concern. He touched her shoulder lightly. "Are you okay?"

Was she? Ellie decided she was. She nodded and slowly and carefully sat up all the way, with Joe steadying her all the while. "Yes, of course."

"Are you sure?"

The last thing he needed was to worry about her. Or anything, really, that could take his mind off one of his life-or-death missions. "Positive," she fibbed. Maybe she did need to see her internal medicine doctor. Find out if she was anemic or something. She'd have to make an appointment, after Joe left, since it always took at least a few days to get in, for non-acute issues. And this was definitely that.

He paused to survey her from head to toe. "What were you doing?"

"Um...stretching out my back muscles," she lied. Pulling herself together the way she always did.

Eleanor appeared in the closet doorway, easing in beside Joe. "Darling, you're so pale!"

Embarrassed heat crept into Ellie's face. She held out a hand for help up, and Joe clasped it. The warmth and strength of his grip was both enervating and reassuring. She looked at him, wordlessly instructing him not to worry her gran. She really was okay now.

He responded with a brief nod that let her know he understood.

Ellie felt her body relax in relief. She forced herself back on task. Pointing to the stack of clothes, she said, "Everything on the bed can go."

Joe assessed the load. "You're going to leave it all on hangers?"

Eleanor and Ellie nodded in unison. Neither of them wanted to do more work than was necessary. Ellie replied,

"It's just going to go from one closet to another, so yeah." She turned back to Gran. "So about your shoes…"

Gran decided to take a dozen pairs, as well as her favorite cowgirl boots. "They have line dancing at Laramie Gardens now, you know."

Ellie had heard. No doubt Gran was excited to partake. Maybe she'd been too quick to judge and this would be really good for Gran after all.

What had started years ago as an assisted living and nursing home had turned into the best senior living complex in three counties. The facilities were beautiful, the staff wonderful, and an hour and a half later, Ellie and Joe had everything moved in to Eleanor's new digs. With her three best friends there to keep her company, Eleanor shooed the couple off, insisting that they needed to go spend time together.

As the two of them walked out through the sprawling complex, Joe took Ellie's hand. "You doing okay?"

Abruptly, Ellie felt on the brink of tears. "Of course." She swallowed around the lump in her throat and quickly changed the subject. "What about you? When are you going to see your family?"

The McCabes had all been at the party at the community center the night before. But he needed to spend time with them, too. Especially since he always bunked with Ellie when he was in Laramie.

"Mom and Dad invited us for dinner this evening."

"What time?"

He squeezed her hand in his, clasping it warmly. "Six."

"The siblings all going to be there?"

Grooves deepened on either side of his mouth. "As far as I know," he said cheerfully.

"That will make your mom and dad happy to have you all together."

He regarded her for a long, careful moment. "They'll be happy to have you there, too. You're like a daughter to them, you know."

Just not a daughter-in-law.

Where had that thought come from? It wasn't like she wanted to get married. Not when she knew she had no affinity for it.

Joe stopped and straightened to his full height, towering over her petite frame. "So what do you say?" he asked. "Do you want to go?"

Ellie nodded, wanting to be as close to his family as he was to her and hers. "Sounds good."

He pulled out his phone and texted their acceptance. "Which means we've got time to do whatever you like."

Intoxicated by his genial, attentive nature, Ellie struggled against the sudden racing of her pulse. "Anything?"

"Mmm-hmm."

She tore her eyes from the sinewy contours of his chest. He radiated sheer masculine strength, and his nearness made her want to make love with him again. Was she starting to depend on Joe too much? Ellie swallowed around the parched feeling in her throat. She forced herself to remember their relationship was about friendship, sex and, most of all, independently pursuing what they both wanted out of life.

"How about we go back to the apartment and hang out?" she asked.

They'd barely gotten through the door when they were in each other's arms again. The passionate lovemaking kept them from concentrating on anything but the moment they were in. For Ellie, whose life had been turned upside down in the last forty-eight hours, the reprieve was exactly what she wanted.

* * *

Joe caught the scent of their favorite dishes the moment he and Ellie walked into his parents' home. Roast chicken for him, mashed potatoes and bacon-sautéed green beans for Ellie.

"So when do you head back to Fort Carson?" Mitzy asked Joe as they all sat down at the dining room table.

Way too soon, Joe thought. The worst part about coming to see Ellie was having to leave her. He had always thought their goodbyes would get easier with time. Instead it just seemed to be harder. At least for him. Ellie—like his family—was amazingly brave and accepting of all his job required.

Noting that Ellie was still looking a little tired and tense around the eyes, he reached beneath the table and squeezed her hand. Giving her the reassurance and affection he sensed she needed. "I have a flight out of Dallas late Tuesday morning," Joe told his mother, "so I'll probably leave here about 4:00 a.m."

"So you and Ellie will still have tomorrow," Mitzy surmised happily.

With a smile, Ellie passed the salad. "Except I have to work."

Mitzy's brow furrowed. "You can't take off?"

"If Gran were still managing the bakery, I could, but now I'm in charge, so…no, sadly. I'm going to have to be there from 4:00 a.m. until noon. Then Ingrid, the assistant manager, can handle it until closing."

"How is the business going?" Chase asked, sounding every bit the experienced CEO of multiple businesses that he was. "Are you enjoying being the new person in charge?"

Looking visibly uncomfortable with the turn the conversation had taken, Ellie seemed to force a bravado Joe sensed she was not yet feeling. "Actually, everything is pretty much the same."

She was starting to look a little pale again. Was something else going on? Was it possible she had some sort of health problem that she either hadn't acknowledged or couldn't? If that was the case, it would be even harder to leave her.

"Do you have any changes planned?" Chase asked. "A way to put your own stamp on Sugar Love? Or things you're thinking about doing in the long run?"

"Well." Ellie pushed the mashed potatoes around with her fork. A new wave of color came into her cheeks, and she gave his dad an earnest look as if wanting his opinion. "I had given some thought to a new look. Doing something to spice up the traditional pink-and-white stripes on all our packaging and maybe update the logo." She exhaled and admitted with visible disappointment, "But when I ran it by Gran and some of our longtime customers a few months ago, the response was overwhelmingly negative. Apparently, the pink-and-white stripes are considered iconic."

"And if it ain't broke, you don't fix it," said Sadie, who also worked at the bakery and had her own business ambitions.

"Right." Ellie smiled at Joe's sister like the very good friends the two were.

"What else would you like to do?" Chase asked.

"I thought about adding some new cupcakes and cookies."

He nodded his approval. "That sounds doable."

"Except we're stretched pretty thin right now just delivering on the walk-in demand and the advance orders we have. Plus, there are the specialty cakes, which are in high demand throughout the entire summer wedding season, and now I've got all the ordering and payroll and stuff to do, too."

"Are you set up on an automated system?" Chase asked.

Ellie shook her head. "Gran liked doing things the old-fashioned way. She felt that was a way to maintain more control."

"Well, maybe that's an area you could modernize to make your life easier," Chase said. "I could help you do that, if you want. It would streamline some of the paperwork for you."

Joe noted that Ellie looked hesitant and overwhelmed again.

"It might be a little soon for Ellie to be making any changes just yet," Mitzy interjected, sending Ellie a sympathetic look. "I mean, I know how overwhelmed I felt when I inherited Martin Custom Saddle from my dad. I didn't know where to begin. Fortunately, Chase was there to step in to help me. And eventually purchase it and take it over completely."

"Except… I can't sell Sugar Love." Ellie toyed with a green bean.

Which wasn't what his mother had been trying to suggest, Joe knew.

"I know our situations are very different," Mitzy returned with a veteran social worker's calm. "I knew nothing about actually running a saddlemaking company. Whereas you've been working at the bakery for years." She paused to let her words sink in, before continuing gently, "I'm just trying to say that accepting help when you need it and are ready to receive it can be a very good thing. In the meantime," she added, a little more casually, "you and Joe can concentrate on what the two of you want to do about the house Eleanor just gifted you."

Chapter Three

It was all Ellie could do not to choke on her bite of perfectly prepared mashed potatoes. She glanced at Joe. He looked as stunned by the comment as she felt.

"How did you find out about that?" Joe asked his mom.

His brother Gabe, who was an attorney, shrugged. "A change of property records—especially the name on the title—is a matter of public record," he said.

Ellie felt even more discombobulated. "But… Gran just did it a few days ago! And told us about it last night after the party. At the same time she announced she was moving into Laramie Gardens this afternoon."

Mitzy nodded with the compassion the McCabes were famous for. "That's been in the works for an even longer while."

"And you knew about that, too?" Joe asked.

Mitzy continued gently, "Social services is always notified when a new resident decides to move in to any of the assisted living communities in the area, in case the seniors need help with anything. So I went by to talk to Eleanor privately, when her name came up on a list, to make sure everything was okay with her. And it was. She said she just wanted to make a change before she *had* to make a change."

Ellie guessed that made sense, sort of. It was always so traumatic when an elderly person was suddenly forced out of their home and into a group living or nursing facility. Still, it seemed awfully premature.

"So everyone knows about this?" Ellie asked, dragging her fork through her potatoes once again.

Sadie shrugged. "Word was starting to get around toward the end of the party last night. Everyone was sort of wondering if the two of you were getting ready to make some sort of big announcement yourselves. If that was why Eleanor was gifting you the house now."

"Big announcement?" Joe echoed, perplexed.

"About your future," Gabe said with his usual matter-of-fact calm.

The front door opened and closed. Then opened again as the doorbell rang repeatedly. "Boys!" they all heard Alex McCabe warn.

The divorced rancher herded his four-year-old quadruplet sons into the dining room. "Hi, Gramma and Grampa!" they shouted in unison.

"Are we in time for dessert?" Marty asked eagerly.

"Yeah, we already had pizza with the soccer team after the game!" Max reported.

"Sorry we're late," Alex said to one and all. He turned to Joe with brotherly love. "But we wanted to make sure we got to see you before you had to head back to base."

"Thanks, man. I appreciate it." Joe smiled and got up to greet his brother warmly. Hugs from all four nephews followed.

"Where is your uniform?" Michael asked.

"I only have to wear it when I'm doing soldier stuff."

Matthew regarded his uncle with a mixture of admiration and disappointment. "Ahhh. We like seeing you in it."

"Yeah." Max nodded. "You look awesome in it, Uncle Joe."

"Well," Sadie drawled, "guess we can't compete with that."

Joe's brother Zach came in shortly after that. A pediatrician, he'd been at the ER, caring for a patient who'd had a skateboarding accident. He helped himself to what was left of the dinner while Chase went to get another of Joe's favorites—lemon meringue pie. And chocolate pudding topped with crushed chocolate cookies and gummy worms for the kids.

"So," Zach asked, looking first at Ellie and then Joe, "is it true what everyone is saying over at the hospital? That the two of you are finally about to get engaged?"

There were times, Joe thought, when the McCabe family gatherings could feel endless. Tonight was definitely one of them.

And the evening was still young, he thought, his frustration with his family mounting. He hated it when they got all up in his business. He knew they thought they were helping—they weren't. Their incessant interest just made him feel suffocated. And now Ellie seemed to be laboring under the excess attention, too.

Sadie looked at Zach, not bothering to suppress her own highly romantic nature. "Apparently, they're still dragging their heels when it comes to making anything formal," she said dryly.

"What does that mean?" Michael asked, his cute little face pinched in confusion.

"It means I need to hear all about your soccer game!" Joe said. He looked at the eager, chocolate-smeared faces of his four nephews, taking them in one by one. Although their faces were each uniquely handsome, and their heights and builds varied slightly, they all had Alex's dark hair and blue eyes. Plus the intense emotional connection and ability to communicate with each other wordlessly that multiples seemed to have. He grinned at them. "Anybody here score a goal?"

"Nah," Max said with a wave of a pudding-smeared spoon. "But Matthew jumped in the air to avoid getting hit by a wild shot, and Marty ran over to help out and tried to kick the ball and missed. And then Michael did a somersault in the grass and jumped back up, and I ran over to do one, too, and everyone laughed."

Alex ran a hand over his face. "True," he said.

To keep the rambunctious stories coming, Ellie stepped in to ask a few more questions. Thankfully, the other topic was not picked up again.

Aware Ellie had to be at work at four the next morning, Joe began to pull them away from the group around nine that night. As they were headed out, Zach said to Joe, "Want to go for a run at 5:00 a.m.?" he asked.

Joe had a lot of energy to work off. He clapped his physician-brother on the shoulder, knowing one thing they both shared was emotionally intense jobs. "Sounds good."

Ellie was quiet on the short drive home. Joe gave her time to collect her thoughts, then gave her the apology he knew she deserved.

"Sorry about the third degree from my family," he said, escorting her up the stairs.

Ellie unlocked the door to her apartment. "It's okay. They were just trying to show their interest about what's happening in my life. Which, admittedly, has been a lot the last few months."

"Not to mention the last couple of days."

Nodding, she reached for a glass and put it beneath the spigot on the fridge. She watched as it filled, then paused to take a small, careful sip.

She was looking a little pale again. Realizing that asking once more if she felt okay would probably not be appreciated, he settled for a more neutral statement. "What can I do for you?"

He knelt to pet Scout, who had jumped off the sofa and come over to him, vigorously wagging her little tail. Still, she seemed to watch her owner out of the corner of her eye, as if she knew Ellie was feeling a little under the weather.

Ellie pressed the water glass against her forehead. Abruptly, looking like she was about to throw up, she lowered the tumbler and pressed her hand to her mouth. Took a slow deep breath. Then, asked, "Could you—" she swallowed hard "—lower the thermostat on the air conditioner, and then take Scout out for her last walk?"

Hoping she wasn't about to be sick, but also knowing it could simply be the suffocating heat of the July evening getting to her, he said, "Be happy to."

She shot him a grateful glance. When he got the AC to click on, she moved to stand beneath one of the vents. Her shoulders slumped slightly with relief as a little color came back into her cheeks. She gave him a weak smile. "Thanks."

Giving her the privacy she clearly wanted, he got the leash and headed out with Scout. The Westie moved slowly, in no hurry to get her business taken care of. And though Joe understood the little gal's need to stretch her legs and enjoy the moonlit summer night and empty downtown streets, he couldn't help but worry over Ellie.

By the time they got back, the apartment was nice and cool. Ellie was already in bed, sound asleep, her color healthy looking once again, her breathing deep and even.

He was a little surprised she had turned in without him.

But that was okay, he thought, as he climbed into bed beside her and curved his body around hers, holding her close. They were here. Together.

And right now, that was all that mattered.

Ellie groaned when her alarm went off five hours later. Joe shared her regret. He hadn't held her close nearly long enough. And their time together was nearly two thirds gone. Unfortunately, she had to be at work soon, and she looked… like she still needed hours more sleep.

Extricating herself from his arms, she got out of bed and disappeared into the bathroom.

Resolved to help her as much as possible, he rose, put on his running clothes and headed for the tiny galley kitchen. By the time she emerged from the bedroom, dressed in a pink Sugar Love chef tunic, jeans and sneakers, he had her favorite latte ready for her. With a smile, he handed it over. It was moments like this that he had the best sense of what it would be like to actually *be* married to her. If she ever wanted to make things legal… But right now, that still did not seem to be the case.

Instead of gulping her caffeine down greedily like she did most mornings, she stood there, holding it awkwardly. She lifted her chin to study him, her lips curved upward in a smile. "Thanks." She lifted her mug in a silent toast. "For making this."

Even though she wasn't drinking it. Yet, anyway. Masculine satisfaction roared through him. "You're welcome."

Their eyes met and held, the air between them crackling with an undefined emotion. He wondered if she was still upset about the interrogation from his family at dinner the evening before. If she was, he couldn't really say he blamed her. They had been…intrusive.

"Actually, I think I'll put it in a travel mug and take it

down with me, so it will stay warm." He watched her rise on tiptoe and pull a stainless steel mug down from the cabinet.

"Good idea." He let his gaze drift over the way her jeans clung to her nicely rounded hips and slender thighs. His body hardening in response, he continued gruffly, "Wish I'd thought of it."

She sashayed closer and kissed his cheek, her bare lips sliding over his stubbled jaw. "You think of plenty, soldier," she murmured.

Joe hugged her back, breathing in the fresh, floral scent of her. He brought her close for a long, satisfying off-to-work kiss. She melted against him, the feminine softness of her body molding to his strong frame. "So I'll see you later?" he asked when they finally drew apart. He wanted to pin down their next opportunity to be together.

She nodded. "I shortened my hours since you're in town. I'll be off work at noon today."

He gave her another quick kiss, then let her go. "I'll see you then."

Ellie headed down to the bakery on the first floor. Joe took care of Scout, the way he always did when he was in town, and then met Zach outside the bakery.

They spent a couple minutes stretching, then headed off at a steady clip. For a while, they ran without speaking. Zach clearly needed to wake up, and Joe was content to exercise in silence. They ran down the length of Main Street, past the new high school and all the athletic fields, then sped by the superstore and on to the old moving and storage company warehouse. The four-story brick building was as empty as it had been the previous summer.

Joe paused to study the big parking lot. "No one has bought this yet?"

"No. You thinking of starting your own moving company?"

A lot of veterans went into the storage and transportation business after they departed the service. And Laramie was a good place to store household goods for people who wanted to work overseas for several years. "No."

Joe had known for a while now what he wanted to do when it came to a second career. This warehouse would be the perfect setting to enact his dream business. He wasn't going to talk about the enterprise he had planned, though. Not even to Ellie. Not until everything was set. And that would not be until he had exited the service and returned to Laramie to live. And hopefully talk Ellie into a more permanent, traditional arrangement than the one they had now.

They turned and began to run in the direction from which they'd come. "Need to talk to you about Ellie."

"Don't waste any more time waiting for the right moment to propose," Zach said bluntly as they jogged side by side. "'Cause it might not come."

His brother had lost the love of his life in a car crash a few weeks before their wedding, five years ago. As far as Joe could see, Zach had yet to recover.

Joe began to sweat in the still, humid air. It was already ninety and set to be another blistering hot day. He concentrated on the sky slowly lightening above them. "Ellie doesn't want to get married."

Zach pushed them to run faster. Rounding a corner and heading on to the side streets, they wound their way through the labyrinth of Laramie residential neighborhoods. "Is that so?"

"Yeah." A motion detector light on one of the houses flipped on suddenly. Joe lifted his forearm to block the light, and Zach did the same. "She doesn't mind being a military girlfriend, but she draws the line at becoming a military wife."

Zach shot his brother a curious look. "The Fitzgerald family curse again?"

Was that the reason? Joe couldn't say. He knew Ellie was superstitious to a point. So was he. It was why he didn't want to talk about his future business plans until they were set in stone for fear it might sabotage them. As far as Ellie's tragic family history went, he and Ellie rarely talked about "the curse" that had kept them from actually marrying. The only time they did was when someone else brought it up. "She just doesn't want to jinx things." He couldn't blame her for that. Not when things were so good between the two of them.

Zach nudged him with an elbow. "What about you?"

Most of the time, Joe was like Ellie, wanting absolutely nothing about their relationship to change. But last night, when his family kept pushing them to legalize their relationship, he'd briefly wished for that, too. Until he saw her looking ill, and then all thought of what-if fled his mind. Her well-being was his top priority.

"I want her to be happy. And well," he said. His thoughts turned to the way she had been looking and acting since he'd been back. "And speaking of her health," he said worriedly, "have you noticed anything?"

Slanting him a look, Zach slowed. "Besides the fact she's stressed out more often than not these days?"

Joe nodded, diminishing his pace, too. Hands clenched, he forced himself to reveal his worst fear. "I think she might be ill."

"Why?"

Joe recited everything that had been bothering him. "She's not eating much, even when it comes to her favorite foods." And Ellie had always been a woman with a big appetite. "She had heartburn the other night so bad she couldn't sleep and had to get up and drink some milk for it."

Zach nodded, encouraging Joe to go on.

Glad to be able to take advantage of his brother's medical expertise, Joe stopped completely and confided, "Sometimes she gets really pale. And yesterday when we were moving her grandmother's belongings, she suddenly looked like she was going to faint."

"Did she pass out?"

"No." Joe frowned, his worry intensifying. "But only because she was already kneeling on the closet floor and put her head between her knees." He remembered how shaky she had been. Which was also unusual.

Zach began to run again. "Did you ask her about it?"

Joe fell into step, letting his brother set their pace. "I tried. She keeps insisting she's fine."

"When you are pretty sure she's not."

"Right."

Zach's brow furrowed. "When did she last have a physical? See a doctor? Do you know?"

"Maybe last summer. Not sure. Nothing recent, at least not that she's mentioned. What do you think it could be?"

His brother shrugged as Main Street came back into view. "A lot of things. Reflux. An ulcer. Anemia. To get a diagnosis, she'll need a physical exam and blood work. Depending on what those show, maybe even an ultrasound or CT scan."

A CT scan? That sounded serious. Hopefully it wouldn't come to that. Joe started his cooldown as they approached the bakery. "I have to go back tomorrow morning. I don't want to leave unless I know she's okay."

Clearly understanding what it was like to want to move heaven and earth to protect the woman he loved, Zach asked, "You want me to call in a favor?"

Joe exhaled. "Can you? If I can't get her in to see her regular doc before I have to leave again?"

Ellie was still at the bakery as noon approached. The morning rush was over, and the single-tier wedding cake she had been working on all morning with Sadie was nearly complete. The forty-four-year-old twins, Sherri and Terri, would be in at noon, and work until closing. Meanwhile, the two assistant managers, Lynette and Ingrid, had been manning the counter in the storefront and baking cookies and cupcakes since 9:00 a.m. and would also stay until closing.

Suddenly, Ingrid tensed. "Oh, no," she moaned softly as she stared out the front door. "There she is."

Ellie turned toward her longest employee, save her newly retired grandmother. It wasn't like the genial woman to disrespect anyone. "Who?"

Lynette, who knew all the hottest gossip in town, came up to stand with them. "Monica Townsend," she whispered in Ellie's ear. "Viv's nightmare daughter-in-law."

Ellie paused. "The one from the Northeast?" Who avoided sugar like the plague?

Ingrid nodded. "Yes, Brad's wife. She's been nothing but mean to Viv since she married Brad two years ago."

"Vivian told you that?" Ellie asked in surprise. Vivian was Gran's longtime friend and one of the most active volunteers in the entire community. She was also famously discreet.

Ingrid shook her head. "Didn't have to. Everyone who has seen the two of them together knows the situation."

Except me, apparently, Ellie thought. Although she supposed it was no surprise, since she wasn't into gossip and never had been.

The bell jingled, and Monica Townsend walked in. Her red hair was cut in a trendy style that just brushed her thin shoulders. She wore a slim black dress and high-heeled rattlesnake boots. Monica sized up the women behind the counter, then focused on Ellie. "You must be Eleanor's granddaughter," she said in a clipped New England accent. "The new owner."

Realizing the two of them were roughly the same age, Ellie smiled. "I am. How can I help you?"

Monica moved as far away from the store entrance as possible. "I want to talk to you privately."

Ingrid and Lynette looked at Ellie, awaiting instruction. She waved them off, and the two assistant managers scattered to the back, shutting the door to the kitchen behind them.

Ellie joined Monica at the end of the service counter and waited.

"I have a special request." The redhead reached into her bag and pulled out a printed recipe. "The Laramie Women's Club is honoring my mother-in-law—Vivian Townsend—at a luncheon in a few weeks. The meal is being catered, but everyone who is invited has been asked to bring a homemade dessert. And I'd like you to make this for my mother-in-law." She handed over a recipe.

Ellie studied the page in surprise, not sure she had ever seen or heard of the dish. "*Mock* apple pie?"

"Yes." Monica nodded eagerly. "It doesn't really have any apples in it—crackers are substituted for the fruit—but it's supposed to taste like it does."

Interesting.

"I thought it would be a fun little surprise for everyone," Monica continued with ingratiating cheer.

Ellie's instincts told her this was about way more than "fun." Not that it mattered, since she wouldn't be party to it. She attempted to hand the recipe back, but Monica refused to take it. Resolutely, Ellie put the paper on the counter and continued, "Well, first of all, we don't bake pies here. Only cakes, cupcakes and cookies."

Without warning, the heartburn symptoms—a mixture of pain and nausea—that she had been battling lately started up in the center of her chest. Wishing she had a glass of milk handy to ease the effects of the acid, Ellie swallowed.

Unaware of Ellie's discomfort, Monica sighed. She propped both hands on her hips. "I know the only place in town who does make pies is the Daybreak Café."

Ellie pushed the printed recipe toward her. "Then it shouldn't be a problem."

Except apparently, it was. Monica tossed her head indignantly. "The café refused to help me. Apparently, they stopped making their pies themselves, years ago, and only bake pre-made frozen ones these days, and only sell those by the slice. They don't do any special orders. Never did. And hence have refused to even consider making an exception for me."

Ellie could see why. This fun little request had disaster written all over it. Her knees were starting to get a little wobbly, and she braced her weight against the counter, eager to get this over with. She looked Monica in the eye and said, as matter-of-fact as possible, "We can't help you, either. I'm sorry." Great. Now she was a little dizzy, too.

Not that Monica seemed to notice the perspiration breaking out on Ellie's brow. She leaned in close. "I'll pay you whatever you deem fair to help me with this."

Why did people always approach bakeries with requests that were impossible to carry out? Ellie shook her head firmly. "It's not the money."

Monica stamped her foot. "I have to have this done for me!"

The tension in the room made her heartburn worse. Ellie

swallowed around the rising bile and tried another tack. "It doesn't look that hard to make," she suggested sympathetically. "Maybe you could do it yourself."

Monica's narrow face pinched with anger. "You don't understand!" she burst out in frustration. "Viv has always looked down on my cooking!"

Ellie found that hard to believe. "Viv openly insults your efforts?"

"Of course not." Monica rolled her eyes. "But I know what she's thinking. She always says whatever I make is wonderful when she clearly thinks it isn't."

"So...you think she's patronizing you?"

"Yes! Anyway, I thought if I played this little joke on her, had you make this pie for me and I pass it off as a real apple pie, ostensibly made especially for her by me, and she said it was really great, then I could tell everyone the filling was really made with crackers and expose her for the fraud she is. And then Brad and I can finally stop arguing about his mother, because he will see that I have every right to resent her as much as she resents me."

Lord Almighty, families could be complicated!

"I see where you're going with this," Ellie said as she heard the kitchen door behind her ease open quietly. "But again, I just don't think Sugar Love can help you."

"You have to," Monica insisted stubbornly.

"Actually," a deep voice behind her said in an intimidating tone, "she doesn't." Ellie felt Joe come up behind her like the warrior he was. "And since she has been very clear with you, Mrs. Townsend, I suggest you leave before I escort you out the door."

Monica's jaw dropped. She whirled on Ellie. "Are you going to let him treat me this way?"

With the bile rising in her throat, Ellie had no choice but

to let him do just that. Hand to her mouth, she pivoted and ran through the door, out of the kitchen and into the alley where she promptly got sick.

Once again, Joe was there. First with just a hand on her shoulder, then when she had finally stopped retching, with a cool, wet cloth and water to wash her mouth with. He handed her some ginger ale to sip while he calmly rinsed away the mess in the alley with a jug of water. Finished, he turned to her. His eyes were full of compassion, and something else she couldn't quite identify.

"Feel like you can go upstairs to change clothes?" he asked gently.

Although her knees were still a little unsteady, Ellie managed, "Yep."

"Good." He wrapped an arm about her waist, bringing her in close to his strong, warm body. "Because we have somewhere else to be."

Chapter Four

"What do you mean, we have some place to be?" Ellie echoed. Although she was no longer nauseated, she still felt a little dizzy and out of sorts.

Joe slid a hand beneath her elbow as they walked up the stairs side by side. "I made an appointment for you with Jayne Landry, the new internist in town."

She stopped on the upstairs landing. *You what?*

"I called your regular doctor. They can't fit you in until Friday."

That much, at least, wasn't a surprise. "Okay. Then—"

"I can't leave town unless I know you're okay, Ellie, and we both know you're not, so...this is the next best thing. Zach helped me set it up." He held her gaze in the way that let her know his mind was made up.

She unlocked the door to her apartment and pushed inside. Eager to get out of her bakery uniform, she headed for her bedroom. Her temper skyrocketing at the way he had just taken over, as if she was a military mission, she stripped off her jacket. Clad in just a bra and jeans, she stalked into the bathroom. Grabbing a washcloth and cleanser, she proceeded to wash her face. "You didn't think to ask me about any of this first?" she snapped in mounting irritation.

"You would have refused my help." His tone was flat.

Ellie brushed her teeth. Finding his penetrating gaze too much for her, she turned back to the sink, rinsed and spit. Blotting her mouth with a towel, she said, "For good reason." She reached for the mouthwash, reminding him tartly, "This isn't what we do for each other."

She swished the minty liquid around, working to get the bad taste out of her mouth.

Lounging in the open doorway of the bathroom, he folded his arms in front of him. He had showered after his morning run and changed into jeans and an open-necked, short-sleeved olive green polo that made his eyes look more green-gray than their usual smoky blue. His attitude was unrepentant, but to her surprise, he concurred with a nod. "Not in the past, certainly."

She smoothed a tinted moisturizer over her face. So he thought they should be more aggressively looking out for each other. She reached for her lipstick. "You're saying you want it to change?"

"I'm saying we need to adapt to whatever the situation requires of us. Without having to constantly worry about overstepping our bounds."

She stared at him in shock. "Is that how you feel?"

He sighed. "Sometimes. Yeah."

She grabbed her mascara and layered it on her lashes. Wiping off a smudge just beneath her left eye, she asked, "Like when?"

He held her glance in the mirror. "Like every time I asked you the past couple of days if you were all right, and you brushed me off. Like it was none of my business."

Guilt rose within her. "I didn't want to worry you."

"Not telling me what's going on worries me more."

Ellie felt an arrow to her heart. She let out a weary breath, her shoulders slumping in defeat. "I'm sorry," she told him softly. That was the last thing she wanted. Turning away from the mirror, she closed the distance between them.

He scanned her head to toe. "So you admit you need to go to this appointment?"

Reluctantly, Ellie nodded.

His handsome features relaxed slightly. "I'll run Scout out while you get dressed, and then we can go."

And then hopefully, Ellie thought as she headed for her closet, whatever this was that had been going on with her the last six weeks or so would turn out to be nothing after all.

Joe wasn't sure what to expect when they arrived at the medical building. Was he going to be relegated to the waiting room while Ellie disappeared inside? But when the nurse that called her name asked Ellie if she wanted to bring "her companion" in with her, she turned toward him, her expression compelling, and said yes.

She was weighed and measured. Her height hadn't changed, but she was down seven pounds, which made her frown. Although Joe couldn't figure out where the weight had come off. She was as enticingly curvy as ever in breasts and hips.

The nurse took Ellie's vitals, had her take a seat on the exam table and told them the doctor would be in shortly.

The internist was roughly their age, fresh out of residency and as cordial and kind as Zach had said. She immediately put Ellie at ease, then got down to business. "How long have you had heartburn, nausea and lack of appetite?"

"Since late May?"

Dr. Landry continued quizzing her affably. "Anything else going on in your life of note?"

Well, now that you mention it, Joe thought dryly, thinking of a major source of his woman's current stress.

Ellie blew out a long breath. "My grandmother retired and gifted me the family bakery business."

"Sounds like a lot of responsibility," Dr. Landry said sympathetically.

"And a lot of change," Ellie admitted, biting her soft lower lip as if just realizing how much she had been dealing with.

Although she rarely articulated her private insecurities, he knew what she was probably thinking. Was she good enough to handle the job? What if she screwed up and the generations-old business failed? What if she disappointed Gran? That would break her heart.

"Which is why I think I haven't been feeling so great," Ellie continued. She waved a delicate hand. "Stress. Anxiety. Whatever."

"Hmm." Jayne Landry looked over the notes the nurse had made and the medical history form Ellie had filled out. "That certainly is likely a contributing factor to whatever is going on. When was your last period?"

Ellie paused, looking a little embarrassed. "Around mid-February, I think. I'm not sure. I've never been regular. If I have three or four cycles a year, it's good for me."

Which was another reason for her not to marry Joe, Ellie occasionally told him when making the case for their continued romantic arrangement. She knew that someday he was going to want kids, like all the McCabes, to whom family was everything. And with her spotty ovulating, the chances of her conceiving were not good.

She always said it like that fact sealed the deal that they would never marry. Discounting the possibility of fertility treatment. Or adoption. Or even continuing on without children. He didn't understand why Ellie did not see that the only thing he needed in his life was the love he and Ellie shared.

Everything else in his life, including his career in the military, was negligible.

Dr. Landry made another note on Ellie's chart. "You've never been on the pill to regulate this?"

"I tried a couple of times. But I didn't like the way it made me feel," she babbled nervously, "and Joe and I are actually physically together only a few times a year, so…"

The doctor nodded, clearly understanding the life of military couples. "What about birth control? What kind of contraception do you use?"

Ellie flushed self-consciously, suddenly aware—as was he—where this line of questioning was going. "Condoms." She looked her doctor in the eye. "I know what you're hinting at, but I'm *sure* that's not it. We're very careful."

Joe confirmed this soberly. "We are."

"Okay, then." Dr. Landry checked Ellie's lymph nodes on her neck and beneath her arms, then asked her to lie back on the table. Joe watched in concern as the internist palpitated Ellie's abdomen. "Anything hurt?"

"No," Ellie answered.

Joe felt himself beginning to relax. Maybe Ellie was right, and he was being overprotective. Maybe this *was* all just nerves. And a little heartburn or…dietary indiscretion. Although he couldn't imagine what she would have eaten that would make her so uncomfortable.

"You can sit up."

Joe moved to give assistance. Ellie leaned into the arm he had slipped around her back, the way she always did when she wanted comfort.

Dr. Landry continued, "I want to run some quick blood work, if it's all right with you."

Ellie locked eyes with Joe, letting him know in that instant how glad she was that he was there with her. He felt the same. "Sure," she said.

The nurse came in, took the blood, then left, promising to have the results in ten minutes or so.

As Ellie sat on the end of the exam table, she looked a little jittery. He understood because it was all he could do not to pace the room. He remained beside her, however, doing his best to exude calm, even though waiting for results sucked.

"How are you feeling now?" he asked, taking her hand.

"Perfect," she said. "Which sort of figures, right?" A new wave of healthy pink color came into her cheeks. "As long as I put off going to the doctor to see what was going on, I kept getting worse. But now that I'm actually here—" she waved an airy hand "—I'm all better."

He grinned. Joking was a good sign. Maybe they'd be lucky, and this was all nothing. They chatted to pass the time, and finally, Dr. Landry came back in.

She was grinning from ear to ear as she regarded them both. "Well, we found out what the problem was. You're pregnant!"

Pregnant! The word reverberated in Ellie's head. "Are you sure?" she croaked, fighting a tsunami of joy, surprise and absolute wonder.

Beside her, Joe looked as if he were feeling the same.

Dr. Landry smiled and reassured them, "The blood test does not lie about this."

Ellie thought about all the times she and Joe had made love when they were in Hawaii that week in late March. How wonderful and romantic it had all been. Still this hadn't been in the plan. Not at all.

Talk about an unexpected turn of events. "But we were so careful!" she blurted.

"No contraception is one hundred percent effective," Dr. Landry said. "But I know you'll both need a few moments to absorb this. Everyone always does. In the meantime, Joe, your brother Zach told me you are headed back to your base in Colorado tomorrow. So if you'd like to hear the heartbeat today, we have a medical student interning in the ER right now who is eager to have more experience with the Doppler. Would the two of you like to go over there and have a listen?"

"Yes," Ellie and Joe said in unison. "We would."

"Give us a minute to get the paperwork together," Jayne Landry said. "And we'll send you over." She smiled again, then the door shut behind her.

Ellie turned to Joe, her heart suddenly pounding. She had always hated the unexpected, but this…this was something wonderful and thrilling.

"A baby," he whispered reverently.

A baby. Our baby. "Yes," she whispered back, her heart filling with bliss in a way she had never even imagined. "We're having a baby, Joe!"

The next thing Ellie knew, his arms were around her, warm and strong. Just the way she always wanted them to be. She surged against him, lifting her face. Their lips connected in a sweet, loving, wonder-filled kiss. A kiss that brought forth all the affection of the last twelve years. One that celebrated the moment. And foretold the future, too.

Ellie's entire body was tingling with happiness when they finally drew apart.

The door behind them opened, and the nurse walked in. "Dr. Landry is sending you home with prenatal vitamin samples, as well as a basic handout on how to handle all the pregnancy symptoms. It should get you through until you can get in to see your OB/GYN—which could take as long as a couple of weeks. Although usually they try to bring the new moms in fairly quickly. And last but not least, here is the order for the ER, asking them to do a Doppler for us."

"Thank you," Ellie said, feeling a little overwhelmed.

"You're welcome and congratulations!" the nurse said, moving to show them out.

Joe took Ellie's hand as they walked through the halls to the elevator. Once downstairs, they stepped outside the medical building and headed across the street to the hospital.

He seemed deep in thought. She was, too, now that the shock and joy were wearing off, and she contemplated what all this was going to mean. How was the pregnancy going to impact their relationship? How did she feel about him being away for months at a time now?

Luckily, the medical student was on the lookout for them, and as soon as they walked through the emergency room entrance, he was there to greet them. He took their paperwork, then led her back to one of the private bays. "I guess they told you I'm new to this," he said. His hands were shaking.

Ellie smiled at the freckle-faced kid in scrubs and sneakers. He barely looked old enough to drive a car.

The medical student gave her the privacy to undress and drape a sheet over herself before returning with the Doppler. As she lay back on the table, she could see he was still as nervous as she was. Her heart went out to him. "I'm sure you'll be great at it," she said. Joe stepped in beside her, taking her hand.

"Let's hope so," the med student muttered. "This will be a little cold." He spread gel over her abdomen, and short moments later, he moved the Doppler over her torso.

At first there was nothing, then an abrupt heartbeat and another, then nothing again. He frowned.

Ellie tried not to panic. She reminded herself he was just getting the hang of finding a heartbeat.

He tried again in the same place and got…nothing. So he moved the Doppler to the other side of her body. Suddenly, the heartbeat was strong and loud and steady.

"There it is!" the med student said happily.

Ellie caught Joe's look of wonder. Her eyes filled with tears as she listened to their baby's heartbeat.

And what had been, up to then, a concept that she was still trying to fully comprehend, suddenly became very, very real.

Joe and Ellie left the ER as quickly as they had arrived. She got halfway across the parking lot when she abruptly came to a full stop.

"What's wrong?" Joe asked. Clearly, something.

She laid her hand across her heart. "We were so caught up with the news we forgot to ask when our baby is due!"

He shrugged. "That shouldn't be too hard to figure out since we know when our baby was conceived."

Her expression brightened. "The week of March 24."

"During a destination wedding slash vacation that will forever be remembered by both of us," he rasped fondly.

Ellie grinned, her mood suddenly seeming as frisky as his. "It sure will."

He held up his hands and playfully ticked off the months. "April, May, June, July—which is where we are now—" he paused to affectionately touch her belly "—then August, September, October, November and December." Even though it was the middle of summer, their baby's birth didn't seem so far away at all.

Ellie's eyes twinkled merrily. "Good counting, soldier, but I'll go you one better." She plucked out her phone and pulled up a pregnancy calculator on-screen. She shifted so he could see, too. "This estimates… December 15 or so." She drew in a soft breath. "Christmastime."

A Christmas baby. Talk about a reason for celebrating. Every year from then on out. Joy filled Joe's heart. "Yup."

"Except." Ellie's lower lip trembled. She shifted away from him, disappointment shimmering in her sage green eyes. "You likely won't be here since that's the hardest time of year to get leave."

Joe couldn't bear to see her hurting. He wrapped his arms around her and drew her close. "I promise you, Ellie. I'll do everything I can to be with you and our baby this year. For both the birth and the holiday."

She wanted to believe him. He could see that. "But…"

"No buts," he cut her off resolutely. "We're going to have a wonderful Christmas come December. Our best ever." He stroked his hand through the silk of her honey-gold hair. "And an even more wonderful holiday right now," he murmured.

She squinted at him. "The Fourth of July has already passed."

"Christmas in July hasn't. It's my understanding that goes on all month long, for those who celebrate. And I do," he told her, "with you." His heart filling with all the love he felt for her, he bent his head and kissed her tenderly. She melted into him, kissing him back so sweetly he wished he could make love to her right then and there.

Slowly, he ended their kiss and lifted his head. "It's all going to work out, Ellie," he promised her. He was going to see to it. Even if she still had some doubts.

Ellie relaxed slightly. She rested her hands against his chest and gazed up at him. "I know that, Joe," she murmured. Her usual confidence seemed to return. "With us, it always does. One way or another. And right now, with a baby on the way, we have even more powerful motivation to bring everything together and make things work."

"We sure do." Joe kissed her again, even more passionately, then let her go. He wished like hell their time together wasn't almost up. That he didn't have to return to base tomorrow. But he did, so he had to take command. Deal with things as they were. Adapt.

"In the meantime," he said, "we have to talk."

Like it or not.

Yes, Ellie thought reluctantly, they did have to talk. Knowing their situation had never been more serious and that their time together was short, she gripped his hand as if her very life depended on it. "I know we do," she told him soberly.

"Want to go to your apartment or your grandmother's house?"

She knew where they would have more privacy: the home they had just inherited. "The house."

He drove them there, then rushed around to open her car door for her as soon as he parked in the drive.

She looked down at the light but proprietary grip he had on her arm. He was treating her as if she were incredibly fragile. "You know, I might be pregnant, but I can still walk," she told him dryly.

He slipped his arm around her shoulders. "I know," he said in a gruff voice that was filled with emotion. He gazed at her, all his love for her gleaming in his smoky blue eyes. "I just want to hold you as much as possible right now."

A new flood of tears filled her eyes. Knowing she loved him, too, so much, she whispered, "I want that, too." Pausing only long enough to kiss him on the cheek, she opened the front door and led the way inside.

The house felt empty, even though her gran had only been gone for twenty-four hours.

Abruptly feeling a little rattled by all the change and uncertainty ahead of them, Ellie went into the kitchen. Wanting to ward off any return of heartburn or nausea, she pulled out some saltine crackers.

Joe followed. His look was all business. "We have to get married," he informed her. "And I'd like to do it before I leave."

"Whoa there, soldier." Calmly, Ellie filled a glass with ice and offered him one.

He refused with a shake of his handsome head.

Giving what she was doing careful attention—mostly so she wouldn't have to react to his inherently commanding nature—she poured ginger ale over the cubes. "You are moving way too fast." And she desperately wanted him to slow down. So this wouldn't all feel so…rushed and reckless. The way their attempted elopement had years ago.

He came closer, inundating her with the brisk, masculine scent of him. "We need to adapt."

"And we will," Ellie promised thickly. Her throat was parched. She took a long swallow of her drink.

"As soon as possible," Joe continued, as if it were already decided. Perhaps it was in his mind. He wrapped his arm around her and held her close.

She knew one of them had to remain realistic. Jumping into marriage as a quick solution to anything, even an unexpected pregnancy, was never a good idea. And as happy as she was to have a baby with Joe, she did not want to do anything to wreck what they already had. Not when their relationship was working so well.

She leaned in to his strength. When her cheek brushed his closely shaven chin, she caught a whiff of his sandalwood and spice soap, and her heart raced even more. "We're already adapting. And it's great that we're both starting to think about the future and how best to arrange things. But—"

she set her glass aside and braced both her hands on his chest "—marriage isn't necessarily the answer."

Joe reached out and tenderly tucked a strand of her hair behind her ear. He exhaled, watching her intently. "Don't you want our baby to be born legitimate?"

She gulped back the acid rising in her throat. Moving away from him, she reached for a saltine, took a bite, then another and another, letting the cracker soak up her discomfort. "I don't think people care about that anymore." She reached for another cracker and offered him one.

He shook his head in mute refusal, pointing out matter-of-factly, "Your grandmother will, and so will my parents."

"You're right about Gran. But as far as your mom goes, I happen to know that she had you and your three brothers on her own, via an anonymous donor and a fertility clinic, before she got together with your dad." Which meant Mitzy understood and approved of a woman having kids on her own. Although how she might feel about her son not marrying his own baby's mother was probably something else entirely.

His gaze narrowed. He watched her sip her ginger ale. "Mom and Dad were still married within months. They didn't waste any time once they knew they were meant to be together."

"I am glad for them, and for the happiness they've found. But we're not your parents, Joe. We both have enjoyed our freedom the last twelve years, every bit as much as we've enjoyed being together whenever we can." At least she frequently told herself that was the case.

He put up a staying hand and came close, filling up the space between them. "But now it's going to be different."

But aside from the baby, was it? "Are you saying you're going to resign from the military and not re-up in a couple of months, when it's time?"

He hesitated. The irises of his eyes turned a smokier blue. That told her all she needed to know. The military still came first with him. Yes, he loved her, but he loved his career, too.

Taking a deep breath, she eased away from him. She folded her arms in front of her, doing her best to keep things practical, rather than emotional. "I don't want you to feel like you're being forced to marry me."

He tensed, but his expression did not change. "I'm not."

She wasn't sure she quite believed that. Ellie forced herself to meet his gaze, then continued honestly, "And I also don't want to be forced into anything, not by a pregnancy and not by you."

He lifted his shoulder in a hapless shrug, then stuffed his hands in the pockets of his jeans. He had the same battle-ready look on his face that he wore whenever he had to go back to his unit. "So what *do* you want?" he gritted out.

That was easy, Ellie thought. "I want," she told him slowly, painstakingly, "to not make the mistake we did the last time we faced a very big change, and rush off to elope only to realize at the last minute it wasn't right and back out."

A brooding look was etched on his face as he, too, clearly recalled that heartbreaking time that almost wrenched them apart for good. His dark brow lifted. "We wouldn't have backed out if your mom and grandmother hadn't intercepted us."

She remembered the looks of disappointment and anguish on their faces. The heart-to-heart she'd had with both afterward that had convinced her marriage wasn't for her. Not then…and not now. At least not to a military man on active duty who could just as easily be killed in action the way her own father and grandfather had been, mere months after they had shipped out.

"That could be true. We might have gone all the way

through with the elopement. But we still would have regretted it. And if you recall, your parents were not at all happy with our antics, either."

He stared at her with his usual fierce pride. "They weren't antics."

Unable to disagree with that, Ellie squared her shoulders and took a deep, bracing breath. "They weren't the actions of mature adults, either."

Silence fell between them, more awkward and disjointed than ever.

She held out her hands imploringly. "Look, I know you have to leave tomorrow. I'm sorry about that. Luckily, nothing has to be decided right this minute. We have plenty of time to figure out how we want to handle this in the long run."

Relenting, Joe added, "We still have to tell our families."

"Agreed."

He took her hand in his, holding it tenderly. "I'd prefer we do that together while I'm still here. And since it is only four o'clock, we've got time to tell them in person."

Ellie nodded. "Agreed."

They went to see her gran first. She was ecstatic.

"Oh my goodness!" She clapped her hands. "I am so happy for you, darlings! We have to start planning your wedding immediately!"

Ellie lifted a palm. "We're not getting married, Gran. At least not right away."

"Well, we *will* talk about it," her grandmother retorted, undeterred.

Joe's parents were next. Mitzy and Chase were equally happy. They were also in favor of an immediate wedding with all their family and friends present.

It was Joe's turn to quash the dream. "We're not walking down the aisle just yet," he said.

His dad frowned. His mom merely nodded. "We under-stand," Mitzy said soothingly, like the social worker she was. "It's been a lot to take in. You need time."

"Yes," Joe said while Ellie breathed a sigh of relief.

"You're still going back to base tomorrow?" his dad asked.

"Yes, I have to." Joe nodded.

After nixing an invitation to stay for an impromptu cel-ebratory dinner, Ellie stopped by the bakery to help close, then went back to her apartment with Joe.

"Are you hungry?" he asked, hunkering down to pet Scout.

Since they had agreed not to decide anything right away, their evening felt surprisingly relaxed.

"Yeah," she admitted with some surprise. "Starved, actu-ally." Now that she knew why she had been feeling so mys-teriously different, her fatigue and sluggishness and lack of appetite had eased.

He rose slowly, towering over her. "Want to go out or order in?" His eyes crinkled sexily at the corners.

Passion roared through her, as fierce as a summer storm. Ellie returned his ornery grin. "In." This was their last night together. She knew they would be making love. Probably till dawn.

Looking every bit as ready to get their evening started as she was, he snapped a leash on Scout. "What sounds good?"

Already tingling with anticipation, Ellie thought it over. "Asian?"

He remained where he was, close enough to kiss her. He smiled and met her eyes, sharing her buoyant mood as only a co-parent-to-be could. She trembled at the raw tenderness in his gaze. "Perfect choice," he replied.

"Okay," she said, wanting to do everything she could to make his life easier, too. "I'll order our faves. It will probably be here about the time you get back from your walk with Scout."

Running a hand down her spine, Joe pulled her against him. He paused to kiss her, slow and lingering. "Sounds good," he murmured against her lips.

They still had a lot to talk about, she knew, but the hard part, breaking the news to his folks and her gran, had been done. Now all they had to do, she thought as she looped her arms about his neck and kissed him one more time, was figure out their immediate future.

Chapter Five

Joe and Scout were returning from their walk when they encountered Gabe standing at the top of the stairs. Looking very much like the workaholic attorney he was, he had a laptop bag slung over his chest. His arms were full of white paper bags from the town's best Asian restaurant.

As Gabe turned to see them coming up the stairs, he grinned in relief. "Thank God you're here. Otherwise, I was going to have to figure out how to ring the bell without dropping something."

Joe chuckled. He shouldered past his brother to unlock the door. Wedging it open slightly, he called in a warning, "Ellie? We've got company!"

Through the narrow opening, he saw her come into view. She had indeed changed clothes while he was gone. She was wearing a pair of white shorts and one of his old denim shirts that came halfway to her knees. Her skin was radiant. She looked spectacularly beautiful.

Was this the special glow pregnant women got? If so, how had he missed it up to now?

"We do?" Ellie echoed in surprise. She opened the door all the way and saw Gabe. Her hands flew to her hips. "Since when did you start delivering food for Chang's?" Grinning, she leaned forward to relieve him of half his bags. Joe took the rest.

Gabe chuckled. "Since I met their delivery guy on the way up."

Ellie looked at Joe's brother affectionately, reminding him how much she adored every member of his immediate family, and they, her. "Ah, well, thank you," she said.

Joe looked at Gabe. He wasn't sure why his brother was here. Nor was he sure he wanted to know, since this was his last night with Ellie for who knew how long. A fact Gabe definitely was aware of. Joe lifted a censuring brow. "Now isn't the best time, bro," he said.

"Actually," Gabe said, ignoring Joe's gruff tone and turning abruptly serious, "now is the *perfect* time."

Ellie's pretty green eyes widened curiously, whereas Joe was just plain irritated.

"In that case, would you like to stay for dinner?" she asked Gabe with a smile, as lovely to his family as always. "I ordered half the things on their menu."

"Love to," Gabe said, ignoring Joe's wordless order to get lost and take up whatever this was later.

Deciding the fastest way to get rid of his brother was to hear him out, Joe filled Scout's food and water dishes while Ellie and Gabe set the table for three.

"So I assume you had a reason for stopping by," Joe said when they had settled.

Gabe helped himself to a crispy eggroll. "First, I want to congratulate you."

Joe went after the beef and broccoli. "Mom and Dad told you?"

Nodding, Gabe passed around the honey chicken. "They notified all the siblings. But they especially wanted *me* to know so I could talk some sense into you."

Some of Ellie's radiance faded. She began to tense. Joe groaned his frustration, which, unsurprisingly, she seemed to share. "If this is about getting married ASAP—"

Gabe spooned rice onto his plate. "It is."

Ellie looked like she wanted to bolt, and Joe wouldn't blame her one bit if she did. Joe reached for her hand and held it tightly. He glared at his brother. "It's none of your business," he said angrily.

"You're right." Gabe remained calm. "It isn't. Which is why I am here only to give you much-needed information. Not tell you what to do."

Ellie leaned back in her chair. She extricated her hand from Joe's and picked up her fork. "What information is that?" she asked.

"The law here," Gabe said plainly. He regarded them both. "In Texas, when a baby is born to parents who are not married to each other, state law does not recognize the biological father as a legal parent."

That was *crazy*, Joe thought.

Gabe continued, "This means that a biological father who is not married to the mother of their child does not have legal rights to the child until he actually becomes a legal parent."

This seemed unnecessarily convoluted, Joe thought. Judging by the way she was wrinkling her nose, Ellie seemed to agree.

"Can't we just put Joe's name on the baby's birth certificate?" she asked with a beleaguered sigh.

"You can and you should, but Joe's signature on the birth certificate creates an administrative relationship between him and his child that is limited to child support." Gabe continued eating like he hadn't had a decent meal all day. "And while that's better than nothing, it's far less than what I think either of you want for him."

"So how do we change that?" Ellie asked.

Joe was happy to see she wanted his participation in caring for their child, as much as he wanted to be involved.

"To have legal rights to his child—which means any say in medical decisions or parenting issues, et cetera—Joe would have to file a paternity suit."

"*Whoa!* Is a paternity suit really necessary? Even if I already claim the baby as mine?" Joe interrupted.

"Yes." Gabe looked from his brother to Ellie and back again solemnly. "Without that, and a positive DNA result and a legal judgment in his favor—a process which could take months, by the way—he doesn't even have any inherent right to have access to your child."

Ellie stopped eating entirely and threw her hands up. "Well, that's ridiculous. I would never keep Joe from our baby!" she declared emotionally.

"Maybe not deliberately," Gabe countered with lawyerly calm, "but the way things stand, if something were to happen to you and emergency care was needed for your baby, Joe would not be able to come in and just take over until you were better or whatever. Instead, the care of the baby would automatically go to Ellie's family, although since Eleanor is now in Laramie Gardens, I don't think it would be possible for her to take physical custody of a child. In that case, it would have to go through social services and the court, and the baby would be temporarily put into foster care." He set his fork aside and took a big gulp of water. "Whereas if you were married, there would be none of that, even if Joe was deployed. The baby would automatically be cared for by his family or yours."

Pink color swept Ellie's cheeks. "I had no idea this was so complicated," she claimed, her soft lips twisting in exasperation.

"And unfair," Joe agreed grimly.

Keeping his promise not to tell them what to do, Gabe shrugged. "Well, there is a simple solution. Stop futzing around and get married ASAP." He paused to let his legal advice sink in. "And then neither of you will have to worry about Joe ever being denied his parental rights."

"Well, I guess that settles it," Ellie said after Gabe had congratulated them again, wished them luck and left the apartment. She closed the partially filled white cartons one at a time. Her earlier radiance had been replaced by an expression that predicted the world—as they knew it, anyway—was about to irrevocably change. She lifted her chin and speared him with a discouraged gaze. "You and I do have to get married after all. At least for a year or two. Or however long it takes to get everything squared away, for you and our baby."

"And then what?" Joe asked. Hating the fact she was already emotionally drifting away from him, the way she always did when things got too difficult.

Ellie shrugged. "Then I guess we go back to the way things were, before we found out we were pregnant, since that arrangement has always worked so well."

His gut twisting, he looked deep into her eyes. "Continue to love each other. Without the constraints of a typical marriage."

For a moment, uncertainty flickered in her sage eyes. She inhaled deeply. "Yes. Of course." Wishing he could just take her to bed and make love to her until everything they had just learned about their situation disappeared, he carried the dishes over to the sink. She looked so distraught, he had to ask, "Do you feel trapped or forced into doing this?"

Wincing, she pulled a clip from her hair. She ran her fingers over her scalp, loosening the silky strands. "A little." She bit her lip and let her hand fall back to her side. "Do you?"

Empathy stirred inside him. This was a lot for her. And he was leaving tomorrow. "Yeah, a little, too," he admitted gruffly. He finished loading the dishwasher, then turned back to study her wan smile. "But I also know that we owe it to our baby to see that they're as protected as they can possibly be."

Arms folded defiantly in front of her, she lounged against the opposite counter. "And that means never risking, even for one moment, that our child could end up in foster care or kept from you."

He came toward her. Leaning in, he braced his palms on either side of her. "So…the next question is *when*."

She tilted her head to one side, thinking. "We don't know when you'll be back again."

She had no idea how much he wished that weren't the case. Especially now. Figuring it would do no good to lament what couldn't be changed, he said only, "No. We don't."

She held his gaze, suddenly the recklessly impulsive girl he had fallen in love with years before. Before she'd become so wary of change of any kind. Ellie shrugged. "Then I say we go back to the plan we had twelve years ago. Ditch the waiting. And elope tonight."

Joe loved this side of her. He didn't trust it, though, not since she had become an adult and hidden that side of her away. Except for when they made love. In the throes of passion, she was always wild and uninhibited, and he couldn't get enough of her. Returning to the matter at hand, he studied her. "You sure you're going to be okay with that? Getting hitched on the fly? Without our families present?"

For a moment, she said nothing. Her expression was maddeningly closed. Her eyes, conflicted.

When they'd been kids, they hadn't wanted their folks

there. They had known they wouldn't approve of a marriage at eighteen. Since then, they hadn't given it any thought because getting hitched hadn't even been on the table. As Ellie had often said, their long-term relationship had all the benefits of marriage and none of the hassle. Most of the time, he agreed.

"I haven't thought about it," she said finally.

He could tell she wanted to bolt, the way she always did when life got too intense. Unfortunately, they didn't have the luxury of a time-out. They had to deal with this immediately. He kept her where she was, caged between his extended arms. "I'm asking you to think about it now," he said softly.

Ellie fell stubbornly silent.

Knowing they both had to be completely honest here whether they wanted to be or not, Joe pushed her a little more. "Have you ever wanted the whole big wedding and reception?"

"Actually, that scares me," she admitted with a disgruntled exhale.

He took in the shiny blond hair spilling over her shoulders in erotic disarray. "Why?"

With one hand on the center of his chest, she pushed past him and began to pace. "Because my mother and grandmother both had big, romantic, formal weddings before their military husbands shipped out, only to have it all blow up a few months later when the men were killed in action. Leaving them widows…"

Joe had felt Ellie remove herself emotionally before she moved away from him physically. "We're talking about the Fitzgerald family curse?" He frowned.

She offered a terse nod, clearly expecting him to understand. And he did. A lot of soldiers were superstitious, too— saying certain prayers, carrying talismans to keep them safe. But he was also skeptical that a KIA incident could happen a third time in a third generation. Statistically, it just wasn't likely. He was pretty sure she knew that, too, in her heart of hearts. Otherwise, she would have worried like crazy whenever he was deployed. She didn't.

"I know we've used it as an excuse, when people push us about getting married," she said. "But now, with our baby on the way, it seems like that should no longer be a driving force. Or impediment." She twisted her hands in front of her.

Joe had been waiting for years to put the damn curse aside. "I agree. My question is...emotionally, can you actually marry me without that worry getting in the way?"

"I think so." Her voice trailed off wistfully. She sighed, coming intimately close again, and tipped her head up to his. "If we dial the whole thing way back, have just the two of us there, and just...you know—" she gestured vaguely "—get it done. For legal reasons. To protect you and the baby."

His body hardened with the need to take her and make her his. He knew that was going to have to wait. "We're talking tonight?" He figured the less time she had to think about it, the better.

Ellie's lower lip trembled slightly. "Yes."

"Well, then, there's only one place to go in Laramie County."

She bent down to scoop up Scout. Cuddling her beloved Westie close, she promised, "I'll be ready in five."

Joe made the call to confirm the justice of the peace could meet with them at 10:00 p.m. while Ellie donned a pretty white summer dress and heels.

Joe ran his electric razor over his jaw, then donned one of his button-downs, khaki slacks and his favorite sports coat.

When he started to grab a necktie, she shook her head. "We don't need that. You look great as is."

He kissed the back of her hand. "Whatever my lady wants," he murmured.

Ellie grabbed her bag containing her ID, he made sure he had his wallet, and they were off.

Although it usually closed at 9:00 p.m., J.P. Randall's Bait and Tackle Shop was all lit up when they arrived. The one-story white building was a popular stop for tourists and locals alike, halfway between Lake Laramie and town. The sign next to the door read:

> *Bait, fresh and frozen, for sale.*
> *Groceries, beer, ice and coolers available.*
> *Spare tires repaired.*
> *Wedding licenses issued.*
> *Ceremonies performed.*

"Looks like nothing has changed since the last time we were here," Joe deadpanned, opening her car door for her. Were they really...*finally*...about to get married? It seemed so.

"Except we don't have my mom and Gran standing sentry just inside the door."

He grinned, feeling much happier now than he had been at the time. "It was a little dramatic."

Ellie made a face. "And then some," she said wryly.

"As well as cloudy and threatening rain."

Tonight, though, a full moon shone in the star-studded Texas sky overhead. Wild flowers bloomed in the fields around them. Beside him, Ellie exuded feminine strength and smelled of her favorite jasmine perfume.

All good signs.

"Ready?" he said.

"As I'll ever be," Ellie promised silkily.

Acute awareness swept through him. He moved toward the shop door, and Ellie followed.

The bell above the door chimed as they entered the beloved convenience shop. A lanky fiftysomething man with spiky red-and-silver hair stood behind the counter. His eyes lit up when he saw them. He turned down the Cole Swindell track playing on the sound system. "Even before you called tonight, I always had a feeling the two of you'd be back," J.P. Randall IV said, extending a hand to Joe.

"I'm surprised you remember us," Ellie said.

Joe wasn't. The kind and compassionate justice of the peace had married many an eloping couple in Laramie County over the years, including a fair number of McCabes.

J.P. grinned. "I recall all the couples I've married since I took over the family business thirty years ago. But some couples stick with me more than others." He shook his head fondly. "You were so in love. I always hoped you two would eventually get hitched."

Standing there, Joe realized he secretly had, too.

"Although it took, what, twelve plus years?" J.P. continued good-naturedly.

"About that," Ellie confirmed, looking happier than Joe would have expected, given how all this had come about.

As before, they didn't have rings, so J.P. fitted them with some basic thin gold bands he had on hand. Then there was paperwork to be filled out. Because Joe was in the military and ordered to be on base in Colorado the following day, they were able to skip the seventy-two-hour waiting period after the license was issued and have the ceremony right away.

J.P. ushered them to the back of the store and opened up the small "chapel," which was essentially a small room with an artificial flower-threaded wedding arbor.

J.P. texted his wife, a pretty dark-haired woman named

Sheila whom Joe and Ellie both also remembered. She emerged from the storeroom and came into the chapel to act as witness.

"What kind of music do you want?" J.P. asked. "You all get to choose one song to set the mood before we get into the vows, and another to wrap things up at the end."

Ellie paused, then turned to Joe as if wanting him to decide.

Joe knew he had to bring back the joy they'd felt earlier in the day and make this a happy occasion. Inspiration hit. "How about the Dolly Parton classic 'A Christmas to Remember'?"

J.P. tilted his head as if he hadn't heard right. "Oh, I get it! You want a Christmas in July wedding theme?"

Joe looked at Ellie, who was suddenly grinning again. "We do," she said.

"And afterward, what would you like to hear?" J.P. asked.

"'Feliz Navidad,'" Ellie said, taking charge.

One of her very favorites, Joe knew.

"All right then." J.P. consulted the tablet that ran the chapel's sound system.

"Did you want flowers?" Sheila asked.

Joe looked at Ellie, suddenly realizing just how unromantic this was all turning out to be for his bride. Which was what she wanted, right? Something fun and sort of casual? That wouldn't feel too confining to her?

Her eyes darkening with an indecipherable emotion, Ellie struggled to decide while everyone waited. "Um...probably not," she said finally.

Joe could guess what she was thinking. A bouquet would make it too much like a real wedding. Except, it was a real wedding. Even if it was an elopement.

Sheila scoffed. "Oh, honey, you have to have them! And don't worry about the cost. They're part of the elopement package." She went to a refrigerator that held fresh flowers and returned with a pretty bouquet of red roses studded with greenery, in keeping with the yuletide theme. She handed them to Ellie.

J.P. started up the sound system, Ellie turned back to Joe, and the ceremony began with surprising solemnity.

They had chosen the briefest set of traditional vows, and the recitation of them passed in a blur. Joe felt steady as a rock, sober and surprisingly content. Ellie's emotions, on the other hand, seemed to be all over the place. She appeared to be scared to death, wildly ecstatic and, like him, in awe that this was happening at all. Her hands trembled as they exchanged rings.

"By the power vested in me, I now pronounce you husband and wife," J.P. said at last.

Satisfaction roaring through him, Joe brought Ellie to him for a sweet and tender kiss to seal the deal. Then it was all over.

"Wow," Ellie said, looking deep into his eyes.

Joe gazed back into hers, grinning.

Together, they drew a deep breath.

"We actually did it," he said.

Chapter Six

Joe hadn't expected Ellie to be particularly chatty on the half-hour drive back to town. It was closing in on midnight, after all, and today had been incredibly eventful to say the least. Finding out they were pregnant. Telling her gran and his folks. Bearing the brunt of familial disapproval about not getting married. Finding out they were going to have to get hitched, after all, if Joe wanted to be a real part of their baby's life. And he sure as heck did.

Now he had a little more than four hours left before he had to drive back to Dallas to catch a flight to Colorado, so he could be back at Fort Carson on time.

"Sleepy?" he asked as he parked in the alley behind the bakery.

She was still holding the wedding bouquet, a gift bag and a folder of impromptu photos the Randalls had taken before they left the chapel. "No." She slanted her head at him. "You?"

He shook his head.

Looking more gorgeous than ever, she unlocked the historic building's service entrance and led the way up the back stairs.

Making no effort to hide the possessive feelings welling up inside him, he caught her hand when they reached the landing. He used his key to open her apartment and then did

what all newly married grooms did—he slipped an arm beneath her knees, swung her up against his chest and carried
her across the threshold.

She gasped in a mixture of delight and surprise. He set
her down, then slowly and deliberately relieved her of all
the things in her hands, setting them just inside the door.
He wanted to make love to his bride, *badly*. He brought her
close and kissed her, ravenous. Only when he felt her sur-
render completely did he pick her up again and hold her
against his chest.

Laughing breathlessly, she wreathed her arms about his
neck. "What are you doing?" she demanded playfully.

Bypassing Scout, who had already put herself to bed for
the night on her cushion in the living room, he carried his
new wife into the bedroom. He set her down on her feet next
to the bed, and another spark lit between them.

"Giving us a wedding night to remember," Joe growled.

He tugged her close. Kissed her. And then there was no
stopping. Joe felt the shiver of delight sweep through her as
she rose on tiptoe, wrapped her arms tightly around him and
pressed her breasts to his chest. Her eyes were a dreamy sage
as she gazed up at him. The corners of her lips tipped up in
an inviting smile. "Then I say go for it, soldier."

"That's husband soldier to you, *wife*," he teased, savoring
the way her heart pounded against his.

She laughed throatily.

Resolved to show her just how much they could have, if she
would only give them—give this hasty marriage—a chance,
Joe kissed her soft and sweet. Slow and steady. And all the
ways in between. Letting her know with every stroke of his
tongue and the pressure of his lips just how much he cared
for her, how much he wanted to be there for her. Now. And
always.

Determined to be as gentle and reverent as this moment required, to honor and cherish her as never before, he kissed her until she was as caught up in all-consuming passion as him. He claimed her lips with his as if he was never going to have to leave again. Like there was nothing but this moment in time.

And she kissed him back, just as meaningfully.

Ellie knew their vows were not supposed to change anything at all. But ever since they had said them and put the rings on each other's fingers, she felt like everything had shifted. For the better.

Something was happening between them. Something that had surpassed her wildest expectations. And she could no more deny it than the need welling up inside of her. She ran her hands over his chest, stripping off his sports coat, unbuttoning his shirt. Her knees weakening, she threw herself into another kiss, smoothing her hands over the warm, satiny muscles of his pecs, discovering his nipples were as hard as hers. Lower still, he was rock-hard, too. She strained against him. Wanting. Needing.

With a low, satisfied sound, he eased the zipper down on her dress. Unfastened her bra and slid his hands over her breasts. She quivered as he palmed the taut, aching buds.

And still they kissed and caressed one another, feelings building until, unable to withstand desire any longer, they finished undressing and joined each other between the sheets. She lifted her hips, he pressed into her, and then they were one, making love until she was clenched around him, gasping his name, and he was whispering hers. They raced to the pinnacle and soared over it, holding each other as they came down, kissing tenderly as heartbeats slowly returned to normal.

Both acutely aware of the ticking clock.

* * *

Her whole body still tingling from their lovemaking, Ellie lounged in bed while Joe got out the bottle of sparkling apple cider and the two champagne flutes from the gift bag J.P. and Sheila had given them.

As he carried the drinks to the bedside table, she let her gaze drift over him, languidly memorizing every inch of his big, hard body for her dreams in the weeks and months ahead. Defiantly, she pushed away the thought of just how much she was going to miss him. He needed her to be strong and independent. And no matter what it took, she would be.

Curious, she asked, "What else is in that gift bag?"

He went back to retrieve it and then, grinning, held up a package of condoms. "Birth control."

Ellie groaned comically as he sauntered back to her, bag of goodies still in hand. "Too late for that. What else?"

He showed her with a flourish. "A package of wedding cookies."

Made out of shortbread. Her favorite, when it came to store-bought. "Cute." She swept back the sheet, making room for him. He slid in beside her and sat up against the headboard. She cuddled against his warmth, loving the way their bodies felt pressed against each other. "What else?"

He brought out yet another gift. "A book…called *How to Have a Happy Marriage*. And—" he laughed "—a sprig of artificial mistletoe." He held it over her head and bent toward her for another sexy kiss.

Bliss blossomed inside Ellie. "Hmm. Well, then." She batted her lashes at him flirtatiously and released a contented sigh. "Sounds like we're prepared for everything."

He put the gifts aside and handed her a glass of the sparkling cider. With all the affection he felt for her in his eyes, he offered a wordless toast. "We've been prepared for everything since the day we fell in love."

Ellie sipped her beverage, and so did he. "Back in high school?"

He shrugged and leaned over to kiss her once again. "When you know, you know," he said in a low, rusty-sounding voice. "And you have always—*always*—been the one for me, Ellie Fitzgerald McCabe. And you always will be."

Ellie and Joe made love twice more, and then it was time for him to grab a quick shower and don his fatigues while she made him a thermos of coffee and a breakfast sandwich to take with him.

She walked him out to the rental vehicle that had brought him from the airport. "I worry about you driving with no sleep."

He squared his powerful shoulders. "Hey. I'm Special Forces. I'm trained to go without. Not to worry, though. I'll grab a little shut-eye on the plane." He slid a hand down her spine, drawing her close once again. "It's you I'm worried about, darlin'."

Ellie swallowed around the growing lump of emotion in her throat. "I'll be fine."

He surveyed her as if memorizing every inch of her, the same way she was him. Softly, he urged, "Tell me you will go in a little late this morning."

How could she deny him anything right now? She forced a trembling smile. "I promise."

He hugged her close, burying his face in her hair. "I'll text you when I get back to base. Okay?"

It was taking all she had not to burst into tears. She nodded.

"And I'll call or email whenever I can," he continued gruffly, still holding her fiercely.

As he always did. It just wouldn't be enough, she knew, given how much she missed him. It never was.

"Hey, thanks for coming in to help me out with the baking this morning," Ellie told Sadie several days later. Usually, Sadie worked five days, from 4:00 a.m. till noon. This week, however, because Ellie was behind on the special orders from spending so much time with Joe, her best friend had graciously added an extra shift.

"No problem. Especially since I need to save as much cash as possible right now," Sadie returned.

Ellie brought out the butter and sugar. "How is the search for a place to put your lavender farm coming?"

Sadie opened up a container of flour. "Very, very slowly."

Ellie measured ingredients. "Is your dad's offer to sell you part of the Knotty Pine still good?"

"Yes. But he's still letting Alex run some of the cattle from Alex's ranch there. Plus, I'm not sure I want to be that close to Mom and Dad. Especially since they've been talking about moving out of their house in town and making the Knotty Pine their base, when they eventually do retire in another five years or so." Sadie turned the mixer on. "I kind of like doing my own thing."

Ellie moved to preheat the ovens. "I can understand that."

"But there is some land coming up for sale soon that might be perfect, so...fingers crossed." Sadie brought out the pans and lined them with parchment paper and softened butter. "Speaking of family, how is your gran?"

Ellie winced. "Ah, she's a little ticked off at me and Joe for the elopement."

Sadie went hands on hips. "I'm ticked off at him, too. He should have gone all out to give you the proper wedding you two deserved ASAP. Even if that meant crawling to his commanding officer on his hands and knees and begging for more time off."

Ellie shook her head. "I don't think that's how it works in the army, Sadie."

Sadie harrumphed. "So Will keeps telling me."

"Where *is* Will these days?"

Her eyes clouded with worry. "His unit is deployed in some unnamed hot spot in the Middle East again."

Ellie gave her friend a brief, compassionate hug. "I hate that he's in danger," she said, holding back empathetic tears.

"Me, too." Sadie looked like she was about to cry. "Unfortunately, it's not likely to change since Will considers the army his only family, since his mom died when he was eighteen."

"He has you and the rest of the McCabe family." Chase and Mitzy had stepped in as surrogate parents for Will at every important graduation, promotion and award ceremony. Along with Sadie and Joe. Will had also spent every holiday he was stateside with them. He was loved as one of their own.

Sadie reflected, "I know that Joe is still his best friend."

The close bond between Sadie and Will was more than that, Ellie knew. Much more. Getting either Sadie or Will to admit that was another matter indeed. "And you're his best gal pal, right?"

"Yeah. I'm the one he can count on to always write him letters and fly to his side if or when he gets hurt."

Ellie didn't know if it was all the hormones from her pregnancy or just that she and Joe had reached yet another level in their long relationship, but suddenly she wanted everyone to not just feel love, but to be *in love*. "Do you want it to be more?" she asked softly. She had always thought that was the case.

Sadie frowned. "Of course not!" Indignant, she waved off

the idea. "We're just friends. Besides, I would never hook up with a military guy who's only going to deploy somewhere far away and break my heart. I want a man who will be here with me, every day and every night."

So did Ellie.

But then she wouldn't have Joe. So...

Ellie slid the first cake pans into the oven to bake. "There are plenty of guys like that in Laramie."

"Yes, but none I could ever see myself falling in love with."

Maybe, she mused, *because you're already in love with someone. You just don't realize it yet.*

"What about you?" Sadie asked in sudden concern. "How are you going to handle Joe being away so much, now that you're having his baby?"

The million-dollar question, Ellie thought. She was already scared about going through labor and delivery without him by her side. Which was, she knew, a very poor attitude for a military wife to have. She planned to work on that.

She stiffened her shoulders. "I'll do fine. Right now, I have to figure out how to make up for Gran's absence here." Without necessarily hiring more staff, which the bakery couldn't afford right now. "So maybe it's good Joe won't be in Laramie," she continued, forcing herself to be practical, "because I don't know that I would have much time to spend with him anyway."

Sadie and Ellie had just slid freshly made cupcakes and cookies into the glass cases and were getting ready to open Sugar Love for the day when a hard rap sounded on the door.

Monica Townsend was back.

Oh no, Ellie thought, turning the dead bolt and opening the door to give the demanding woman entrance.

Monica strode in with what looked like a multipage legal document in hand.

"How can we help you?" Ellie asked, as her two other employees arrived for work. Twins Sherri and Terri grabbed their aprons and walked into the front of the shop.

Sadie, sensing trouble, stayed right where she was behind the display case, too.

Favoring Ellie with a bright smile, Monica said, "You want to help me? Then you can do what I asked you last week."

Play a mean trick on her mother-in-law? The untoward request had been made in confidence, so Ellie responded carefully, "As I told you then, we don't bake pies here."

Monica continued to smile persuasively. "I don't think you understand. You are my mother-in-law's favorite bakery."

Ellie knew that to be true. Vivian Townsend was a loyal customer. "We would be happy to bake her any cake that is currently on our menu, and we can customize that however you like." Or in any way at least that wasn't meant to be a nasty prank.

Monica waved off the offer. "That won't work. The Laramie Women's Club specifically asked me to bring Viv's favorite dessert, which happens to be apple pie. I am supposed to bake it myself, of course, but as I told you before, Viv does not care for my cooking. So this is the compromise I have come up with."

Wow, did Monica know how to spin things untruthfully, Ellie thought. She stared at the woman, hardly able to believe her gall.

"And furthermore, I know for a fact that you have baked a pie on special order before. The bakery did it for Calvin Barrett's wife, about fifteen years ago. I confirmed it with Calvin. It was cherry crumb. He said it was wonderful, and your grandmother was so sweet to do it for them." She furrowed her brow. "I don't know why you won't be sweet to Vivian, too." Monica's lips thinned. "Which is why I have decided not to stand for such horrible treatment and file a lawsuit if you don't backtrack and agree to help me out."

If it had just been a simple pie instead of a mock apple pie meant to be some sort of embarrassing prank, Ellie might have relented just to get rid of Monica. But there was no way she was going to be part of any effort to hurt or humiliate Viv. Or anyone else for that matter.

In the foreground, Ellie could see the shocked, disapproving looks of her three employees.

"I'm sorry, I still cannot do what you're requesting," Ellie said again.

Monica scowled and let out a long, breath. She stared at Ellie furiously. "You're really going to do this?" She handed over the document for Ellie to peruse. "You're really going to force me to *sue* you to get what I want?"

"Looks like," Ellie said.

Monica left her with the papers and stormed out.

These were the kinds of times she really wished she had Joe's strong shoulders to lean on. But with him back on base in Colorado, Ellie had no choice but to go to the bakery's lawyer, Joe's brother Gabe.

He was in court all morning but was able to stop by the bakery on his way back to the office. Ellie picked up some sandwiches from the bistro a few doors down. She snapped a leash on Scout, and they went over to the park to sit on a bench in the shade.

"So catch me up to speed," Gabe said, as the July breeze wafted over them.

"Read it and weep." She handed over the document.

Gabe perused it with ease. "Doesn't look as if this has actually been filed," he said finally.

Ellie sighed her relief. "It hasn't. Yet. Monica is giving me until the end of next week to change my mind."

He opened up his sandwich. "She won't win. Thanks to some recent court decisions, private businesses can no longer be forced to perform services outside their comfort zone. And if this *is* merely an attempt to hurt or humiliate her mother-in-law, as you told me on the phone earlier, then it really won't wash in a Texas court."

Finding her appetite had vanished, Ellie sipped her decaf iced tea with lemon. The cool beverage eased the parched feeling in her throat. "What about the fact that the bakery made a pie for Calvin Barrett's wife fifteen years ago?"

Gabe started on the second half of his ham and Swiss. "It could complicate matters, but it was just the one time so far as we know, and your grandmother no longer owns or works for the bakery. So although you never know what will happen in court, it's unlikely a judge would consider that a deciding factor in whatever ruling they might make."

Ellie reflected silently and, still feeling a bit confused, asked, "So then why is Monica threatening to file this lawsuit if she and her attorney know they can't win?"

Gabe shrugged and leaned against the back of the park bench. "They're probably banking on you not wanting the bad publicity or the expense and just folding like a house of cards." He flashed her a sidelong grin, in that second reminding her very much of Joe. It made her miss him all the more. "Obviously, they don't know you."

Pushing aside the pang of loneliness she felt whenever she thought of her military husband, Ellie released a long breath. And forced herself to concentrate on the matter at hand. "What do you suggest I do?"

Gabe swallowed his last bite of sandwich. "You can try to reason with Monica."

"I already did. And failed miserably." Ellie toyed with her chicken salad croissant. "I got the sense when she first made the request that she feels like she has some sort of moral high ground in the matter."

"How so?"

"She seems to think that by playing this prank, she'll be teaching her mother-in-law a lesson and forcing her to be wary of her in the future or something like that."

Gabe still looked perplexed.

Ellie put her sandwich away for when she was hungry later, as she knew she would be eventually. She waved a hand. "It's all *Mean Girls* stuff. Adult level. With dysfunctional, family-by-marriage dynamics and an apparently clueless husband slash son thrown in."

"Ah. Well," Gabe said finally, as if thinking that on that level at least he was way out of his league. "You have a little time," he advised kindly. "Maybe you should talk to your gran, see what she suggests you do."

"I really didn't want to bother her about this." Especially since her grandmother seemed so happy with her new life at Laramie Gardens.

"I can understand that," Gabe said with brotherly concern. "But Eleanor is probably going to hear about it sooner or later anyway, and better it come from you. Besides, she ran the bakery for over forty years. Maybe she's come across a situation like this before and found a way out."

The two of them gathered their trash and stood.

Gabe regarded Ellie seriously. "Certainly it couldn't hurt to ask if your grandmother has any ideas about the best way to prevent a lawsuit and keep this out of out of the newspapers, as well."

* * *

Ellie had just taken Scout back to the apartment when her cell pinged with a FaceTime request. Seeing who it was, she let out a big sigh of relief and answered the call. "Joe!"

He looked tired and filthy from head to toe. He hadn't shaved since he had left Laramie earlier in the week, and he had a big scratch on the lower side of his face. Which was, she knew, typical for a soldier coming back from some sort of training exercise out in the field.

"Hey, darlin'!" A smile as big as Texas split his wind-burned face. "How's it going?"

This was the part where she usually fibbed and told him everything was just fine, so he wouldn't worry about her or be distracted by her problems. Today, she just couldn't do it.

Without warning, everything that had happened that day came spilling out.

Joe shook his head and scowled. "Monica Townsend is a piece of work."

"I know."

"But Gabe is right. You should share this with your gran. She'll have some thoughts about what you should do."

Ellie nodded. She knew that, too. She was just dreading it because it seemed like yet another sign she wasn't meant to run the bakery on her own.

Joe's expression softened. "Baby okay?"

Ellie's hand fell to her abdomen. There was no way to tell, really, since she hadn't felt the baby move yet. But there was nothing wrong, either, so... "Yes." She drew on the happiness she felt about the fact they were having a baby together and smiled.

His gaze scanned her lovingly. "What about you, sweetheart? How is the heartburn and morning sickness?"

"A little better actually," she was able to say honestly.

"Then why are you looking so down?" he asked gently.

Because I miss you, she thought. *And I wonder how I'm going to manage all this without you by my side. Or go through another Christmas and perhaps the birth of our baby without you, too.*

Unable to say that, however, she turned to the first excuse that came to mind. "Your parents are really pushing for us to have some sort of big party to celebrate our marriage as soon as you do come home again. So was Gran the last time I talked to her."

Joe paused, his expression maddeningly inscrutable. "You don't want a wedding reception?"

Given the rushed way they'd gotten hitched, it seemed like a reception would be tempting fate in some weird way. As if they would be pretending their union was more than a legal maneuver meant to give Joe all the paternal rights he deserved under Texas law.

Ellie hitched in a breath. Not sure yet how she was supposed to act now—as a new bride? Or as if nothing of import had changed between them? "Do you?"

He remained motionless. Behind him, there was a sharp rap. Another soldier came into view. "Better get cleaned up," the man advised gruffly. "The CO wants to see you in fifteen."

Joe nodded and turned back to her, his expression etched with purpose and regret.

"I know, you have to go," she said.

"We'll talk later," he promised.

The call ended.

And once again, Ellie was alone in Laramie, Texas, miles from the man she loved. Left to deal with both their families and prepare for the birth of their baby on her own.

Chapter Seven

"So you're married," Joe's commanding officer remarked as the meeting commenced.

Joe settled in the seat indicated. "Yes, sir."

Major Jax Wilson's brow arched. Happily married and the father of four himself, he was understanding of familial responsibility. "Shotgun wedding?"

A roundabout way of asking if Ellie was pregnant. Joe toned down the joy he felt bubbling up whenever he thought about *their* child. He kept his expression military-inscrutable. "We're expecting a baby, yes."

Rocking back in his desk chair, the major steepled his fingers. He continued to study Joe. "Was that the only reason you married her?"

Another tough question, but Joe understood why his superior officer was asking. A lot of people in the military married on the fly when on leave only to quickly regret it. And that regret led to all sorts of difficulties that could impact a soldier's ability to do their job. "I love Ellie, and I'm happy about the pregnancy, unexpected as it is."

The major's glance narrowed. "Which doesn't answer the question."

Joe knew that. But talking about the fact that he and Ellie had had no desire to marry until now, when they had been pushed into it for legal reasons, would mean answering more questions about their relationship than he cared to. Inhaling sharply, he finally said, "I want to take care of them to the best of my ability. That means marriage. Ellie and I both realized that."

The CO's unflinching expression hardened even more. "So she was the one being pushed into legalizing your relationship?" he guessed correctly.

More so than him, yeah. Unwilling to admit that, Joe remained silent for a long moment, then said finally, "I don't think we would have chosen to get married this way, but it was the right thing to do. And I don't regret that for one moment. Nor does Ellie."

At least he hoped she didn't. She had seemed stressed and unhappy when he talked to her earlier. But that was mostly about the bakery and Monica Townsend's antics, wasn't it?

His expression serious, the major asked, "So how does this change your plans to reenlist in two months for another tour of duty?"

Another question Joe didn't quite know how to answer. He kept his back ramrod straight. "I was planning to do that."

"But…?"

"Word is we are going to be deployed overseas again, in November."

"Word is correct. Can't tell you where yet, but you won't be able to come back for the birth of your baby if you go."

A litany of swear words went through Joe's mind. He had never minded being deployed before. Now the idea was every bit as unappealing as leaving his teammates shorthanded in what could end up being a very dangerous mission.

"You've honored your commitment and served your country well, McCabe. I'll understand if you want to be with your family now." His commanding officer paused. "I just want to make sure you've thought it through. That you know just what you will be giving up, if you decide to leave."

The lifelong military career he had pictured for himself.

"I also want you to understand what we expect of you if you decide to re-up. One hundred percent of you, one hundred percent of the time. No whining about all you're missing stateside."

Self-pity was the fastest way to get himself or his fellow team members killed, Joe knew. "Understood, sir."

"And then there's the matter of your promotion to captain and team lead. That will happen if you reenlist."

Which was something else Joe had worked hard for.

A long silence fell.

"So what're you thinking?" his CO asked finally. "Are you leaning one way or another?"

"Honestly, sir," Joe admitted reluctantly, acutely aware of just how torn he was, "I don't have a clue right now."

Was there a way he could remain in the Special Forces and still keep the promise he had made to Ellie, to be there for the birth of their child *and* Christmas this year?

Right now, it didn't seem so. And even if he managed to work around the orders he was about to receive, how would she feel when he left again? Was it time for him to move on, career-wise? Would he regret it if he did?

Joe looked his CO in the eye. "I wish I did."

Major Wilson exhaled in disappointment. Brusquely, he said, "Then there's only one thing you can do."

"Hi, Nora!" Ellie greeted the energetic sixty-year-old nursing supervisor. A former military nurse, she had worked at Laramie Gardens for the last three decades.

"How is Gran doing today?" Ellie was hoping to talk to her before dinner was served at six.

"Busy. By the way, I wanted to congratulate you on your marriage to Joe McCabe. And the baby you two have on the way."

"Thanks." To her surprise, Ellie was starting to get used to the idea that the two of them were now husband and wife with a little one on the way.

"Will Joe be staying in the service? Or coming home to stay?" Like Nora's Special Forces husband, Zane Lockhart, had after they married.

"Um. Staying, I think."

"Are you okay with that?"

"I knew Joe was a lifer when I first got involved with him a dozen years ago. So…" Ellie didn't know what else to say.

Nora accompanied Ellie down the hall toward the wing that housed Gran and her friends. To her surprise, Ellie saw Dr. Claire Lowell, the community's newest cardiologist, coming out of her gran's room, medical bag in hand. Shock went through Ellie. She turned to Nora. "Is everything okay?"

For a moment, the nursing supervisor stood there, seemingly also at a loss. Then she shook her head and said, "Yes. Of course. We would have called you if it weren't."

Ellie hurried down the hall just as Gran stepped out of her room, looking pretty and chipper as could be.

"Darling! What a surprise?" Gran wrapped her in a hug. "You remember Dr. Claire?"

Dr. Lowell took in Ellie's anxiety. "I just stopped in to say hello while I was here, checking on another patient," she explained.

"That's the only reason?" Ellie persisted. Something seemed amiss.

Gran beamed. "Well, Dr. Claire did want to know if I thought the bakery could come up with a heart-healthy line of goodies that would taste as good as our usual butter-rich treats."

"That's a tough one," Ellie admitted with a wry grin. "Although whoever does top that challenge will be wealthy beyond their wildest dreams."

Everyone laughed.

Gran gave Dr. Lowell a meaningful look. "I'll think on what you said," she promised.

Dr. Lowell sobered. "I hope you do."

"And in the meantime," Gran continued, "maybe Ellie could send over some special treats for you and your toddlers to enjoy."

Dr. Lowell smiled. "We'd love that." She walked off with Nora.

Ellie looked at Gran. It was now or never. And she really needed the help. "Can we talk?" she asked.

Minutes later, Ellie had updated her grandmother on Monica's latest ploy and the subsequent conversation with Gabe. "She also said you had once baked a special cherry crumb pie for another customer."

"That was years ago, and he and his wife were friends. I don't think I even charged them for it. But I did do it in the bakery kitchen." Gran frowned. "That complicates things, I suppose."

"Not to worry, Gran. Gabe didn't think that would be a deciding factor if Monica decides to actually file her lawsuit. I'm still hoping she won't."

Eleanor's eyes were knowing. "Well, either way, darling, it'll be fine. Something like that won't deter our loyal customers in the slightest. In fact, once word gets out, it might increase our business. Since you know how people in this community like to rally round one another."

"That's true." Ellie settled next to Eleanor on the settee beneath the bay window. "I still wonder if maybe you shouldn't talk to Monica yourself. Or help me find another solution."

"Oh, honey, you're doing just fine on your own!" Her grandmother reached for the candy dish on the side table and offered a butterscotch.

Ellie took one and unwrapped it slowly. "It doesn't feel like I am," she said honestly.

Eleanor scooted closer and patted her on the knee. "That's because it's all still so new to you."

Ellie snuggled against her grandmother's vanilla-scented warmth and laid her head on her shoulder. "I just don't want to make a mistake."

Eleanor tucked her into the curve of her arm. "Well, that's unrealistic, sweetheart. We all make mistakes. What is important is learning from them."

Ellie sucked on her butterscotch, considering. She supposed that was true. Except… "I don't recall you or Mom making any when it came to the bakery."

Eleanor's pale blue eyes sparkled. "That's because you were too busy mooning over Joe McCabe to notice."

Ellie rolled her eyes. "Ha, ha."

Gran's expression gentled. "How is your new hubby by the way?"

Way too far away. "Fine." Ellie folded and refolded the wrapper in her hand. "I talked to him earlier."

"When is he coming home again?"

Not soon enough. Not nearly! Ellie shrugged and adapted the casual demeanor of a military wife used to being without her spouse. "Don't know."

An announcement came over the loudspeaker, letting residents know dinner was being served in the dining hall. Ellie got up to walk with her grandmother, their arms linked. Pausing at the entrance to the dining room to say goodbye, a wave of homesickness swept through Ellie. She missed spending time with her gran so much.

"You sure you don't want to help out with the Townsend situation?" Ellie asked.

Her expression suddenly pinched and reluctant, Gran shook her head. For a moment, she looked tired and worn-out, making Ellie feel guilty for even asking. "I retired so I wouldn't have to deal with these kinds of things," Eleanor admitted soberly. "But not to worry." She patted Ellie's arm and smiled. "You've got this."

"Why is it," Ellie asked Scout later that evening as they headed up the stairs to the apartment after their last walk of the day, "that the only time Gran or even Mom ever really had absolute faith in me was when it came to something I really didn't want to do, or even thought I couldn't do, for that matter?"

Scout wagged her short tail. Head cocked, she listened intently, loving their heart-to-heart girl talk as always.

At the top of the stairs, Ellie paused to pick the Westie up and cuddle her in her arms. She buried her face in Scout's silky white fur, breathing in her sweet doggy essence, then looked her in the eye. "Like the time I had to give that speech to the PTA about the importance of extracurricular activities for the students?" She'd been terrified to stand up in front of so many people. "Or the time I entered my first original recipe in the bake-off at the county fair?" She came in dead last in the junior chef category.

"But when I needed them to believe in me, to really think I could do something that scared me—like elope with Joe at eighteen—they had zero faith in me and my ability to be a competent wife to a soldier."

"Probably had something to do with our ages," a low voice said. Joe swung open the apartment door. "And the fact we were barely out of high school. And way too sheltered."

Not sure she could believe her eyes, Ellie splayed a hand across her chest. *"Joe!"* she whispered.

Scout let out a happy bark.

If it was a dream, it was a happy one! Ellie stepped into his waiting arms. "What are you doing here?"

He enveloped her in a tender but exuberant hug. "My commanding officer sent me."

Confused, Ellie tilted her chin. "To do what?"

He hesitated. Then said, "He wanted the two of us to have a little time together and get things settled."

"Is your unit being deployed overseas again?" Ellie asked in concern.

His expression suddenly taut and unreadable, Joe said carefully, "There's nothing concrete—no specific dates or locations—right now."

"But anything can happen at any time," Ellie said reluctantly. "And when it does, you don't have a choice. You have to go." She had always accepted that. She would continue to do so, no matter how hard it was.

Because that was what military families did.

Joe nodded. "But let's not talk about that tonight," he said. Escorting her and the madly wagging Scout inside, Joe soon had her backed up against the wall, his hips pressed into hers.

"Now, where were we when I left?" he murmured. His hands came up to cup her shoulders. Engulfing her with the heat and strength of his body, he lowered his head and delivered a breath-stealing hello kiss.

Sensation rippled through her with the force of a Texas windstorm. Her knees wobbled, and she moaned, wanting more. She lifted her arms and encircled them about his broad shoulders.

He kissed her again, shattering what little reservation she had left. Her lips parted beneath the pressure of his as his tongue swept her mouth with sensuous strokes, and she reveled in the unique male flavor of him.

His hands roamed down her body, molding her curves through the fabric of her clothes. It felt so good to be wanted and touched again. To be loved like this. To feel the barriers that a long-distance relationship created coming down again. Her whole body was alive, quivering with sensations unlike any she had ever felt. Desire trembled inside her, and she melted against him.

"Oh, Joe, I want you," she gasped. "So much..."

"I want you, too, darlin'," he whispered, raining kisses down her throat, across her cheek, her lips. He tunneled his hands through her hair, tilting her face up to his. Kissed her with surprising tenderness. A roguish smile tugged at the corners of his sensual lips. "I also...don't want...to rush."

The next thing she knew he had swept her up in his arms and carried her into the bedroom. She had left the covers undone, thinking what did her messiness matter? Joe wasn't here. But he was here now, and she couldn't get enough of him.

"Ah, look," he teased, slowly removing her shirt, then her jeans. "Our bed is all ready for us."

She eased off his shirt, not wanting to admit she hadn't washed their sheets since he left because they still smelled like him. Inhaling the scent of his cologne and soap and the aroma unique to him made her feel a little less lonely. And not quite so adrift.

She ran her palms over his shoulders, loving the satiny smooth skin over the strong muscle. "Wistful thinking on my part, I guess. I always want to be ready for you."

* * *

He slid off her bra and panties. Her whole body was quaking as he let his glance drift sensually over her, taking in the new, maternal curve of her stomach. "Same here. You are so beautiful, so sexy...so...radiant..."

So amazingly radiant, Joe thought.

Her skin was glowing. Healthy color flushed her high, sculpted cheeks. Her honey-blond hair tumbled over her shoulders as if it hadn't seen a brush or comb since morning.

Wanting to remember every second of every homecoming, the way he always did, he stripped off his own clothes and joined her in the rumpled covers on the bed.

He knew the immediate future was uncertain. They should be talking about how the baby had changed everything, what they both wanted out of this hasty marriage and, most of all, what should come next. Because his CO was right. He and Ellie couldn't keep drifting from one reenlistment period to the next. He had to commit himself one way or another to what came first in his life. The military. Or Ellie and their baby and life here in Laramie.

He knew what *he* wanted. To jump forward to the days when he and Ellie and their child never, ever had to endure long separations again. For him, like it or not, their baby had made him reevaluate his life plan.

But so far, Ellie didn't seem to be feeling the same shift in priorities. Whether that would change as her pregnancy progressed, he did not know. He was willing to give her time to figure it all out, just as he was planning to do over the course of the next thirty days.

Meanwhile, they had this, he thought, as he slid down her body, letting his mouth move feverishly over her breasts. She quivered in response, softly calling his name. Her desperate entreaty filled him with pleasure. He kissed the rounded slope of her stomach, stroked the insides of her thighs. Traced her navel with his tongue and then moved lower still to deliver the most intimate of kisses. Again and again, until she was as awash in pleasure as he wanted her to be, shuddering with her need.

Achingly aware of every soft, warm inch of her, Joe rolled onto his back. He brought her on top of him, and she straddled his hips. Easing down on him ever so slowly, taking him all in, she rode him gently until they found their perfect rhythm.

Giving. Taking. And giving some more. Until there was no doubting how much they needed each other, needed *this*. And then they were both lost in the ecstasy, free-falling into pleasure, unlike anything either of them had ever known.

Long minutes later, they remained in bed, their bodies tangled intimately together.

"So how long are you going to be here?" Ellie asked, loving the safety and security of being held against him this way.

"I've got thirty days emergency family leave," Joe said.

Ellie paused to take that in. Long weekends together like they'd just had were rare. Monthlong rest periods were even rarer, and only came once a year, if then. And usually after, not before, a deployment.

"Thirty days!" she echoed. Her eyes filled with tears. She ducked her head so Joe wouldn't see just how overcome she was. She had been needing him. Wanting him here with her, so much. She could get used to this. But on the flip side, every time he headed out to go back to his unit, it got harder and harder to pretend she was okay letting him go.

Gazing back at him, she murmured thickly, "Oh, Joe! That's…"

"Long enough for us to figure everything out," he promised, holding her closer.

She sighed with contentment, knowing in her heart of hearts that his CO was right. She and Joe couldn't move forward without having a more viable plan for their future than simply taking things day by day, reenlistment by reenlistment. Now that they were married and having a baby, they had to decide what their future held.

Chapter Eight

The alarm went off way too soon. Wishing Ellie didn't have to get up so early—especially when she was pregnant and clearly exhausted—Joe went in to put a pot of decaf coffee on for her. He had just started to warm the milk when he heard her groan loudly in the bedroom.

"Ellie?" Alarmed, he rushed to her. "What is it?"

She was sitting on the edge of the bed in tears. A pair of jeans was on her lap, and several more were strewn across the bed. She threw up her delicate hands in dismay. "I can't get any of these zipped, that's what!"

"Don't you have any sweats or…yoga pants…or something?" Those had enough stretch in them to fit. And Ellie looked incredibly sexy and feminine in them, to boot. Not that he didn't love her in denim. Or in nothing at all.

Oblivious to the amorous nature of his thoughts, she exhaled in frustration. Her soft lips formed an inviting pout. "Yes, but I can't wear those when the bakery opens for business. As you very well know, our uniform is jeans and pink chef coats."

He settled beside her, gently curving his arm around her shoulders. "I don't think people will care."

"That's not the point!"

He studied the indignant spark in her eyes. "Then what is?"

"I'm the boss now. I have to set an example." She pulled

on the jeans closest to her and drew them up her still slender thighs and over her hips. They were at least an inch from fastening.

With another growl of pure outrage, Ellie stood and pulled on her chef coat over her tank top. It, too, was straining seductively at the seams, especially around her breasts and hips. "I'll just have to hope my top covers the fact I can't get my pants zipped until I can get to a maternity store." She shook her head in aggravation. "Maybe this weekend…"

The problem had to be solved sooner than that. Joe pulled out his phone and did a quick search. "The closest maternity shop is in San Angelo. It opens at ten this morning and doesn't close until nine this evening."

Briefly, she looked hopeful. "I'm not going to have time to do that today."

"Not even after work?"

"Well, normally I could, but today I have to do payroll."

"How long does that take?" he asked.

She lifted her shoulders. "Three hours or so, depending."

He stepped nearer. "For six employees?"

"I have to calculate each person's hours and taxes and so on for the two-week pay period, and then write all the checks."

He inhaled the sweet, floral scent of her perfume. "I thought that stuff was all automated these days."

Twin spots of color emphasized the elegant bones of her cheeks. "It is for a lot of businesses. But my grandmother and mom were never that comfortable with the computer, never mind accounting software."

He narrowed his gaze, struggling to understand her thinking. "But you have an online ordering system for the bakery, right?"

"Yes. The other employees and I all manage that. But we

print out the order and work from a paper copy when we're making the actual cake. And walk-in orders are usually hand-written to begin with."

He paused to carefully measure his words. "I didn't realize that part of the business was so labor-intensive for you."

Ellie shrugged, as if to declare it was what it was. "Anyway, we also had a last-minute order for an anniversary cake for two hundred people come in last night. They need it today, and they were willing to pay the rush fee of an extra eighteen percent, so I'm going to be helping with that as well."

Joe looked back at his phone, still searching for a quick solution. "It says here that you can order clothes online and pick them up in the store or have them shipped. If you tell me what you want, I'll go pick it up for you."

Ellie sipped her decaf latte. He could tell by the way she was looking at him that the independent side of her wanted to decline his assistance. Finally, she said, "You wouldn't mind?"

He wrapped his arms around her and brought her in close for a hug. He pressed a kiss to the top of her head, glad she was letting him play the role of a doting husband, at least for today. "Darlin', it's the least I can do."

To Joe's relief, Ellie took him up on his offer. She ordered a pair of maternity jeans and a pair of black pants, insisting she pay for them herself. When she went down to the bakery to get started with the day, Joe took care of Scout. At around 9:15 a.m., he headed toward San Angelo.

As he drove, he thought about what life would be like if he were to live in Laramie permanently. Money wasn't going to be a problem. He had savings from his years in the military and the trust his parents had given him, which he had always planned to use to underwrite his next venture. He knew he would be happy if he could make his dream come true of building something of his own…something that would help the community. He wasn't sure Ellie would be on board with it, though. She might think it was all too much of a risk.

Which was why he had to get it all worked out before he told her. Then he would hope she would be as supportive as he was going to need her to be.

"I'm happy you stopped by," Chase told Joe when he walked into the executive suite at McCabe Industries at noon.

The corporation his dad had spent the last forty-five years building included McCabe Fine Leather Goods, Martin Custom Saddle—his mom's family company—as well as two dozen other manufacturing organizations scattered across the Southwest. The two initial companies, however, were located here in Laramie County, as was Chase's executive office that oversaw it all.

"I wanted to get some business advice," Joe said.

"For yourself?"

Yes. Eventually, probably. "For Ellie." Joe went on to explain Ellie's situation.

"I'm happy to help her in any way I can," his dad said when Joe had finished. "But I can't just barge in."

"I know. I'm planning to talk to her first."

Chase nodded. "Let me know how it turns out. In the meantime, have you given any thought to coming to work for me when you do leave your soldier days behind?"

Joe hated to hurt his dad's feelings. "Sorry, Dad. I really respect everything you've built, all the failing manufacturing businesses you have saved, but I can't see myself being happy taking over for you."

Chase rocked back in his chair. Hands clasped behind his head, he exhaled. "I figured. With Gabe going into law, Zach medicine and Alex ranching, you were kind of my last hope."

"Don't forget Sadie. She's got one heck of a business acumen, from what I've seen."

"True. Unfortunately, all her energies are directed toward starting a lavender ranch. And now that the land she's had her eye on is coming up for sale soon, I'm afraid that ship has likely sailed, too."

Joe settled comfortably in his seat. "You worried about retiring? What'll happen then?"

"No. That's still a few years off." Chase turned reflective. "I had just hoped to have family taking over for me when I do leave, is all."

Joe nodded. "Understood."

He had his own dreams with uncertain endings. He wanted to forget reenlisting and build a life here, in Laramie, even if doing so put him a few years ahead of schedule. That way he could be here for Ellie and their baby. See that they wanted for nothing. They would always have him around to offer love and support, and he could accept theirs in return.

But he also knew it might all be too much for his wife. She was used to being independent and had only married him for legal reasons. Would she really want him around twenty-four-seven?

"But," his dad continued, matter-of-fact as always, "if it's not meant to be for you to come back now and work for the family company, then so be it."

It might actually be time for Joe to come back and do something else. Something that would financially support his family. Help others. And challenge and engage him.

That night, Ellie barely made it through dinner before tumbling into bed at 8:30. Joe held her close until she fell asleep, then got back up and went into the dining area to do a little research online.

He knew he was going to have to be competitive to make his venture a success. Wanting to know what similar facilities offered, he researched everything in Texas, making detailed notes of all he found. And then he went beyond that, to the top ten organizations in the country. What he discovered was illuminating. There was a lot involved to build something state-of-the-art. But it was something he could definitely do, if he used his trust fund and the wages he had saved.

The only problem was the timetable. He had the feeling Ellie would not like a work-in-progress that went on too long. He sensed that she would see it all as too much of a gamble and feel stressed. Which was why he had to get all his ducks in a row first.

Still, reassured that he was on the right path, he worked a little more, then climbed into bed at two in the morning. This time, when the alarm went off at four, he was the one who was bleary-eyed.

She handed him a cup of coffee when he came back into the apartment with Scout. "What would you think about the two of us going clothes shopping tonight after work?" she asked with a flirtatious batting of her eyelashes.

He hunkered down to unhook the leash from Scout's collar. Standing, he quipped, "You know it's my favorite thing in all the world, darlin'."

She wrinkled her nose at his teasing tone. "I know." She sighed. "My need for more maternity clothes isn't really the kind of thing you came home to handle during your emergency family leave. And I don't want you to be bored with me, or life here, so if it really is out of your realm, especially after you already drove to San Angelo once to pick up a few things for me, then…"

"Hey!" He cut her off before she could come up with more

reasons for them not to spend time together. "You can't retract an invitation once it's given."

She slipped on the jeans he had picked up for her at the maternity store the previous morning. They hugged her tummy and rounded buttocks in a way he found very enticing. She reached for her pink chef tunic and slid it on over her white tank top. "I can if it doesn't fit my adrenaline-junkie husband."

Whoa. Had she really just called him that? Joe thought, surprised. Her adrenaline-junkie *husband*? Like this was for real, instead of a temporary legal arrangement? She had. More surprising, he did not mind.

"And helping me purchase clothes is not your responsibility," she continued, a little more soberly.

Injecting a little levity back into the situation, he winked. "Actually, unless we want you walk around naked, it kind of is my responsibility to see you have a wardrobe that fits."

She flushed and sauntered back into the tiny galley kitchen. "Ha ha. Very funny."

He chuckled, too. It always amazed him how hard it was for her to ask for even a tiny bit of help. "So. Back to your proposed plan for this evening…"

"Well, it won't be as easy as what you did for me yesterday. This time, I want to actually try the clothes on."

Leaning against the opposite counter, he helped himself to more coffee. "Makes sense."

"I also want to spend as much time as possible with you while you're home."

"Ditto, sweetheart." He set his cup aside and pulled her into his arms, trapping her body against the kitchen counter.

She put her mug of tea aside, too, and splayed her hands across his chest. Gazing up at him hopefully, she asked, "So, what would you think about us leaving here at six when the bakery closes, driving to San Angelo, hitting the maternity store and then having dinner afterward? My treat."

He teased, "Damn, Ellie. You drive a hard bargain."

"Don't I?" She wreathed her arms around his shoulders and delivered a sweet and soulful kiss that he took his time returning. Finally, wistfully, they drew apart. "So what is your answer, soldier?"

He felt her heart beating in tandem with his and smiled. "Sounds good to me."

It had seemed like a good idea this morning, Ellie mused. Now, with Joe trailing close behind her, insisting on holding anything she thought she might want to try on in his strong arms, it felt a little…suffocating.

She always did her serious shopping alone. No distraction. No one else's opinion to consider except her own.

Joe still hadn't offered any advice. But she could tell from the subtle change of expression on his handsome face that he thought she ought to splurge and go with the more expensive, peach silk maternity top and tailored white slacks, or the pretty floral print summer dress with the cap sleeves. Or the sexy black cocktail dress with the low neck and the flounced hem.

And honestly, if he were going to be here to take her out on date nights, she would have thought about getting all three. But he wasn't. And most of her evenings were going to be spent curled up at home with Scout or at Laramie Gardens, visiting Gran. So she forced herself to be practical and concentrate on comfy clothes and pajamas, as well as another pair of jeans to wear to work. A casual summer dress, perfect for running errands. And a classic scarlet wrap dress that could be dressed up or down. And worn even after the baby was born.

"Well, I guess I better try these things on," she said, when she had finished her tour of the big store.

Joe grinned. As he gazed down at her, she knew he wanted to kiss her again.

Worse, she wanted to kiss and hold him, too. Which would be a bad thing right now. Kissing would lead to touching. And touching would lead to more intimate kisses... They'd wish they were somewhere else—somewhere private— where they could take things to their natural conclusion. And while she had no doubt that would be oh so pleasurable, she also knew acting on their ever-escalating need to be intimate as much as possible while they had the chance would circumvent their errand, not to mention dinner afterward.

Smile widening, he waggled his brows mischievously. "Want some help?"

Not, she reminded herself, if they wanted to stay on task. Ignoring the sizzling chemistry arcing between them, she shook her head and disappeared into the dressing room.

"You are so lucky to have your baby daddy here with you," one of the other pregnant women said.

Ellie had noticed the statuesque brunette perusing the racks alone. Most of the other women in the store had a companion—either their mom or husband. But this thirtysomething woman was alone. And from the swell of her belly and the fatigue rimming her amber eyes, clearly nearing her due date.

Ellie smiled, not sure what to say. "Joe's great."

The other woman smiled back. "He seems very involved— in the best way."

He was. Ellie knew—and appreciated that—so much.

"You know," the brunette continued, moving to the mirror at the end of the fitting stalls. "Supportive but not overbearing."

Again, true. At least for now. There were times, however, when Ellie first learned she was pregnant that Joe had been a little too take-charge for her comfort. Pushing that memory aside, Ellie looked at the other mom-to-be. "How is your guy?"

"Long gone." The woman's eyes filled with sadness. She mounted the pedestal in front of the three-way mirror. "He split as soon as we learned I was pregnant."

Compassion filled Ellie's heart. She couldn't imagine how much that would have hurt. She reached out to give the other woman's hand a squeeze. "I'm sorry."

"I'm not." The brunette drew a deep breath and marshaled her strength. "He probably would have made a lousy father." She examined her profile in the mirror, then stepped down off the pedestal. She turned back to Ellie, confident again. "Not to worry, though. I have friends and family who will be there for me. And the baby."

Ellie smiled again. "Glad to hear it."

Apparently satisfied with the way the maternity outfit looked, the other mom-to-be went back into her dressing room. A second later, she popped back out, holding another garment in front of her. "I forgot to ask. When is your baby due?"

"Ah… December." Ellie was still getting used to saying that.

The brunette smiled. "That's about when I found out I was pregnant. I was so excited! That part made the holidays so happy for me. But you! You and your husband are going to be able to welcome your child into the world and celebrate the holidays together!"

They would if Joe got his wish and was able to be there for both. But as Ellie had told Sadie, that wasn't really the way the military worked. Orders came and had to be obeyed.

Oblivious to her thoughts, the brunette held up another

outfit in front of her as she looked in the mirror. "Christmas this year is going to be so nice for you. Are you going to buy presents for the baby?"

"Um." Something else she and Joe were going to have to discuss. "I imagine we will."

"Well, don't tell anyone," the brunette stage-whispered with a smile, "but I've already started buying gifts for my little one."

Ellie understood that temptation. She had already started looking at layettes, dreaming about the day she and Joe would take their baby home from the hospital. Assuming all worked out as they wanted, of course.

"I'm thinking it's easier to shop now, you know, before the baby gets here," the woman went on.

"Absolutely," Ellie agreed.

"But I know I can do this," the brunette said. "Plenty of women do. I just have to be strong."

"And you will be," Ellie reassured her.

"Thank you for saying that." The woman inhaled. "It helps."

She disappeared back inside her dressing room.

Ellie went in to hers to change, too. While she went about trying on the things she had picked out, she couldn't help but think how hard it was going to be when Joe left again. She had friends, too, and plenty of family if she counted all the McCabes as well as Gran.

But none of them could take the place of her husband.

Forty-five minutes later, she and Joe were settled into a booth in a Thai restaurant. "What were you and all those other guys talking about so intently when I came out of the dressing room?" she asked after they had ordered. Beef pan-ang for him, and Thai chicken with basil and ginger for her.

"They were telling me about the birthing classes they were enrolled in with their wives," he said.

"Oh." She suppressed a sigh. That was something else Joe would miss out on, she realized sadly.

He gazed over at her, as protective as ever, and covered her hand with his. "Have you signed up for those?"

Reluctantly, Ellie admitted, "When I had my first OB appointment."

His brow furrowed. He let go of her hand and sat back. "You didn't mention it."

Regret swept through her. "You were back in Colorado, out on training maneuvers."

He looked hurt. The muscles in his jaw flexed. "I still would have figured you'd tell me about it."

Her guilt over her lapse increased. She hadn't meant to shut him out. She'd just been trying to be as independent as always. So he would know that even though they were temporarily legally married with a baby on the way, nothing really had to change.

She drew a bolstering breath. "I had planned to, but our first conversation when you got back from maneuvers was so short, because your CO wanted to see you right away. And then the next thing I knew, you were back here in Texas, and we got caught up in making love and being together again. And then I had to do payroll, and…"

Joe gave her another long, assessing look. "Speaking of payroll." He was all business now. "I spoke to my dad. He told me that getting set up on an automated system is not all that expensive and will save you a lot of time, effort and headache in the long run." He paused, giving it a moment to sink in. "He offered to have his payroll person come over and help you."

"I'm not sure…"

Undeterred, he continued persuasively, "It would only take a few hours to set up. Then everything would be automated for you."

The server set their plates down in front of them. "I don't think Gran would like that," Ellie said.

"Gran isn't running the business. *You* are. And she gave you carte blanche."

Ellie spread her napkin across her lap. She picked up her fork. "I don't know. It just doesn't seem like a good idea."

"Because it was my idea?" he chided her in exasperation. After taking a bite of curried beef and jasmine rice, he added, "Or because it involves change?" He speared a red pepper slice and green bean. "Which you hate?"

There he went. All take-charge, problem-solver extraordinaire. Ellie stared at him, mutinous, her appetite all but gone. "I wasn't aware any of this was your problem."

He seemed caught up short. "Sorry," he told her brusquely. "You're right. I shouldn't be commenting or going behind your back to find solutions for your business problems."

Suddenly, Ellie felt near tears. Those darn pregnancy hormones. She swallowed hard around the rising knot of emotion in her throat. "Then why did you?"

"I was just thinking ahead."

"To?"

"When you're busy with the baby and the business. And your employees still need to get paid."

That *would* be a lot. Damn it, she hated it when he was right. Sighing, she asked, "Did this payroll person agree to help, or are they just being drafted?"

Joe smiled. "It's Tom Ryan, and he agreed. He said he could come over tomorrow and get you all set up."

"All right." Ellie reached across the table to take Joe's

hand again. It felt as warm and reassuring as his strong and steady presence. "Set it up and thank him, and your dad, too."

Joe's regard turned even more tender. "No problem. So back to those birthing classes… When is the first one?"

She didn't even have to look at her calendar to know. The date was engraved in her memory. "Tuesday evening, next week."

"Then I'll go with you."

Something else to feel guilty about. She glanced at him hesitantly. "Um, actually, I'm not sure that is possible."

He tensed. "Why not?"

Wishing their situation were a lot more traditional and that Joe could be there for her and their baby every single step of the way, Ellie took a deep breath. "I need emergency backup in case something happens and you get deployed or you simply can't get here from Colorado in time for the birth. I asked Sadie to attend all the birthing classes with me. So she—we—will both know what to do."

He nodded, accepting her logic. He still looked as if he felt left out, and she could hardly blame him.

"I had no idea you would get an emergency thirty-day family leave to figure things out," she said. "Otherwise, I certainly would have scheduled the first obstetrics appointment to include you." As far as the birthing classes went, though, that was a much trickier situation to navigate.

"What about your next doctor's appointment?"

Ellie sighed. "It's not for another four and a half weeks. That's when they're going to do my next ultrasound." She pulled up her calendar on her phone. "Here it is. August 14, 4:00 p.m."

He grimaced. "Which is the day after I'm supposed to report back to Fort Carson."

Briefly, Ellie felt as disappointed as he looked. For a moment something flickered in his expression, then disappeared. "Is Sadie going to attend that, too?"

Ellie nodded. "She was, but... I'll call the doctor tomorrow and see if we can't move the ultrasound up a few days so you can go with me."

"That would be great, thanks," Joe said, entwining his fingers more intimately with hers.

She relaxed into his grip as the mood between them lightened once again. Gently, she reminded him, "You are the baby daddy, after all."

"Baby daddy." Flashing a crooked smile, he leaned across the table to kiss her. "A*nd* longtime lover and now husband."

Temporary husband, she reminded herself as she leaned into their sweet kiss. She had to remain as practical and matter-of-fact as their unexpected situation required her to be. Because unbeknownst to their family and friends, their deal had not changed. No matter how much she was beginning to secretly wish that it would.

Chapter Nine

"Thanks for coming out to help," Alex told Joe the next morning.

A section of pasture fence had gotten knocked down. The cattle had found it overnight and scattered. Joe's brothers and the cowboys who worked for Alex were all out on horseback, rounding them up one by one.

There to do the same, Joe tightened the cinch on his saddle. "This your idea or Dad's?"

Alex grinned and climbed up onto his horse. "He thought I might sell you on the idea of running cattle on the Knotty Pine again, at least for a few years. There's room for more than the ones I have running there now, you know. Plus, me or some of my men would always be nearby to show you the finer points of cattle ranching."

Joe swung himself up into the saddle with the expertise he'd learned as a kid. "Yeah, well, that's not going to happen." He slid his boots through the stirrups.

Alex gripped the reins and took off at a lazy clip. "Don't see yourself a cowboy, hmm?"

Joe kept pace with his brother. "Not full time. No." He slanted the brim of his Stetson a little lower across his brow, shutting out the brilliance of the morning sun. "Although I don't mind occasionally lending a hand when you need one," he confessed.

"Good to know." Alex flashed him a grateful smile. Spying a mama cow and her calf, he turned his horse in their direction and picked up the pace.

When they were riding side by side again, Joe asked, "Did you go to birthing classes with your ex?"

Alex got on one side of the mama and baby, and Joe on the other. Together, they steered the pair back in the direction they wanted them to go. "Yep."

"Do you think I'd be missing out on a lot if I weren't here to take the instruction with Ellie?"

Alex gave him a look that said he knew what Joe was really asking. Would it be a mistake to re-up the way Ellie expected him to and miss out on pretty much everything about their baby's early years? Let her handle it as independently and single-mindedly as she handled everything else?

But wouldn't that also be letting her shut him out—even if that wasn't her intention?

"You'd probably be missing out on some important stuff, not going to those classes with her. But if you're not going to be here when Ellie gives birth, I don't know that it matters. Why?" Alex herded a few more strays while Joe kept track of the two they already had. When all four cattle were in a single group, Alex prodded, "Are you thinking about letting your current tour be the end of your military service?"

Why did everyone keep looking at him so skeptically, asking him that? Joe knew what he wanted to do, if he could get it all worked out in time. He also knew that Ellie wasn't exactly begging him to stay. More like, she still had one foot out the door, the way she always had since their botched elopement years ago.

Ignoring his brother's question, Joe said instead, "What about the actual labor and delivery? Did the classes help you and Tiffany with that?"

Matt frowned. "Yes and no. I was able to keep my ex-wife calm during early labor. But because she was having quadruplets, we also knew a C-section was going to be necessary. So in the end, I was relegated to standing on the sidelines, keeping her calm, while the four teams brought the babies into the world. So it was pretty chaotic, to say the least."

Joe imagined it had been.

"But you're just having one kid, so Ellie will probably have a natural birth, and she will want someone with her. Sadie, if you're not there."

Joe and Alex added a fifth heifer to the herd. "What about after the quadruplets were born?" Joe asked. "Did the babies need you specifically, or would any caring, decent person have done the job?"

Alex shrugged. "I'd like to think I was irreplaceable, that I was their daddy to them from the start. Especially because Tiffany, as you know, was never all that maternal. Plus, because she didn't have enough milk to feed all four boys, we were exclusively bottle-feeding all of them. Which meant they associated me with food and diaper changing and holding them and all that. So I guess you could say we were bonded pretty tight from the very beginning."

Joe respected all his brother had done. "And you were able to do all that *and* work the ranch?"

Alex nodded. "I had hired hands by then, so they picked up the slack for me, and I paid them overtime. Sadie and Mom came over to help with the kids until they were sleeping through the night and could eat some solid food." Misinterpreting the real reason behind Joe's worry, he flashed him a reassuring smile. "I'm sure they would do the same with your son or daughter and give Ellie whatever help she needs for as long as she wants. So if you need to keep on doing what you're doing in the military, you can rest assured, Ellie and the baby will be okay."

Joe believed that. But did he *need* to keep on with what he was doing? Being promoted to lead a Special Forces unit for the first time would be both an honor and a challenge. Since his group specialized in extraction, there was no doubt he'd be saving lives. But he would be risking his own, too. Would it be worth it if something happened, and his child had to grow up without a dad? Was it okay to even be thinking like that? The risks associated with his military service had never entered into his decision-making before. It had never kept him from giving one hundred percent of himself to whatever task was required.

Interrupting Joe's thoughts, Alex said, "You want my advice?"

"Yeah. Very much."

"Go to those classes while you're here. Even if Sadie goes, too. Also, get some books and read up on the birth process and newborn childcare as much as you can. You can give Ellie the emotional support she needs, even if you aren't here physically all the time, and when you are here, you'll know what to do."

Joe nodded, listening.

Alex's gaze narrowed. "As far as cattle ranching goes, I think Dad already knows it's not for you. But something else might be."

How right his brother was about that, Joe thought, feeling a little less torn than he had been.

"And thanks to the trust funds Dad set up for all of us kids, you've got a considerable nest egg to help get you started in whatever post-military career you might decide to pursue."

A contemplative silence fell.

Finally, Alex slanted him another empathetic glance.

"Bottom line? You have to do what is going to make you *and* Ellie happy. She is a strong woman from a line of strong women. She will handle whatever life hands her, which is why you two have done so well the past twelve years. She understands you both have to be who you are, and you can still come together and love each other. Even after long stretches apart. And that, bro," Alex concluded with admiration, "is a fact that makes you one lucky couple."

Feeling less stressed out than she had in what seemed like forever, Ellie met Joe at the door with a big kiss and a hug. Still holding on to him, she drew him all the way inside. "Oh, Joe! You were so right!"

He was dusty and sweaty from a day spent working cattle at Alex's ranch. She didn't care. She was happy to see him. Happier still that they had the entire evening ahead of them.

He toed off his boots and left them next to the door. Sunburn covered his ruggedly chiseled cheeks and the bridge of his nose. He studied her as if he found her as endlessly fascinating as she found him, then prodded her with a lift of his dark brow. "Right about what?"

She squared her shoulders. "The payroll system! Tom came over to the bakery this afternoon and helped me set it all up. It was *so* much easier than I ever imagined!" And every bit as liberating as her husband had promised her it would be.

Stripping off his denim shirt, Joe flashed her a smile. "I'm glad."

Ellie followed him around, admiring the view of his wide shoulders and muscled chest. "Now it'll take me less than thirty minutes to do payroll every two weeks, instead of several hours," she informed him with relief. "The state and federal taxes are all being calculated and paid automatically, too. So I won't have to worry about that, either!"

"Sounds great." He shoved his filthy shirt in the empty stackable washer. His pants, T-shirt and socks followed.

Enjoying the mouthwatering sight of him in just his briefs, Ellie went to the fridge and got him a cold beer. She opened it and handed it over. "I sent Tom home with a dozen cupcakes for his wife and kids, but I need to do something nice for your dad, too. As a thank-you."

Joe guzzled the icy cold beer. "I'm sure he would appreciate cupcakes, too."

"What's his favorite?"

"Dad likes them all." Amusement glimmered in his blue eyes. His gaze drifted over her, taking in her pretty cotton blouse, maternity jeans and bare feet as if he were already mentally making love to her. His smile widened. "If you want to hedge your bets, you could send a variety."

"Good idea. I'll get on it tomorrow morning."

Trying not to think how cozy and domestic this all felt, never mind how much she secretly would like the situation to continue, Ellie asked, "Are you hungry?"

"Starved." He paused, looking longingly at the dinner ingredients spread over the apartment's tiny counter space and compact four-burner stove. "Do I have time to get cleaned up?"

She could only imagine how badly he wanted to get rid of the grime and sweat. "Yes. The potatoes are in the oven. I'll wait to cook the steaks until you're out of the shower. And I still have to finish making the salad. So…" Her heart racing, she gave him one last lingering look. "Take your time."

"Thanks." He kissed her again and headed into the bathroom.

Ellie waited until the water started and she heard the curtain pulled across the rod. Then, feeling bolder than she had in a long time, she stripped down and went in to surprise her man.

Joe had just finished lathering up when the bathroom door opened, and a beautifully naked Ellie joined him in the shower. Like everything else in the historic building's apartment, the tiled enclosure was just barely big enough for two.

Not that it mattered, with Ellie pressed up against him. Her breasts were fuller from the pregnancy, ripe and luscious. As was the rest of her.

This was the *old* Ellie—the recklessly romantic woman he had fallen in love with and adored all these years. Sexy, exciting, fun. Living happily in the moment. Keeping him there, too.

"Hey," he said, glad to have her join him. He bent to kiss her throat.

"Thought you might need some help washing up," she murmured.

He handed her the bar of soap and watched, his body hardening, as she lathered her palms and then spread the suds over his shoulders and chest and finally down to his burgeoning arousal. He groaned as her fingers trailed delicately over the length of him, making him even harder. He rocked into her tantalizing touch, loving the feel of her seductive ministrations. Closing his eyes, he pressed a kiss against her temple and felt her shudder in response.

"Just remember what comes around goes around," he growled.

Her eyes glinted with devilry. "Mmm, soldier." The corners of her mouth quirked upward. "I like the sound of that." She took the handheld sprayer from the wall mount and rinsed his shoulders, back and chest with such deliberate precision he was driven wild with the same desire that shone in her smile.

"I bet you do," he said as she pressed in close. The warm abundance of her breasts rubbed against his chest. He cupped her mounds in his palms, then laved the tender pink tips with his tongue. She writhed in pleasure.

Long moments later, he took the handheld nozzle from her and put it back on the wall. He picked up the bottle of lavender liquid soap he knew she favored and, appreciating the way she quivered when he touched her, he moved his hands from her hips, across her ribs and...lower. She gasped as his sudsy hands dropped to the apex of her legs. As she arched against him, he found her, *there*. He stroked her intimately before rinsing her with the same sexy languor she had done for him.

Her face lifted to his.

He set the showerhead in the overhead cradle, so the warm water sprayed gently over both of them. She gave him a soft smile, her gaze sliding over his features, before lingering on his mouth a beat too long. That was all it took for him to know that playtime was over, for both of them.

He wanted her as much as she wanted him.

"Oh, Joe," she whimpered, wreathing her arms about his neck, bringing him even closer.

"I know, darlin'..." He moved her against the tile wall, trapping her in place. They came together with shuddering impact. Her eyes were dark with passion, her fingers tangled in his damp hair. She moaned as she wrapped her legs around his hips and kissed him with a slow, ardent precision that told him just how much he meant to her. He settled in as she opened for him, pressing closer still. The water sluiced over top of them as he claimed her with everything he had.

His body throbbed, and she clung to him even tighter, her nipples taut and hot against his chest. Fire swept through him, turning him inside out. Making the intimate connection all the sweeter.

She had been his from the very first time they had kissed. And he had been hers. The years of distance and reunion had only sweetened their need for each other.

But this was different.

Maybe it was the fact they were married. Or the fact they were having a baby. All he knew was that he couldn't imagine his life without her—or their child, Joe thought, as their passion soared and sent them hurtling into oblivion.

And that wasn't going to change.

No matter what their future held.

"So how did the rest of the Sugar Love staff take the payroll change?" Joe asked over dinner an hour later. He had helped make the meal, cooking the steaks in a cast iron skillet while she fixed a salad.

Her blond hair still adorably damp from their shower, Ellie paused, as if savoring the tartly dressed romaine. "They were really happy." She shifted in her chair, her knees brushing his beneath the kitchen table. "And surprised, I guess."

Because they knew their new boss did not like change any more than her mother and grandmother had, he reflected silently, at least when it came to the family business. He noted the troubled expression on her face. "You worried about telling your grandmother?"

Ellie added butter and salt to her baked potato, then said, "No. I'm sure Gran will be fine with it since she gave me autonomy to run things as I see fit. Especially when I show her how easy it's all going to be for me from here on out."

Gently, he ran his thumb across her lower lip. "Then why the frown?"

"Well, I had the sense that now the door has been opened

to altering something about how the business is run, the staff would like to see other changes made as well."

Joe polished off his last bite of steak. "Like what?"

"I didn't ask." Sighing, Ellie went back to fiddling with her potato.

"Why not?"

"Because there's enough going on right now."

Ignoring a potential problem never made it go away. But he figured Ellie was right about one thing—she had enough on her plate at the moment without inviting further tumult into her life.

Her mood brightened. "How did the cattle herding go with Alex?" she asked.

"Good. We were able to find the last few strays while his hired hands moved the rest of the cattle and repaired the broken fence." Plus, he'd gotten good advice from his previously married sibling. Who was also a great dad to his boys, the way their own dad had been to them.

The silence stretched between them.

She looked at him from beneath the fringe of thick honey-gold lashes. "Didn't want to make you want to be a cowboy in your next life, though?"

It was a light, teasing question. Meant to give him an opening into discussing what his plans might eventually include, once he ended his military service.

He'd like to tell her. Would, if he thought she would take it well. Unfortunately, he knew that the turmoil of trying to start something from scratch and the uncertainty of half-baked plans would just stress her out. She had enough stress, managing Sugar Love, looking in on her gran and taking care of herself and the baby.

"No," he quipped honestly, smiling at her. "No riding the range for me. So how about some dessert?"

She pushed her empty plate aside, admitting wistfully, "I wouldn't mind some butter pecan ice cream."

Wanting to do everything he could for her, to make her life easier, he grabbed their dishes before she could help and deposited them in the sink. With a wink, he promised, "Coming right up."

She propped her elbow on the table and rested her chin on her fist while he got the ice cream out of the freezer.

"By the way," he asked. "Did you see our joint invitation from your grandmother for lunch tomorrow at Laramie Gardens?"

Ellie nodded, her expression sober once again. "I did. Are you going to be able to make it?"

Joe scooped ice cream into two dishes. "Sure. Any idea what this is about?"

Ellie shook her head as he settled opposite her. "Just that it must be serious. Otherwise, she would never ask us to come at noon in the middle of a work week."

Chapter Ten

"So what's up?" Ellie asked Gran. She and Joe had met her in her room a few minutes before they were due in the Laramie Gardens dining hall for lunch.

Gran gestured for them to take a seat on the sofa, next to the bay window.

Joe settled next to his wife. He gazed at his grandmother-in-law, waiting. He knew the elegant former businesswoman well enough to realize she was on a mission that he and Ellie might not like.

Eleanor folded her hands on her lap. "I want Joe to talk to Nora's husband, who also used to be part of the Special Forces."

This, Joe hadn't expected. He squinted. "That was a while ago, wasn't it?" Zane Lockhart was in his early sixties.

Eleanor nodded. "Yes. That was thirty years ago. He was about Joe's age now when he left the military and moved here to be with Nora and her infant son. Like the two of you, they'd had a long-term relationship but never married until he settled down in Laramie and started his own very successful business."

"Lockhart Search and Rescue."

Eleanor's smile spread. "You know it!"

Of course he did. They trained the fire and rescue crews from all over Texas, as well as deployed for emergencies near and far. "They're the team to call when people need help," Joe said. Working for them was an adrenaline junkie's dream—if a person didn't mind being on call twenty-four-seven and away from family whenever and wherever duty called. Which was something Zane's wife, Nora, and their now grown three children understood.

Eleanor beamed. "His organization employs a lot of ex-soldiers like yourself. So—" she leaned forward urgently "—I was thinking…"

"Gran!" Ellie chided. "You really have to stop pressuring Joe!"

Funny, Joe didn't *feel* backed into a corner by the suggestion. But his wife clearly did.

She continued in the temperamental tone he knew so well, "He and I have a deal. Joe is career military, a lifer, and I accepted that from the get-go. He has work he loves. I have work I love. And we are just fine, seeing each other when we are able."

Were they? Joe knew they had been. But now with their baby due sometime in the next five months or so, it didn't seem like enough to him.

Ellie obviously had a different point of view. Even pregnant, she didn't seem to want to see him more than she already did. The realization was like a dagger to his heart. Prodding him to stay and help her see just how wonderful things could be for them.

Oblivious to Joe's hurt, Eleanor splayed a hand across her chest, imploring, "But the baby, sweetheart…"

Yes, Joe thought. The baby. *Our baby…*

Ellie sat up straighter. "He or she will have tons of love here, Gran. From you and your friends here and all the Mc-Cabes and everyone at the bakery. You know as well as I that the baby will never want for affection or attention."

Joe knew that to be true, too.

Eleanor studied her granddaughter. "Every child needs a father, Ellie," she reminded her.

Crossing her slender legs at the knee, his wife tossed her curtain of honey-blond hair. "And our child will have one. Whenever Joe is stationed stateside, I will get on a plane and take our baby to see him." She lifted a hand before anyone could interrupt her, making it clear she had thought long and hard about this. "And to make traveling to him more economical, I just signed up for a frequent flyer credit card that will earn me miles with every purchase. I am going to put everything on it starting now. Gas. Groceries. Diapers. So I can get more points."

Joe hadn't known that.

He had one of those cards. He made routine purchases on it, paid them off at the end of the month and then used the points to fly home to see Ellie whenever he could.

Up to now, though, he had always been the one going to see her. With her working at the bakery six days a week, it was near impossible for her to travel to see him. At least that was what she had said, when they discussed it early on in their relationship. He had accepted that, and stopped bringing it up. Now he had the feeling it went a little deeper than that.

Eleanor sighed. Disappointment etched her beautiful, lined face. "Well, what about the house?" She looked from Ellie to Joe and back again. "When are you two moving in there?"

"I don't want to do that while Joe is home, Gran. It can all be done after he leaves."

"That doesn't make sense," Gran countered, pulling out a folder with photos of remodeled kitchens and bathrooms, paint samples and a decorator's business card. "You're pregnant, and he is here to help with everything now. If you're worried about the cost, I'll foot the bill."

"That's not necessary," Joe interjected politely yet firmly.

"Gifting us the Fitzgerald family home was more than enough. And we do appreciate it."

"Then why," Eleanor wanted to know, "haven't the two of you moved in? You would have to be more comfortable there."

Why indeed, Joe wondered. Part of it was that Ellie was still getting up at four to start work, and it was easier for her if all she had to do was go down to the first floor of the building, where the bakery was located. The other had to do with her holding on to what she had, stubbornly resisting any and all change.

He knew this wouldn't work once their baby was born. She was going to have to be more flexible. They both were.

With a sigh and shake of her head, Ellie shut the folder her grandmother had handed her with a snap.

Eleanor frowned just as a shadow appeared in the doorway. Nora rapped lightly on the open door. "Okay if I interrupt?" she asked breezily.

"Absolutely," Ellie said with a bright smile.

Nora approached the wing chair Eleanor was sitting in. She held a small tray with several small white paper cups. "I've got your noon meds."

Eleanor smiled and picked up a cup of water from the table beside her. She swallowed five pills, one at a time, then handed the paper cups back to the nursing supervisor.

"I'll see you later," Nora promised with a caring smile.

"Thanks, Nora," Gran said.

"That was a lot of pills," Ellie remarked with a frown.

Joe was thinking the same thing. Maybe because he had never seen Eleanor take any, at least not on a regular basis.

Eleanor waved an airy hand. "It's no big deal."

"Uh-huh." Ellie nodded but her face registered disbelief. "What were they?"

"Calcium with vitamin D for osteopenia. Blood pressure medication. Antihistamine for allergies. A blood thinner to guard against heart attack and stroke. And another to keep my heart rate from getting too high."

Ellie did a double take, their earlier difference of opinion forgotten. She leaned toward her gran urgently. "Have you been having issues with your heart?"

Eleanor remained unconcerned. "Not when I take my medicine as prescribed," she returned lightly. Seeing that her granddaughter still looked upset, she continued more gently, "Relax, darling. Nora and the staff keep an eagle eye on me. And speaking of Nora, you really ought to get her husband's phone number from her, Joe. Zane really is a wonderful man. It would be a good personal connection to have."

Joe figured Eleanor was right. There were surely some things an ex-military entrepreneur like Zane could advise him on. "Of course," he said affably. "Why not?"

Luckily for them all, the lunch bell sounded soon after. They all went down to the dining hall together and spent the rest of the visit talking to Gran's friends and other residents. The tension between Ellie and her grandmother had been eased somewhat by the time they said goodbye. They hugged each other tightly, and Ellie's eyes were misted over with tears as she walked away. It was a reminder of just how hard the new separation was on her. Bottom line...she missed her grandmother.

Did she miss him the same way after he left?

He missed *her* like hell. And even though they'd been going through the separation routine for over a dozen years, it wasn't getting any easier. Just the opposite. He hated to think of Ellie's heart aching with loneliness the way his did.

As the moment passed, she managed to pull herself together. "I'm sorry about the familial interference," she murmured softly as they walked across the parking lot. It was a beautiful summer afternoon. The oleanders were all in bloom, as were the flowers in the meticulously maintained landscape beds.

Joe caught her hand in his. "It's okay. We should probably brace ourselves anyway. Now that we're married, people are bound to feel we need their advice."

She turned to him with a beleaguered sigh, her blond hair glinting in the sunshine. "You really think so?"

"Yep." A wave of affection rushed through him, deeper than ever. He brushed a kiss across her brow. Then said soothingly, "It's nothing we can't handle." Needing her closer still, he wrapped an arm about her waist and guided her against him. She leaned into him, as if needing his emotional backup more than ever. When they reached his pickup truck, she rolled her eyes. "At least she didn't ask about the Monica Townsend situation."

Joe paused next to the passenger door. "What's going on there?"

Ellie's lower lip shot out. "Nothing except a voicemail or two every day reminding me to make a decision."

"*Have* you made a decision?"

The misery in her expression matched the unhappiness in her low tone. "I can't make that mock apple pie and let her use it to embarrass Vivian Townsend. So I guess I will have to hope she's bluffing and won't sue me at the end of the day. Maybe she'll accept some fancy cupcakes or a cake gratis to make up for her disappointment."

Joe considered the situation. He had never understood the feuds women sometimes got into. He did know that societal pressure could work both ways. And whatever Monica was hoping to accomplish was likely to blow up in her own face instead.

"Do you think her husband knows what she is doing?" he asked curiously. Brad Townsend had been a good guy, back when they had all been growing up. None of this would set well with the guy he had known back then.

"Doubtful. Monica probably doesn't want him to know, either, since she's intent on playing the victim here."

"Victim or villain?" Joe countered. He was still wondering if there was anything he could or should do, now that he and Ellie were husband and wife and not just longtime lovers.

Ellie slanted him a glance, signaling she did not want his help. Even though he would love to step in and defend her. "Not to worry, I've got it," she said firmly.

Joe hoped that was the case. Stress like this was not good for his wife. Whether she wanted him to or not, he was going to do everything he could to protect her and the baby. No matter the sacrifice. All he could do was hope, when the time came, she would understand.

"I need a favor," Joe told Sadie the next day at noon, just as she was leaving the bakery.

"I'm way ahead of you." Sadie paused beside her parked pickup truck, a vintage fire engine red Ford F-150. She gave him a sympathetic smile. "I already told Ellie she should let you come to the birthing class with her this evening since you're in town, and this may be the only part of her pregnancy you really get to share in."

He should have known his little sis would have his back. Gratitude filled his heart. Curious, he lounged next to her and asked, "What did she say?"

"Well, at first she was worried that if I missed the initial couple of sessions that I wouldn't be up to speed. And since they only want one coach to come with each mom-to-be..."

"You and I both can't go," Joe surmised.

"Right. But then I found out all eight sessions have been recorded, and can be watched online."

"So you and I can both get *all* the information that way."

"Yes!"

Sounded like the perfect solution to him. "And Ellie's on board with this?"

To his dismay, Sadie hesitated before saying, "Yes."

Confused, Joe waited, hoping his sister would further illuminate him. When she said nothing else, he asked, "Does she *not* want me there?" That would really blow.

Sadie tilted her head. "It's not that."

"Then?" Joe asked impatiently.

"I think she's afraid having you there will make her want you there with her when the baby is born, and she knows that's not likely to happen unless for some reason your unit doesn't get deployed overseas again. Which is probably the plan, isn't it?"

Not wanting to borrow trouble when it seemed like there was already so much coming his way, Joe shrugged. "There's really no way to know for sure at this point."

"Isn't there?" Sadie countered skeptically. "I mean Will is usually overseas when you're stateside and vice versa, unless a war happens or something. And thank God that's not the case right now."

He could tell from the look on her face that her feelings for his fellow Special Forces officer went far deeper than she was letting on, but she was right about one thing. Peacetime brought its own set of challenges.

"And since Will is set to return to the USA in another three months or so, it makes sense your unit will be heading back out to the Middle East."

"So Ellie is worried about me being deployed overseas before December?" Joe asked.

"She's always concerned about your unit being sent to some hot spot, Joe."

"She doesn't act like it."

Sadie threw up her hands in frustration. "Because she doesn't want you to worry about her! And how she is handling things. When you already have enough to deal with. Regardless, since there is no concrete way to know what your future military duty holds, unless you leave the service at the end of this tour the way our entire family is secretly hoping you will," Sadie said pointedly, "you need to savor every single second you have with your wife and baby and be at that class tonight."

Hours later, Ellie sat on a comfy yoga mat on the floor of the birthing classroom. Joe was behind her. Her back was to his chest, her head against his strong shoulder, her thighs cradled by the warmth of his. His palms were resting on her belly.

The feel of him so close and caring was blissful as all get-out.

"All right, let's do one last round of thoughtful breathing," the instructor told the class.

Wishing they could stay this way forever, Ellie closed her eyes.

"Breathe in through your nose. Slow, deep breaths. That's it," the instructor said approvingly. "Then let it out through your mouth. A little bit at a time. Partners, be sure you're breathing in tandem with your baby mama. We want this to be a team effort. It's really important for the baby trying to make his or her way into the world to know that everything is exactly the way it needs to be."

Except it *wouldn't* be, Ellie thought, as tears suddenly pressed against the back of her eyelids. Because if he reenlisted, Joe likely wouldn't be here with her. Not when the baby was born. And maybe not for a while after that, either.

"You okay?" Joe asked as the two of them walked out to his truck a short time later. His voice was a low, sexy rumble.

She stumbled slightly as they stepped off the curb. "Why?"

He steadied her with a hand to her elbow. "You got kind of tense there at the end of class."

The corners of her lips tightening, she turned away from his scrutinizing look. The last thing she wanted was for him to try to psychoanalyze her. "I think I was just tired," she said, knowing that was only partially true. "I had a very long day."

Getting up at four to go to work. Having lunch with Gran. Finding out she was on all those medications and, worse, not pleased that Ellie and Joe weren't nesting in the house she had so generously given them.

"Is that all it was?"

Ellie felt the tears prickling her eyes again. She shook her head, blinking the moisture away. What was *wrong* with her? She knew the score. She always had. It must be the pregnancy hormones, pushing her emotions so close to the surface so often.

Determined not to show the weakness welling up inside her, she twisted her lips into a rueful smile. "I guess I've been thinking that we—er—I had plenty of time to get things ready for the baby, but when the instructor gave us that list of things that needed to be done before the birth, I realized it wasn't going to be as effortless as I thought."

Looking relieved that this at least was something he could tackle, Joe asked, "You want to get on it and knock it all out?"

Did she? Ellie wasn't sure.

All she knew for certain was that whenever they dealt

with the reality of their pregnancy, she also had to deal with her feelings about everything Joe would be missing out on. Which made her wonder if the baby would feel his absence and miss him, too.

Mistaking the reason behind her indecision, Joe hastened to add, "I mean I don't know much about layettes and stuff, but I could always ask my mom to help us with that if you want. And you could ask Gran. I'm sure she knows all about that stuff, too."

It was sweet, the way he wanted to include their families. "Actually, I think I've got that," Ellie told him wryly. "Or I will, once I visit the appropriate baby goods stores. It's preparing the nurseries that I am going to need help with."

"*Nurseries?* As in...plural?" Surprise etched his handsome face.

"Well." Ellie gestured vaguely. "I figure I'm going to need a crib in the apartment over the bakery, as well as a chair to nurse in. A place for our baby and a babysitter to be, when I'm working."

Joe's brow furrowed. "But that apartment's awfully small."

Ellie nodded. "Way too tiny for everything a baby needs. So I'm going to have to get a room ready in the house, too."

He tucked a strand of hair behind her ear, then caged her in the warmth of his strong arms. Leaning down, he kissed her temple tenderly. "What do you need me to do?"

Feeling stronger now that she was focused on a task they could do together, she gazed up at him and said, "Help me clear out a bedroom and at least get the nursery furniture in."

And once that was done, they could figure out their plans for Christmas this year. One, if he was actually with her and their baby. Another, if it turned out he was not.

Because one way or another, this was a very special year for them, and they were *not* going to let it go uncelebrated.

Chapter Eleven

"So, I'm finally being let into the inner sanctum," Joe drawled late the following afternoon.

Ellie stood blocking the closed door to her bedroom. Her entire face flushed a self-conscious pink that made him all the more curious as to what she—and her mother and grandmother—had been hiding all these years. All he knew was it had been against the rules for him to be on the second floor that held the bedrooms when they had been dating as teenagers. And there had been no reason for him to be up there once they became adults, since she no longer lived there. Her apartment was where they spent time together now.

Even on the day they had moved her gran out, the door to that room had been firmly closed. And still was.

Ellie wrinkled her nose. "My bedroom isn't the *inner sanctum*," she retorted.

He tugged playfully on a lock of her hair, then grinned, unable to help teasing her. "Well, it certainly feels like it since I've been with you for how many years now…thirteen… fourteen?" Trying not to think about what he would really like to do, which was forget the room-clearing-out, at least for the moment, and spend another leisurely evening making love to his new wife again and again, he tamped down his desire with effort.

The color in her cheeks deepened, making him wonder if she could read his mind. "Fourteen, if you're counting from our first date."

He grinned, having known she would correct him. He countered, in return, "Fifteen—if it's from the first moment we shared a seat on the school bus. And I knew I was in love with you."

She smiled, remembering, too. Her expression turned as loving and tender as her soft voice. Gazing up at him adoringly, she ruminated, "It's funny, isn't it? How you can sort of know someone your entire life and yet not really know them until *kazaam*." She mimed a cupid's arrow to her heart. "You get hit with all the feelings you never knew you had."

Yet another wave of sizzling chemistry arced between them. "Nothing like young love." He brought her close for a kiss.

Their gazes meshed and held.

"Nothing like love at any age," she murmured back, melting into him.

One kiss turned into another.

"But we digress," she said when they finally came up for air. Her chin taking on that stubborn tilt he knew so well, she lifted a hand as she continued blocking his way into her childhood bedroom. "I need to warn you about what you are about to see."

Joe chuckled. "Let me guess." He blotted the moisture on her soft, kiss-swollen lips with the pad of his thumb. "It hasn't changed since you left for college."

"Pretty much." She sighed, looking embarrassed again. "I moved right into the apartment above the bakery when I came back to Laramie, and I've lived there ever since."

Joe inhaled the flowery scent of her hair and skin. He

drank in the sage green of her eyes. "And never got around to changing things here at the house?"

"Well, my mom and gran were pretty attached to the time warp aspect of my childhood that you get when you walk in there. They really liked remembering me that way."

This was all so cute, Joe thought, revealing a side of Ellie he didn't yet know. But he wanted to. *So much.* He braced a forearm on the door above her and leaned closer. Waggling his brows, he asked, "Do *you* like remembering you that way?"

Ellie leaned against the wood, one hand tightly clutching the knob. She lifted her slender shoulders in an elegant shrug. "Honestly, it seems like another life and another person inhabited that space these days. Which is why I'm finding it so difficult to let you in there."

Joe could see that, too. Fortunately, the kid in her brought out the kid in him. "Maybe I should carry you across the threshold then," he told her playfully.

Ellie's lips formed a round O of surprise. "What?"

He swung her up into his arms. "Let's give it a try." Cradling her against his chest, he pushed open the door and, ripping off the Band-Aid, strode in.

"Wow. You must really like glitter," Joe drawled seconds later as he set her carefully on her feet. "And shades of purple."

Ellie tried to see her old bedroom the way he must be seeing it. At one time it had been a little girl's dream, with a white canopy twin bed and matching dresser. Ruffled purple-and-white gingham decorated the windows. A lacy white bedspread with a deep purple chenille throw and matching pillows, laid on her bed. The pièce de résistance, however, was the fully outfitted Barbie Dreamhouse in the corner.

Parked next to it was Barbie's pink convertible and vinyl carrying cases stuffed with clothing for Barbie and her friends, while the dolls lounged around inside the town house.

"I don't see a Ken doll," Joe remarked.

Ellie ran a hand through the tousled strands of her hair, pushing it off her face. It was hard to explain, but… "I wasn't in to Ken."

He whirled back to her, asking curiously, "How come?"

With effort, Ellie fought back another embarrassed flush. "I had other romantic heroes in mind."

Like the dream of grown-up him…with her all grown-up, too.

He walked over to an old boom box atop a stand crammed with CDs. Above it a bulletin board was plastered with pictures of popular boy bands from the time.

"Like these guys?" He pointed to a couple of very young, shirtless guitarists with shoulder-length hair and six-pack abs.

Joe could not stop grinning, Ellie noted in consternation.

She turned to another bulletin board, this one above the desk where she had done her homework every night. Many photos adorned it, all of them of her and her girlfriends, and her and Joe. "If you want to know the truth, this guy has always been more my style," she said, pointing to a picture of him standing on the high school track in his cross-country uniform, holding a fistful of first place ribbons. She stood next to him, smiling with all the blissful innocence of youth.

He ran his finger beneath the photograph, clearly remembering that sunny day. "Damn, we were young."

"Yep."

It looked like he couldn't take his eyes off the pictures. "You really had these photos of me in here all these years?"

She shrugged. What could she say? "I never wanted to

take them down." Still didn't, really. But they needed the nursery space. She frowned and, biting her lip uncertainly, admitted, "The problem is, I don't even know where to start."

Which was not, she quickly realized, a problem for her husband. Like all soldiers, he was all about completing the mission, whatever it was.

She watched as Joe sprang into action mode, just the way she expected. He sized up the amount of stuff in the room. "You planning to keep all the toys or donate them?"

Suddenly, Ellie found herself on the same page as her late mom and gran. There were so many memories attached to every single thing, she didn't want to part with any of it. Plus, wouldn't it be fun to share all this stuff with her daughter if she had one? Ellie inhaled. "Retro is always in, so… I thought I'd keep this stuff for our kids."

He lifted his brow. *"Kids?"*

She hadn't meant to give away the entirety of her romantic dreams and wishes. Her pulse suddenly jumping, she replied, a little breathlessly, "Well, you know what I mean."

Blue eyes twinkling, he lifted his hand to her face and let his thumb sweep gently over her cheekbone. "Not sure I do."

Already aching for another kiss, she locked eyes with him. "We had one surprise. I guess we could have another." So their child would grow up with siblings, like he'd done, not an only child like her.

His gaze drifted over her thoughtfully. "We'd need to stay married for that to happen."

Open mouth. Insert foot. Wishing she could withdraw the faux pas, yet knowing she couldn't, Ellie lifted her hand in an airy wave, wordlessly dismissing what she had said and any further conversation about it. Instead, she said matter-of-factly, "Bottom line, we have to get this room completely cleared of all furniture and belongings so we can

get it painted a more neutral color and set up the nursery."
As soon as they purchased furniture for it.

He nodded in agreement, then opened her walk-in closet to
find it also packed to the gills with all sorts of school memo-
rabilia, old dance recital dresses, cheerleader uniforms and
glitter-decorated shoeboxes. "So where do you want to put
everything?" he asked, turning back to her.

Ellie envisioned the hours it was going to take, going
through all this, and immediately felt overwhelmed. At least
until she realized it was one thing that could keep her occupied after Joe left again. "How about the living room?
There's plenty of floor space down there. If we both carry
stuff, it will only take a few hours to clear this space out."

Joe went all protective on her once again. "You're not carrying anything, darlin'. The heavy lifting is for me. All you
need to do is stay up here and organize things into stacks."

He set off with an armful of infant-size baby dolls and a
buggy from her preschool days.

Ellie spied a small white rubber cap with multicolored
streamers on one end sticking out from beneath her bed. It
was the kind of thing usually attached to a bike. But there
was no way she had a bike under her bed. Those were all
in the garage, and occasionally loaned out to the neighbor's
visiting grandkids.

Wondering what the cap and streamers were attached to,
Ellie got down on her knees and lifted the white eyelet bed
skirt.

Her baton from dance class! And the sparkly tiara she'd
worn at the recital.

With a cry of delight, Ellie retrieved both, sticking the
tiara on top of her head. She hadn't touched a baton in years.
It took a moment to remember how to hold it, in the center, her fingers placed just so. But after a few awkward at-

tempts, she was able to twirl the silver wand up and over and around her wrist.

Standing, she twirled her baton in front of her, doing fancy figure eights, then behind her back. She brought it forward again and again, then gave it a flip and sent it skyward.

With, as it turned out, a little too much force. It bounced against the ceiling and came back down right toward her face.

Ellie ducked out of the way, saved by her quick action.

The hero stepping quickly—and unnecessarily—in to rescue her was not.

The end of the baton caught Joe on the top of his head just a second before he reached up and coolly clasped the offending "weapon" and brought it down to his side.

Ellie couldn't help it; she started to laugh. It was all so silly. He guffawed, too. "Whoops," she said.

His smile said *whoops* was right. After carefully setting the baton on her desk, he came back to circle her waist with his hands. He let his gaze drift over her appreciatively, then leaned down to whisper in her ear. "You were putting on quite the show."

Her skin already heating at his light, possessive touch, Ellie sucked in a breath. "How long were you standing there?"

He drew back just far enough to peer into her eyes. "Long enough."

She splayed her hands across the sinewy hardness of his chest. Felt his heart beating in tandem with hers. "Why didn't you let me know you were there?"

He hooked an arm around her waist, bringing her even closer, and threaded a hand through her hair. Then he kissed her. "Because I'd never seen you twirl a baton." He grinned down at her indulgently. "And I have to say, it was quite the sight."

Ellie giggled despite herself. "I suppose that's what I get for goofing around instead of working hard."

"Oh, there's a lot to say for goofing around," he murmured, dancing her ever so slowly back toward her canopy bed.

Ellie knew where this was going. Her heart kicked hard against her ribs, while the rest of her went all soft and melty. The back of her thighs hit the edge of the mattress. "Joe..."

His eyelids were heavy with desire. "I can finish carrying stuff downstairs tomorrow while you're at work," he said, kissing her brow, her cheek, the nape of her neck. "But right now, I want to make love to my wife."

Emotion swept through her like a typhoon, followed by a wealth of need. Lower still, a tingling warmth spread and built. Sex with Joe had always been wonderful, but her pregnancy hormones added a physical and emotional intensity unlike anything she had ever imagined. Every kiss, every caress, every touch set off fireworks inside her.

Wordlessly, impatiently, they divested each other of all their clothes, drew back the covers and tumbled onto her narrow bed. Trembling with pleasure, she wound her arms about his neck. Their breaths mingled as their lips locked together, their tongues tangling, the kisses hot and hard, then soft and sweet and tender yet again.

His hands cupping her breasts, he teased her taut nipples with his thumbs. She arched against him, feeling like making out was the most intimate thing they could ever do. And then his hands and mouth began a languid downward journey. She fisted her hands in his hair, afraid he would stop. He didn't. Not until she was opening herself up to him impatiently, drawing him closer, shuddering with sensation and crying out his name.

Feelings sweeping through her, she watched as he moved up her body, settling above her. Both hands cradling her bottom, he held her right where he wanted her to be, and then there was no more thinking, only feeling and wanting... needing and loving. Their wet kisses turned into hotter pleasure. He caught her sounds with his mouth, and then he was moaning, too. Whispering her name. Shuddering and plunging ever deeper.

Their passion escalated until, together, they surrendered to each other and their marriage and whatever else their future held.

Chapter Twelve

"Thanks for meeting me so early," Joe told Skip Carlton the following morning.

It was 7:00 a.m., and Ellie had already been working at the bakery for a couple hours. Joe had taken Scout for a run, showered and then driven to the edge of town where the old moving company warehouse was located.

His former high school classmate smiled. "No problem." The commercial real estate agent unlocked the door to the four-story brick building. "I'm happy to show you around."

The two men walked inside. Skip hit the light panel, enabling them to look around the huge space.

The cement floor bore markings where four levels of steel shelving had been, but there wasn't much else to see. The walls were plain gray cement blocks with no windows and a loading dock with big double doors. A couple of restrooms and a set of stairs led to a glass-walled office that looked down on the floor.

"You thinking about going into manufacturing like your dad?" Skip asked. "Or leasing it out to a moving company storage facility again?"

Joe shook his head. "No to both."

"Then?" Skip arched a brow, waiting.

"I'd rather not say what I have in mind just yet. There's

too much yet to be worked out. In the meantime," Joe said as he paced the wide-open space, imagining all it could be, "I don't want anyone else knowing I'm looking into purchasing this property." Especially Ellie and his family. "I'm going to need your complete discretion."

The respected businessman nodded. "No problem."

"I also need the tax and utility history, zoning restrictions, an estimate of how much it will cost to quadruple the size of the parking area. And what you think the property is worth, given that it's stood empty for the last eighteen months."

Skip typed the details into his phone. "I'll get all this to you by the end of the day."

"Thanks."

"Want to see the loading dock in the back?"

Joe nodded.

To Joe's surprise, although the brick in front was still like new, the brick in back was scratched up, even broken in a few places. There were holes in the grout, where hooks or pegs had been put in. "What's been going on here?"

Skip frowned. "Kids used to just climb up the sides of the water towers for fun, but now it appears they've started trying to scale the building exterior, too."

"That's pretty dangerous." As well as one hell of a liability.

"Which is why the sheriff's department has been patrolling the area twice hourly, twenty-four-seven." Skip paused, as if realizing he might have just curtailed Joe's interest in the property. "I think it will stop if this place is occupied and a new security system is put in."

Joe nodded. "Let's hope so." Because this place was perfect for what he had in mind.

"Ellie?" Ingrid came into the back of the bakery where Ellie was putting the finishing touches on a three-tiered wedding cake. "Vivian Townsend is here. She'd like to talk to you privately."

Vivian was Monica Townsend's mother-in-law and a beloved community volunteer. Ellie had known her since she was a kid. She imagined if Viv was here that the woman knew something of what was going on with her daughter-in-law. Just how much, though, was anyone's guess. "Sure. You can have her come on back. Just do me a favor and keep everyone else out until we're done talking?"

Ingrid nodded. "Will do."

Ellie's second-in-command disappeared. Seconds later, Vivian Townsend walked in. The fifty-eight year old brunette was dressed, as always, in mom jeans and a pastel button-down cotton tunic. Her hair was caught up in a youthful ponytail, and light makeup highlighted her pretty features.

She was not, however, as laid-back as usual. In fact, she looked downright tense as she got straight to the point. "I understand my daughter-in-law, Monica, has been threatening to sue the bakery."

Caught off guard, Ellie carefully piped violet flowers on the top of the cake. She would prefer to keep Vivian out of this mess. "How did you hear about that?" she asked carefully, moving to add more petals to the other side of the cake.

Vivian folded her arms. "It doesn't matter." She regarded Ellie stoically. "Is it true?"

Ellie felt caught between a rock and a hard place. She wished Gran were still here, because she would know how to handle this. "I...our customers...expect a certain level of privacy."

Vivian frowned. "*Is* Monica a customer?"

Ellie inhaled a deep breath. "Not yet."

"Which is why she is threatening to sue you, because she'd like to be one?" Vivian surmised.

Ellie figured if the woman knew this much, she might as well know the rest. "Let's just say your daughter-in-law had a special request that we can't honor."

"Well, actually, I am here to tell you that you can give her exactly what she wants you to make for the Laramie Women's Club luncheon in my honor."

Ellie paused, stunned. Finally, she admitted, "It's a pie…"

Another scowl. "Probably apple."

Too distracted to put any more finishing touches on the cake, Ellie put her piping bag aside, grabbed two bottles of water from the fridge and sat down on one of the stools, inviting Vivian to do the same. "Ah, yeah. And she wants you to think she made it especially for you."

Vivian seemed more emotionally worn-out than surprised as she settled next to Ellie. "Then just make two of them. Make them identical, only leave out the ghost peppers or whatever she is asking you to include in hers. I'll do a switcheroo at the luncheon, her plans to embarrass me will be foiled, and that will be that."

Ellie struggled to take it all in. Laramie had always been the kind of place where neighbors helped neighbors. It wasn't usually a venue for dirty tricks. "I don't understand why she wants to do something like this."

"I do." Viv sipped from her bottle of chilled water. "She hates the fact that Brad is still close to his family and wants to live here in Laramie."

"But she had to know that when she married him."

"He was at Harvard Medical School when they met. And even though he always maintained that he intended to come back to Texas to practice, I think she thought she'd be able to convince him to stay in Boston, so they could be close to her family." Vivian paused for a beat. "And when that didn't happen and Brad took a job at Laramie Community Hospital instead, she began acting out. Doing everything she could to undermine our relationship with Brad, claiming I insulted her cooking and so on."

"I can't believe you ever did anything like that."

"I didn't. But she can really turn on the waterworks for him, and more often than not, he buys it and blames me for hurting her feelings, so…" Vivian sighed and buried her face in her hands.

Ellie reached out to briefly touch Vivian's shoulder, offering what comfort she could. Not sure what else to do, she simply waited.

With a shake of her head, Vivian straightened. "Anyway, I've been trying really hard to stay out of their marriage and not let our family come between them, but when I caught wind of the fact she was trying to sue the bakery, that was the last straw." Her jaw set. "I decided to thwart her plans and show her that my days of being her scapegoat are over, once and for all."

"Wow," Joe said when Ellie told him what had transpired with Vivian earlier that day.

They were back at Eleanor's old house, sitting in the floral wall-papered living room and attempting to sort through the toys and mementos Joe had carried down from Ellie's bedroom while Ellie was at work. Ellie was sorting the books into age groups, figuring they could put away all but the baby and toddler stories for now. Meanwhile, Joe was putting together cardboard storage boxes.

"Mrs. Townsend is one of my mom's close friends," he confided. "They've worked together on a lot of different service projects. I've never known her to lose her temper or be mean."

"I know." Ellie ran a hand lovingly over one of the Frances books she had loved so much growing up. She looked back at Joe.

The late July day had been excessively warm. He was clad in running shorts and a quick-dry athletic T-shirt. His face was lightly sunburned, his short dark hair tousled, his face rimmed with evening beard. He looked sexy and approachable. As she remembered their passionate lovemaking the night before, a river of desire swept through her.

Determined to do a better job of staying on task, she turned her attention back to the Townsend family problem that was spilling over onto her bakery. "But it sounds like Vivian's had it with all the underhanded troublemaking from Monica. And wants to send her daughter-in-law a warning shot that will put an end to it."

Joe handed Ellie a black marker so she could label the boxes. "You think it's going to work?"

Ellie thought about Monica. The big city girl from Massachusetts now trapped in a small Texas town. Desperate to get out. "I don't know." She wrote across the side of the cardboard, then the top. Recapping the Sharpie, she handed the box back to Joe. "The whole thing bothers me, though."

Their hands brushed warmly during the exchange. His dark brow knit. "Because?"

Ellie tried to explain how bamboozled she felt. "I never would have expected this of Monica. At least not three years ago, when she first came to town when she and Brad were engaged. Back then, she seemed really sweet and personable, happy to be here and continue to work virtually as a marketing rep for a Boston software company. Everyone liked her and thought she was a great match for him. Including me." Ellie winked, joking lamely, "Even if she was a Red Sox fan."

Joe chuckled, knowing as well as she that Laramie was

a bighearted place where everyone was welcome. "So what happened?"

Marriage, Ellie thought. It changed everything. Raised all the stakes to an uncomfortably high level. Knowing Joe didn't share her wariness of the institution in general, she kept her feelings to herself and said only, "They got married. And stayed in rural Texas, I guess. Vivian mentioned that Monica didn't expect that."

Which was something that Joe, who had hightailed it out of his rural hometown the moment he graduated high school and never returned for more than a visit, no doubt understood.

"She probably figured after being at Harvard, Brad would get restless practicing pulmonology here and want to go somewhere he could do lung transplants and be big time, you know." She sighed. "Instead, he happily settled in. I mean he is super busy. He's the only pulmonologist in two counties. Before he came back, patients had to go to Dallas or San Antonio to see a lung specialist. So folks are happy he's here."

"Except Monica."

Ellie nodded in affirmation.

She wondered if Joe would eventually feel just as trapped as Monica did in rural Texas, if and when he retired from the military and returned to be with her full time. True, they would have a baby here, which was a good reason to stay. And his entire family, whom he loved dearly, lived in Laramie. But would there be enough challenge here for an adrenaline junkie like him?

Or would he eventually feel bored, restless and unhappy, too?

Ellie returned her attention to the problem at hand. "The whole situation certainly has taken a toll on Monica." Especially since her new husband was such a local hero.

Joe worked on putting together another box. "What about Brad? What is his opinion of all of this?"

Good question. Ellie shrugged. "If he's unhappy in his marriage, he hasn't said. Although since this all started, I've heard through the grapevine that Monica has been very careful to try to keep all this bakery drama from him. She must figure he wouldn't approve of her publicly pranking his mother."

"The guy we went to school with certainly wouldn't have."

They both fell silent.

"So," Joe said eventually. "What was your final decision? Did you tell Monica you're going to make the mock apple pie?"

"Yep. Since it's the surest way to keep her from suing the bakery, I called her after Vivian left and told her I decided to honor her request."

Joe sat down beside her on the sofa. He took Ellie's hand in his. "What was her reaction?"

She leaned into his comforting grip while she tried to figure out how to describe it. "She was victorious, I guess. Kind of snotty and arrogant." Ellie sighed. "She said she's going to drop off a plastic pie-carrier in advance, because she wants to pass the pie off as her own."

Joe's usual inscrutable expression turned disapproving. He stroked the inside of her wrist with his thumb. "Are you glad or sad you won't be there to watch what happens next?"

She groaned and fell back against the cushions of the sofa. "Actually, I *will* be a witness." She turned to take in his ruggedly handsome face. "Gran is part of the women's club and wants to attend, as well as gift the club with cupcakes to add to their dessert buffet. So I'll be picking her up at Laramie Gardens next week and taking everything over to the public library annex where the celebration is being held. And then maybe I can put this whole mess behind me." Or at the very least Monica could go torture someone else.

Blue eyes darkening, he shifted her over onto his lap in a way that encouraged her to wreathe her arms about his broad shoulders. "Never a dull moment here, hmm?"

She thought once again about the way they had made love the evening before in her twin canopy bed. She wished they could forget all about the problems at the bakery and sorting through her old stuff and do it again. "Not with you here, soldier, that's for sure."

He kissed her temple, then the curve of her cheek. "It's because I have such a loving and wonderful wife."

Wife.

Funny, how she was getting used to him calling her that. After years and years of avoiding just such a connection.

She was beginning to think of him as her *husband*, too.

He stroked a hand through her hair, pushing it off her face. "Oh, and did I tell you that my mom said you weren't the only one with childhood treasures needing to be sorted?"

Ellie turned to him, her bottom settling more intimately on the hard cradle of his thighs. She blinked, realizing she had never been in the private lair he had grown up in, either. "Your old bedroom still looks like mine did before we—er, you—cleared it out?"

"No. It was turned into a guest room when I joined the military. But she did save my favorite toys when I was a kid, figuring I might want them when I had children of my own. So…" He made the sound of a drum roll, then reached over and opened up a cardboard box with his name on it.

Ellie gazed inside. She wasn't sure what she was expecting. Certainly not her pink Barbie convertible with Barbie sitting behind the wheel and a camo-clad G.I. Joe doll riding shotgun beside her.

How did he know that this was *exactly* the way she would have paired the two, if she'd had her own G.I. Joe doll back then?

She turned to him. "Cute."

"Aren't they? I think they look a lot like us."

Ellie laughed. "The soldier and his woman?"

"Now all we need is a doll-size pickup truck that can also carry Scout and a baby. Or two or three."

That would be great, Ellie thought, if she weren't already so overwhelmed, weathering her first pregnancy more or less on her own. At least, she would be as soon as Joe headed back to his unit again. As well as caring for her gran and managing a business, it was all a whole lot more than she had bargained on.

Plus, they had a deal. They had agreed before they eloped. They were only staying married for a year or two, until Joe's legal rights as their child's father were established.

They had talked about staying together permanently, when they were teasing each other about having more than one child. And Joe had stated they would have to be married to do that. But that hadn't been a serious or deal-changing proposal. More of a tentative what- if that allowed them to continue doing what they had always done, live their lives one day at a time, without constraint. Determined not to want more than she should for fear they would wreck all the happiness they already had, she eased off his lap. "Simmer down, handsome."

She started to rise, then froze as something really weird happened inside her midriff.

What was that?

It felt like a kick or a flutter. Was that their baby moving?

"Ellie?" Joe was on his feet, too. "What is it?"

She put her hand over her stomach.

Gently cupping her shoulders, he gazed at her face. "Are you okay?"

And there it went. Again. A gentle, deliberate flutter, like a wave.

Wordlessly, she took his hand and put it over her belly. Pressing it against her.

Suddenly he felt it, too. "That's…?"

"Our baby," Ellie whispered. "Moving." Tears of happiness blurred her eyes.

Joe looked overcome, too. And she knew that for whatever reason this had all come about, it was all meant to be. She wouldn't trade this time of happiness for anything in the world.

And neither, apparently, would he.

Chapter Thirteen

Joe stopped in front of Eleanor's suite at Laramie Gardens. Ellie's seventy-year-old grandmother was standing in front of the window overlooking the beautiful courtyard. Clad in stylish workout clothes in her trademark pink and white, she was by turn wiping sweat from her silver brow and gulping bottled water. He rapped on the door frame. "Got a minute to talk?"

Gran turned, a welcoming smile on her face. "Well, if it isn't my favorite grandson-in-law." She motioned him in.

He ambled toward the wing chair she indicated. "Your *only* grandson-in-law."

With a grin, she sat, too. "What brings you by, darling?"

"Ellie. And the push present I am supposed to get her. I don't know what to buy. I know it's usually jewelry but…"

"Ellie's not really a jewelry gal," she interjected.

"Right."

Eleanor studied him. "What do you think she likes?"

"Cooking. Baking."

"So get her something related to that."

"Like a new stove for the house?" Joe asked. All the other kitchen appliances had been replaced in the last five years or so, Ellie had said.

Eleanor shrugged. "If you think she would enjoy that."

"I know she would, but isn't gifting a wife an appliance the kiss of death for any husband?"

Gran laughed even as she wiped her brow again then took another long, thirsty sip of water. "For most. But then, Ellie's not like most. Is a new stove what you really want to get her?"

"Yes, but maybe not as a push present, more like an 'I love you' present."

Eleanor nodded approvingly. "A present for no particular reason except you want her to be happy. I think she'd really appreciate that."

"I kind of want to do it before I leave again." So his wife would be reminded how much he loved her every day.

"Then go for it," Gran said, suddenly setting her water bottle down with a thud. Her face turned white, then red, then pale again. She splayed her hand across the center of her chest. Her lips worked, but no sound came out.

Joe was up and at her side in an instant. "*Eleanor!* What is it?"

"My...pills..."

He looked around, not seeing any.

Gran seemed in even more distress. "Nurse..." she finally gasped.

He raced to the phone and called the front desk for help.

Nora was there in a flash. She had a blood pressure cuff in one hand, a vial of pills in another and a stethoscope around her neck. She looked at Eleanor. "Angina?"

Gran nodded weakly.

Nora doled out a small pill. Gran put it under her tongue. Relief came as quickly as the attack had come on.

"You know you're supposed to have your pills on you at all times," the nursing supervisor scolded kindly as she sat beside Eleanor, wrapped the blood pressure cuff around her arm and inflated it. She watched the results, declaring them "a little high, not bad," then listened to Gran's heart. "That's good, too. What happened to trigger this, do you know?"

"I think I worked out a little too hard in my senior aerobics class."

"Well, this is your body telling you that you need to dial it back a notch," Nora said. "In any case, I'm going to give your cardiologist a call and let her know that you've had another angina episode." The nurse stood. "Let me know if you need anything else. Or if you can't find those pills that are supposed to be on you at all times." She looked at Joe. "Would you help her look for them, please?"

Joe nodded, and Nora left. He turned back to Gran. "Want to tell me what's going on?"

"Obviously I have a heart condition."

"Does Ellie know?" he prodded gently.

"No! And she doesn't need to, either, so I forbid you to mention any of this to her. Do you understand me?"

"Yes, I do." Joe's lips flattened into a hard line. "But I think you're wrong." He thought a moment. "Is this why you retired and moved into Laramie Gardens so suddenly? Because you needed full-time nursing care?"

Turning away, Eleanor looked through her handbag but came up with nothing. "I will *eventually* need full-time nursing care," she corrected archly. "Right now, I only need occasional care for my mild heart arrhythmia."

The episode she had just had said otherwise, Joe thought. Ellie and her gran were very much alike in this regard. Both of them fiercely independent, resisting help or advice.

"But." The old woman rose and surveyed all the surfaces in the room for the missing pills. "I figured I would just go ahead and get things set up now. Since I knew Ellie was going to have enough to manage, taking over the business and moving out of the apartment and into the house. And then, of course, she found out she was pregnant and married you, so I am doubly glad I made permanent group living arrangements when I did. Otherwise—" Eleanor searched through the sofa cushions "—if something like this happened and I needed to call a neighbor or God forbid 911, Ellie would have gone bonkers and insisted on being with me all the time, instead of living her own life. And I couldn't have that. She has sacrificed far too much as it is."

The disappointment in her low voice stung. Joe stood back to give his grandmother-in-law room to maneuver. "Are we talking about my military career here?" The sacrifices Ellie had made for him?

"No." Eleanor opened her bedside table, frowning in annoyance as she spotted a small flowered metal pill case. With a sigh of relief, she picked it up and tucked it into the edge of her bra for safekeeping. She shut the drawer and went back to reclaim her water bottle. "Believe it or not, I understand your devotion to serving your country, since my late husband felt the same way. I'm talking about our Ellie and how she keeps putting off for tomorrow what could easily be done today. On every level."

Mostly, because she resisted change. "Speaking of that," Joe said gruffly, "you should tell her about your heart."

"No."

"She'll be really hurt if she finds out any other way," he reminded her.

"I know. Which is why neither of us are going to tell her. And thanks to the medical privacy laws, everyone else here is sworn to secrecy, too."

Joe studied her, knowing he needed to ask. "You're okay for the moment?"

"Hopefully for many years to come, yes, which is why Ellie does not need to know."

Joe relaxed. Realizing they hadn't come to terms on what he should get for Ellie, he said, "About her push present."

"You're the husband, darling. You figure it out."

* * *

"You really should take the rest of the week off," Ingrid said as they wheeled a wedding cake into the walk-in refrigerator, then went back to cleaning up the worktables. "You know I could handle it."

Better than me, sometimes, Ellie thought. In addition to being one of the two assistant managers and having twenty-five years of experience at Sugar Love, Ingrid had also studied baking and pastry in culinary school. She was great with all the customers, too.

"I'm sure Sherri and Terri and Sadie and Lynette would all pitch in a few extra hours each, if needed," Ingrid went on. "Then you would have all that extra time to spend with your new hubby."

Ellie was definitely tempted. "I feel like it would be a bad precedent to set. Given the fact I just took over the business."

Ingrid cut her off with a shake of the head. "Everyone knows how much you love Joe and how little time you two have together. No one will think you're skipping out. They'll think you have your priorities straight."

Was her husband first in her life? Ahead of or equal to her baby? Ellie didn't know.

She did miss Joe. The only contact she'd had with him since this morning was a text asking her to meet him and Scout at the house again as soon as she got off work.

Ellie turned to Ingrid. "You sure you wouldn't mind filling in for me on Thursday and Friday and maybe Saturday, too, if necessary? We really have to get the baby areas set up before Joe leaves again…"

"Not a problem." Ingrid hugged her. "Consider it done."

Feeling lighter and freer than she had in longer than she could recall, Ellie soared through the cleanup, dashed up to the apartment to change and then drove to the house. Joe's truck was in the driveway.

He and Scout were already headed into the foyer to greet her when she opened the door. She hugged him warmly and petted Scout. Then turning toward the living room, she could only stare.

"What happened here?" she asked in shock. There wasn't a toy or keepsake in sight!

"I nixed the cardboard. Boxed it all up in clear plastic storage containers and put it in the garage."

She curved her hand around his biceps. "All of it?"

"Every last thing," he told her proudly.

"Why?" She suddenly felt a little unsteady.

"Because we've already spent two nights trying to sort through it. And it's something that can wait and be done at leisure. So I put it where it will be safe, nearby, easily accessible, yet out of the way for now." He peered down at her. "You're not mad, are you?"

Was she?

Sort of, she realized. Shouldn't he have at least asked her before he undertook all this on his own? Then again, it was half his house, too, thanks to the way Gran had gifted it to them. Which meant he had just as much right to make changes and decisions about things as she did.

Although she would have preferred it if they had done so together.

"I could carry it all back in and store it in here, if you want," he finally said, looking as disappointed in her as she felt in him.

"No. It's fine." Ellie didn't want to fight with him about this. It was too silly. Besides, he was right. She could sort through all this when he was gone again. Which had been her plan, anyway.

"I also called that interior decorator Gran suggested the other day, and she stopped by, took some photos and measurements. She's going to send us some suggestions. Apparently she can get high-quality baby furniture at a deep discount and arrange for delivery and setup, too. And she can hook us up with a good mural artist, if you want to go that route."

He had said *if you*, not *if we*. Ellie looked at him, not sure what any of this meant except that Joe had never been one to mess around. He liked to get on things and get them done. Ellie blinked. "You don't have an opinion about that?"

"Well." He shrugged his broad shoulders affably. "Besides having G.I. Joe and his military jeep, and Barbie and her pink convertible and fancy Dreamhouse worked into the wall painting somewhere? Maybe along with a little nod to Christmas in July—and December, too? No."

Ellie laughed, not sure if he was serious or not. One thing was for sure. It really did feel like Christmas, more and more. "That's not usually what goes on baby room murals."

Joe grinned, undeterred. "The right artist might find a way."

His cell phone buzzed with an alert. He pulled it from his pocket and glanced at the screen. "I have to take this." Expression sober, he walked away before answering, "Second Lieutenant Joseph McCabe. Yes, I'll hold." His voice became even more professional and deferential. "Sir." He listened, his back still to Ellie. "Tomorrow?"

Oh, no, Ellie thought. *No, no, no!*

Joe continued, "I'd be honored to help." He paused, still listening. "Yes, I can do that, too." His broad shoulders flexed. "Thank you, sir." He ended the call and turned back to Ellie.

Her heart sinking in her chest, she tried not to cry in disappointment. Instead, she asked, as crisply as possible, "Have they cut your leave short?"

Chapter Fourteen

Not sure what he should, or could, tell Ellie at this juncture, Joe remained where he was. Standing with his back to the living room windows. "No."

She sat slumped in an overstuffed chintz club chair and continued staring at him. Waiting. As pale as if the world were ending.

"That was my commanding officer. The San Antonio public schools are having a career fair, and they want Special Forces officers there to help answer questions and get kids interested in the army as a career. So of course I said yes."

"And it's tomorrow," Ellie ascertained, jerking in a breath.

Joe nodded and began walking toward her. "I have to be there at noon. It's a three and half hour drive there, so I'll need to leave early. Not sure when it will end, but I should be back tomorrow evening. Probably not in time for dinner, obviously, but…why is this upsetting you so much?"

"No reason." She shook off her low mood and stood.

Had she found out her gran had a heart condition? It hadn't seemed so. He thought about the other chores she had wanted to complete before he left for Colorado again.

"Are you worried about me not getting the nursery painted? Because I can get the paint and do that as soon as I get back, once we decide on a color."

Ellie wrinkled her nose, color coming into her face again.

"I'm not sure we can really do that until we find out if we're having a girl or a boy at the ultrasound."

Excitement poured through him. "You want to know?"

"Yes. As soon as possible. Don't you?"

He nodded, glad they had the same view on that.

"And I did get that rescheduled, by the way. It'll happen three days before you're supposed to leave. The doctor's office staff was very nice about it."

"Good to hear. Back to the paint color, though. I don't think we can wait until then to decide on that, if we want to get everything set up for the baby before I leave again."

The troubled frown was back on her face. "Let me think about it," she said slowly.

Eleanor was right not to tell her about the angina just yet, Joe realized. Ellie probably couldn't handle it right now. Any kind of stress was bad for her and their baby.

"Or I can arrange for the decorator to have a contractor come in and paint for us, if you want to wait a little longer." He had just wanted to be here and do this together.

Abruptly, Ellie seemed to be on the same wavelength. "No. I don't mind hiring her to help us get discounts and shipping arranged for the furniture and help us find a mural artist. But I still want to do the things we can easily accomplish ourselves."

Independent as always.

"And you're right. I am making this too hard." Ellie got to her feet. "None of the samples I've seen so far have seemed exactly right." She paused to look him in the eye. "But the paint store will have something perfect, I am sure. I'll go over there tomorrow evening while you're gone, and check it out."

"Ellie! What are you doing in?" the twins asked, when they arrived at the bakery at nine o'clock the following morning.

Sadie and Ingrid had asked the same thing when they'd found her there at 4:00 a.m., shortly after seeing Joe off.

Terri said, "I thought you were taking the next three days off!"

That *was* the plan, but obviously things had changed. "Joe had army business in San Antonio."

"For how long?" Sherri asked.

"Just the day." Ellie explained what had happened.

"Bummer," Sadie said. She seemed to think Joe'd had a choice. That he should have stuck to the plan and done his recruiting when his leave ended.

Secretly, Ellie wished he had been able to do that. That wasn't how the military worked, however. She looked at Joe's little sister, determined to change the subject. "Do you know of any other uniform suppliers where I could try to get a pink maternity chef coat?"

Sadie looked surprised. "The ones you ordered still aren't in?"

Ellie shook her head. "I emailed the company yesterday. Customer service wrote back this morning and said they're on indefinite delay. A problem with the manufacturer."

"The sewing shop in town takes special orders," Terri informed her. "You could just get some pink aprons made up, wear them with white T-shirts underneath and the usual jeans and sneakers."

"Yeah," Sherri added. "It would be easier and likely more comfy, too. Since you could wear short or long-sleeved tees."

"Actually we could *all* do that," Ingrid said. "I think it would be fine as long as the entire staff had an identical look."

Ellie didn't want to even ponder what Gran—who had been every bit as tied to the pink chef coat uniform as her late mom was—would think about that.

One thing was sure…it was too much change, too soon.

Sadie exchanged looks with everyone else. "Actually, I think it's probably not really the right time to talk about this, when we have those two new wedding cake orders to fill. Meanwhile—" she patted Ellie on the shoulder "—I'll make some calls and see what I can do about finding another source for your pink maternity chef coats."

Thanks to a very busy day in the bakery, Ellie had little time to wonder how Joe's day was going and when exactly he would be home from San Antonio.

He didn't call or text her.

She didn't call or text him. As per their usual arrangement. But that didn't mean she didn't miss him. Terribly.

Too tired to go to the hardware store to look at paint, she took Scout for a walk in the lovely summer evening instead. Scout seemed a little sad, too. Like she was also missing Joe.

A harbinger of things to come?

Ellie couldn't help but wonder.

Around eight thirty that night, Ellie finally did get a text from Joe.

ETA for my return now tomorrow afternoon. See you then.

"Well, great," Ellie told Scout. "He was as effusive as ever."

The Westie jumped up beside her on the sofa, where she had been listlessly thumbing through the paint swatches she already had.

"Not that I should expect anything different. He is who he is. Marriage is not going to change that."

Scout put her head on Ellie's thigh and gazed up at her balefully. Ellie stroked her pet's silky white head. "I know you miss him, too, sweetheart," she soothed. "But the two of us have to buck up and get used to it because before we know it, this is just the way it is going to be. For weeks and months on end. And there's not a thing either of us can do about it."

"Ellie, are you okay?" Ingrid asked when she walked into the bakery shortly before it opened the next day.

Lynette slid a fresh batch of strawberry cupcakes into the display case. "Yeah, you look like you didn't sleep at all."

Ellie hadn't. She and Scout had both tossed and turned all night.

Sadie shook her head, clearly as worried as her other employees. "I tried to get her to take the whole day off. Rest up. Or at least start coming in at a more humane hour than 4:00 a.m."

Ellie scowled at Joe's sister. "You're doing it, too."

"Only because I need the extra cash if I'm ever to get my lavender farm up and running. Once I actually buy the land, that is. Also, I'm not pregnant. *You* are."

"She's also a newlywed." Lynnette, who was still passionately in love with her own husband of thirty years, winked. "So maybe there's a good reason she's looking so tired."

Sadie shook her head. "My brother is still in San Antonio. Not due back till later today. And I mean it, Ellie. As your best friend, as well as your sister-in-law, I am telling you, you have got to take better care of yourself. You need to take the rest of the day off and tomorrow, too. Put your feet up and get some sleep, so you can enjoy what time you have with Joe."

Romance-laced smiles abounded as everyone nodded in agreement. Almost as if they knew something she didn't, Ellie thought.

"Sadie's right. We've got everything covered here," Sherri said, taking the mixing bowl out of Ellie's hands and practically pushing her out the door.

Ellie thought about going right back into the bakery and arguing her case. After all, she *was* the boss.

But she also knew they were right. She did need to take better care of herself. And first on her list of things to do was go and see Gran.

Fifteen minutes later, she was on her way.

Gran met her in the Laramie Gardens courtyard. The landscaped area was beautiful, tranquil and shady. "Look who came to see you," Ellie teased.

Tail wagging, Scout hurried over to Gran's side. She reached down to pet Ellie's beloved Westie. "I have missed you," she cooed. "Both of you!" she added with a warm, welcoming smile.

Ellie bent to hug her grandmother, than took a seat at the table beside her where a glass of decaf iced tea with lemon was already waiting. "I have missed you, too," Ellie said hoarsely. "I'm so used to seeing you every day at work."

Gran patted Ellie's forearm gently. "You'll get used to me not being there."

Ellie knew that was true as far as the bakery went. She was simply too busy running things and filling orders to mope around, wishing everything hadn't changed so drastically, so fast. And even if that weren't the case, her separation anxiety wasn't a burden her aging grandmother should have to carry. She covered Gran's wrinkled hand with her own. "Still, I feel like I should be here every day, and I haven't been."

Eleanor squeezed her fingers and gave her a gentle, reassuring look. "I have plenty of company, darling. Lots of activities to keep me busy. Plus, Joe was here on Wednesday. And now it's Friday. And the three of us are still scheduled for Sunday brunch again, right?"

Ellie nodded. "Yes. We will be here." At least *she* would.

Who knew where Joe would be off to if the army called? She told herself to grow up and get a grip—if she weren't careful, she'd turn into one of those resentful wives who made their military husbands miserable. Instead, she focused on what her grandmother had just revealed. "You said Joe was here to see you?"

"Yes." Gran smiled and sipped her drink. "He didn't mention it?"

"No. He didn't." Ellie tried to pretend it was no big deal. Even though it felt like it was. "Was there a special reason he was here?"

"He just wanted to stop by and see if I needed anything, which I didn't. But of course," she continued cheerfully, "I always love seeing my new grandson-in-law."

That was true. Ellie also knew that Joe usually didn't do anything without a specific reason. So what was it? Gran's benign expression gave no clue. "How long was he here?" she asked curiously.

Eleanor smiled as Scout curled up at her feet. "Oh—" she waved an airy hand "—maybe an hour."

That was a long time for idle chitchat. Especially for Joe. Feeling more off-kilter than before, Ellie asked, "What did you talk about?"

"Mostly? You."

Unable to tamp down her curiosity, Ellie waited. There had to be more.

Gran paused, as if choosing her words carefully. "He wants to make sure you're happy and that you and the baby have everything you all need, whether he is here or not."

So her husband's mind was on departing for duty again, Ellie thought, depressed. She'd always had a hard time dealing with him leaving. She usually was better at covering her sadness, though. "What did you tell him?"

Gran flashed a maternal smile. "To follow his instincts. He's always known what to do when it comes to you."

That wasn't quite true, Ellie thought. Otherwise, he would be doing *a lot better* job of communicating with her.

Leaving Gran to her midmorning pottery class, Ellie walked out of Laramie Gardens. She was still feeling glum when her phone rang. Transferring Scout's leash to her other hand, she answered.

Mitzy McCabe was on the other end of the call with an invitation that just added to Ellie's stress.

"A family dinner at the ranch sounds wonderful," she fibbed, because she really wasn't feeling like it, not at all. "But I'm going to have to talk to Joe..."

"Where is he, by the way, do you know?" Mitzy asked, sounding as frustrated as Ellie privately felt. "I can't get him to answer my calls or my texts."

Ellie opened her car door and stepped back to allow Scout to hop inside the passenger compartment. "San Antonio. Army business. He was supposed to be back last night, but that didn't happen."

There was a long pause. "When is he coming back?" Mitzy sounded even more unhappy.

"This afternoon. Hopefully," Ellie couldn't help but add.

Her mother-in-law made an indistinguishable sound, then cleared her throat and said pleasantly, "Please let him know the two of you have got to be at the Knotty Pine Ranch for dinner this evening. It's important."

"I will," Ellie said.

She just hoped he was back in time.

Ellie got in the car, backed out of the space and headed back to the apartment with Scout. Once there, she looked in the mirror. She didn't look all that great, given the paleness of her skin and the dark circles under her eyes. In fact, she looked so worn-out, she was surprised her grandmother hadn't mentioned it. Eleanor was probably just being kind and discreet.

She stifled a yawn, fatigue moving over her in a wave. Her employees were right—she needed to be taking better care of herself.

Kicking off her shoes, she grabbed a throw blanket from the sofa and headed for her queen-size bed. She closed her eyes and, still thinking about Joe and wondering if he would actually be home when he said, fell fast asleep.

Chapter Fifteen

Joe walked into the apartment at four thirty that afternoon, expecting to find it empty.

Scout was on her cozy dog bed, sleeping away. Ellie was on theirs, curled up atop the covers, a white chenille throw drawn across her body. Also sound asleep.

He set his duffel down, wishing he'd had time to change out of his camo utility uniform and boots. He walked over to the bed and sat on the edge of it. As he stared down at her, his heart swelled with love for her and their unborn baby.

Her lashes fluttered open. She gazed up at him, more gorgeous and feminine and alluring than ever. She was going to be such an incredible mother to their child. She was already a great partner and wife to him.

"Hey there, sleeping beauty," he said.

"You're home." Her low voice trembled with emotion.

"I sure am." He gathered her in his arms and kissed her hello, letting her know how much he had missed her. She surrendered to him sleepily. When he let her go, the desire in her gaze eased, replaced by the complex welter of feelings he knew he deserved to see.

Soft lips twisting, she raised up on her elbows. "Why didn't you come home last night, like you promised?"

He unlaced and pulled off his boots, then stretched out on the bed beside her. "Long story."

"Luckily for both of us," she told him impatiently, rolling onto her side to face him, "I've got time."

Joe watched her shiny blond locks fall loosely over one shoulder but tamped down the urge to run his fingers through the soft, silky strands. "Well, you know when my commanding officer called, he asked me to appear at the career fair for the San Antonio Public School system."

Her gaze narrowing, she propped her elbow on her pillow, her head on her fist. "It went on for two days?"

Trying not to think how pretty she looked with her flushed cheeks and mussed hair, Joe told her calmly, "No, just the one."

Indignation flared in her green eyes. "Then?"

"When the instructions came in by email yesterday morning, there was also an order for me to meet with the Special Forces recruiting group in the area. That was supposed to happen on Thursday evening after the job fair, but it got pushed to this morning. So I had to do that before I could leave."

"Why did they want you to meet with them?"

"Because," Joe informed her, enjoying the challenging nature of the conversation, the way he always did when they went toe-to-toe on a subject, "my commanding officer has arranged for a temporary one-year assignment as an army recruiter, if I want to take it, starting when I reenlist. I'd be stationed in San Antonio."

Hope shone in her eyes, replaced quickly by the reality of the distance. "That's three and a half hours from here."

Joe caught her free hand in his. "It's also an easy drive, and I would have a lot of weekends where I could come to Laramie during that assignment." He tightened his grip on her delicate skin. "And the group promised me I could come home for the birth, if we knew about when it was going to happen. Otherwise, I could just get in the car and drive here right away when you went into labor."

"And then you'd be a recruiter from now on?" Twin spots of color appeared in her cheeks.

"No." He drew in a long, calming breath. *Now for the downside.* "I'd go back to my company when the time was up. And finish out my next enlistment that way."

She studied him, her mood shifting, just the way his had when presented with the offer. She withdrew her hand and sat up all the way. "You don't want to do it, do you?"

Joe knew he owed it to her to be honest. "I can't see myself sitting at a desk in an office forty hours a week. It's just never been me."

"You're right about that. A recruiting office is no place for an adrenaline junkie."

His wife was absolutely correct in that, yet she still looked hurt by his disinterest, Joe noted guiltily.

"Have you turned it down?"

"Not yet," he replied.

"But you want to."

If everything he was trying to accomplish worked out, hell yes, he would turn it down. As well as another three-year enlistment, too. But with his plans for a new business still in flux, he kept silent.

The tension between them continued, broken only by the ring of his cell phone. Seeing who it was—again—he groaned. "Sorry." He sent Ellie an apologetic glance. "I have to get this, or my mother is going to kill me. Hey, Mom."

"Please tell me you're not still off doing military stuff," Mitzy said, sounding more stressed out than he had heard her in a long while.

Joe grimaced. "That's done for the moment. I'm back in Laramie."

"Great, because we need you and Ellie at the Knotty Pine Ranch in an hour for an important family dinner."

Joe looked at his wife. He covered the phone speaker. "There's a family dinner at the ranch this evening," he said.

"I know," she mouthed. Clearly, she wanted to beg off as much as he did. Given that the two of them were in the middle of something important, it was probably wise they did. He turned his attention back to his mom. "Could we have a rain check?"

Her answer was immediate. "No."

Joe blinked in surprise. Generally, his mother was the most reasonable person he knew. "No?" he echoed.

"There are times when family comes first, and this is one of them!" she snapped, before going on in her firmest tone, "So we will see you and Ellie soon. And next time…pick up the phone or answer your texts!"

"Yes, ma'am." Joe ended the call. He turned back to Ellie in shock. "Wow, she is hot under the collar."

Ellie got off the bed and stood, propping her hands on her hips. "I don't blame her. This not answering your phone or replying to your messages is getting old, soldier."

From her tone, this resentment had clearly been simmering for a while. Yet she had always acted as if she were oh so chill, not expecting more of him than he was willing to give or demanding unnecessary things from him.

He ambled closer. "Why didn't you say something if it ticked you off?"

She stood still as a statue and glared at him.

"I thought we had an understanding. That if something changed, I would let you know. Which I did. And if you don't hear from me, then—" he shrugged calmly, not about to make more of this than they should "—whatever I last told you still holds."

"Joe…" She put both hands on her head, as if she felt a giant headache coming on, and moaned so loudly Scout got up off her cushion and came over to see if she could help.

"What?"

"We're having a baby now," she blurted out, seemingly unable to stop herself. "And that means *everything* has changed! Or at the very least," she fumed, "it certainly should!"

Ellie regretted the words the moment they were out.

Joe dropped his hand from her shoulder and stared at her as if he could hardly believe what she had just said.

The heat of embarrassment came into her face. She had just broken every promise they had ever made to each other. About loving each other fiercely but also living their own excessively independent lives.

"That, um, didn't come out right," she said, heading for the bathroom sink.

He lounged in the doorway, arms folded. "It sounded pretty direct to me. You agree with my mom then. That I don't communicate enough? Although to be fair, when I'm off on any kind of army assignment she'd prefer I send proof-of-life pics every hour on the hour just so she knows I'm okay."

Ellie grabbed the face soap, spreading it over her skin. "She's a mom. That's the way mothers are. And just because she wants it," she continued, grabbing a washcloth and wetting it before rinsing off the cleanser, "doesn't mean she thinks it's a sensible request. She knows it's not."

Joe grabbed the electric razor he kept at the apartment and ran it over his jaw. "And yet you agree with my mom on some level," he retorted. "That I should have called her back a whole lot sooner, even though I had my hands full the entire thirty-six hours I was gone."

"Doing what?" Once again, the words were out before Ellie could stop them.

She could have sworn she saw Joe wince, but the next second his expression was as impassive as ever. He looked in the mirror, focusing on the other side of his jaw.

"You went to the job fair in the afternoon and met with the recruiters this morning. What were you doing the rest of the time?" Ellie demanded.

"I had some things there I wanted to look at," Joe said gruffly.

"Like what?"

"Potential improvements for the house. Baby furniture for both the nurseries. A new king bed for us. Stuff like that."

Improvements for the house? Nesting sounded so unlike him. "But you hate shopping." Why did she have the niggling feeling that wasn't the only thing he had done while in San Antonio?

"Yeah, well." He frowned again in obvious frustration, clearly hating her third degree. "Sometimes getting it done early means it's the only way you can get it done at all."

True. He was only going to be here a couple more weeks, and thanks to everything else they had going on, they were woefully behind on getting ready for the baby. "Did you buy anything?"

"I was tempted to buy a king bed for us, but the delivery costs would have been ridiculous, so if we want to do that, we need to purchase it around here. And for the record, I *do* want to do that. So that at least the nursery and the master bedroom will be set up for us at the house."

Her apartment only fit a queen bed. Gran's bed was just a double. Her mom's was long gone and of course now so was her old twin bed.

"I'm sorry," she said. "I didn't know that bothered you."

But like she had realized earlier in the week, the house now belonged to both of them. Which meant the two of them should be able to make improvements. Although it would be nice if they did it together. Instead of having him go off and take the lead, solo, the way he seemed to do almost everything else!

He exhaled. She saw regret—mixed with something else she couldn't identify—on his face. When he spoke again, his voice had softened. "You're pregnant, darlin'. I want you to be comfortable. I want us both to be comfortable when we are together."

Once again, he had seen things others had missed. "I want that for you, too."

He studied her tenderly, all the emotion she felt reflected in his blue eyes. "Then, since you had already planned to take the day off from the bakery, do you want to go shopping tomorrow morning?"

The Ellie of two weeks ago would have said it was way too much too soon. Then she would have reminded herself their marriage was a temporary legal construct and that Joe would be here with her rarely, if at all, once he reenlisted and returned to duty. Baby or no baby.

But the Ellie of right now wanted to live in the fairy tale of all her secret dreams finally coming true. Even if it was only for two more weeks. "Yes," she said.

Half an hour later, Joe and Ellie were on the way out to the ranch. He was driving the beloved pickup he'd had since high school and kept in Texas for his visits home. An unusually quiet Ellie was buckled into the passenger seat. Scout was stretched out on her cushion in the cargo area behind them. Country music playing on the radio added to the laid-back ambiance.

Or *should* have.

Ellie still seemed tense. Reluctant for the evening ahead. He could hardly blame her. After his prolonged unexpected absence the last couple of days, he really wasn't in the mood for making nice at a McCabe family dinner at the ranch, either.

Mostly because of the guilt still twisting his gut into knots.

He hadn't told her everything about what he had been doing lately. Secretly and unsuccessfully shopping for a push present was just the tip of the spear. There was so much more he was still keeping to himself.

Joe had always hated withholding information from Ellie. As a rule of thumb, he wanted to tell her everything. But he couldn't do that when it came to his work in the military, and he couldn't do it when it came to his future plans, either.

Part of it was worked out. He had a location. Funds from his trust to secure the purchase. And thanks to his visits to two similar successful businesses in San Antonio last night, he now had a very good idea what it would take to be competitive in the current Texas market. But a lot of other issues remained, and he couldn't tell Ellie or anyone else what he wanted to do until they were resolved.

That had to be done in the next two weeks.

He knew he could make it all happen. Their future happiness and security depended on it.

The only question was, could he keep Ellie in the dark until he could finally tell her his plan?

They saw the rows and rows of cars and pickups as soon as they turned into the lane for the Knotty Pine Ranch.

Ellie turned pale. "Unless your parents invited every McCabe in the state of Texas—which would admittedly be quite a few—it doesn't exactly look like a simple family dinner. Does it?"

"No," Joe said, frowning. His thoughts returned to a conversation he'd had with his dad a few weeks prior. And the sense he'd had, given his mother's tone, that he and Ellie needed to be semi-dressed up for this important family meal. "It does not."

Deciding his pregnant wife didn't need to embark on a mile-long hike in her dress and heels, he bypassed the last available space and kept right on driving toward the house his parents had used as a country retreat for years.

Ellie's face was turned toward the hundreds of guests milling over the lawn. "And...is that a band and a dance floor?"

He turned off the radio. Music continued faintly in the distance.

"Yes. I think so," he said.

Damn. Damn. Damn.

Ellie whipped back around to face him, perplexed. He couldn't help but note how gorgeous she looked in her new scarlet wrap dress. "Did you forget an anniversary or something?"

He squinted, wishing lamely that were the case. "Well, Alex got married in springtime, but he's divorced, so we don't celebrate either of those two occasions. And my parents were married at Christmastime. Which was months ago..."

Except, now that he took a closer look, he could see there were holiday decorations strewn about. Garlands threaded with sparkling white lights and bows were strung everywhere. The dinner tables were covered with red cloths and sported hurricane lanterns and vases of red roses.

"Then I don't get it," Ellie said as Joe steered onto the lawn next to the house and double-parked.

But she did as soon as he shrugged on his sports coat, and helped her and Scout out of his truck. The band started up a familiar Dolly Parton tune. It was the one J.P. Randall had played during their elopement. Only the lyrics were a little different this time.

"Let's make this a reception to remember. Christmas feelings in the middle of July," the band sang.

Ellie turned to Joe, her lips parted in a soft O of wonder and surprise. Delight sparkled in her eyes, and Joe couldn't help but be moved, too.

The throng of people headed toward them, yelling, "Surprise!" and showcasing a big banner that read *Best Wishes, Joe and Ellie.*

Chapter Sixteen

Gran came through the crowd, flanked by Mitzy and Chase. "Congratulations, darlings!" she said, offering Ellie and Joe both warm, effusive hugs.

"We know you didn't want a big wedding or even a formal reception," Chase told them.

"But we couldn't let such an important commitment go uncelebrated," Mitzy said. "So we arranged a casual outdoor gathering instead."

"With a Christmas in July theme," Ellie said appreciatively. She was a little surprised by how sentimental the event was making her feel. Maybe because with her and Joe married, albeit temporarily, and a baby on the way and him actually here with her for an entire thirty days, it did sort of feel like Christmas.

She could tell he was touched, too.

"Well," Mitzy said with a grin, "we really wanted to make it a special celebration for you."

Ellie hugged her mother-in-law. "And you have," she told her thickly.

"Even if I had to nag you both to get you here?" Mitzy asked.

"We admit," Joe teased his mom right back, "your behavior did seem uncharacteristically demanding."

"Puzzlingly so." But Ellie smiled, too.

"Was there a plan B if you couldn't get us to cooperate?" Joe asked curiously, hugging his mom.

"She was going to send me to bring you here for dinner," Chase said, embracing Joe and Ellie, too. "But it turned out not to be necessary."

As if on cue, half a dozen of the area's most popular food trucks came down the lane. Chase directed them where to park on the grass.

And then Joe and Ellie were swarmed with family and friends. The entire bakery staff was there, grinning from ear to ear because they'd been in on the secret, too. All of Joe's siblings were also in attendance. Plus lots of people they had both grown up with, and others they had recently come to know.

When the initial hullabaloo had cleared, Mitzy appeared at Ellie's side, a cold lemonade in hand. "How are you doing? Do you need to sit a while?" her mother-in-law asked, while Joe continued indefatigably greeting and chatting with their guests.

"Yes, actually," Ellie replied.

Mitzy steered her over to the covered front porch of the ranch house and into one of the rocking chairs. The older woman took the one next to hers.

Ellie glanced over at the sleigh, parked near the entrance to the party. It was brimming with wedding presents and early Christmas gifts. There was also an evergreen tree with sparkling lights, and a wedding bell tree topper. The live holiday music added to it all, and the food and the people... "You did an amazing job with this party," Ellie said. "Thank you so much!"

Mitzy smiled. "It's not every year we have Christmas in July. Although maybe now we should."

That actually would be fun, Ellie thought.

"Anyway, it didn't start out to be this extravagant," Ellie's new mother-in-law confided wryly.

"But like for Gran's retirement bash," Ellie guessed, "everyone wanted to come?"

"You got it." Mitzy smiled proudly.

Ellie watched Joe continue to work his way through their guests. He looked so happy. So content. One would never know how restless he sometimes got when home on leave from the Special Forces. "I can see Joe is loving it, too."

Mitzy's brow lifted.

She continued, "I go to so many local gatherings and see so many people coming in and out of the bakery every week. I think I sometimes take the sense of community Laramie offers for granted." Ellie regarded her husband, unable to help but note how handsome he looked in a dark sports coat, pale blue button-down that brought out the hue of his eyes and jeans. "Watching Joe tonight, it's clear how much he loves having everyone here for him."

"Here for the two of you," Mitzy corrected fondly. "For the happy future we all hope you have. Although, for the record, for a short while there, I was afraid I wasn't going to be able to pull off this surprise party."

Ellie took another sip of tart lemonade and sympathized, "It must have been nerve-racking."

Mitzy laughed and shook her head. "Yes, there were a few tense moments when I found out Joe had gone to San Antonio and not come back. But all is well that ends well." She leaned over to give Ellie a warm hug, promising, "And tonight is going to be spectacular!"

Joe noticed Ellie and his mom sitting down, deep in conversation, and thought maybe Gran should be taking a break, too. Spying her in the crowd, talking to Nora and Zane, he walked over to join them.

"Joe! Have you met Zane Lockhart?" Eleanor asked. "You two really should get to know each other since you're both Special Forces. Or in Zane's case, *was* before he started his now very successful business here."

Hint much? Joe smiled.

"Actually, we've been playing telephone tag," Zane told Eleanor. "But I hope to get together with Joe next week. Show him around Lockhart Search and Rescue."

Gran clapped her hands. "That's fabulous!"

Joe sent the couple, whose kindness was legendary, an appreciative glance. "Looking forward to it," he told Zane, knowing there was much he could learn from the entrepreneur.

Then he turned back to Eleanor. From what he had been able to see, the seventy-year-old had been on her feet since he and Ellie had arrived. "Your granddaughter is taking a little break with my mom. Would you like to go join them?"

Nora looked at Joe. "I think that would be a great idea," she said.

Eleanor frowned. "You don't have to fuss over me," she huffed. "I'm fine. You, either," she told Joe, but nevertheless allowed him to take her elbow. They headed for the covered porch where Ellie and Mitzy were still sitting.

"How are you feeling?" He dropped his voice to a whisper only she could hear. "Any more episodes of angina?"

"No, and not to worry, I have my pills tucked right here." She patted her bosom.

Guilt flowed through Joe. This was not a secret he should be forced to keep. Although he would honor the confidence out of respect. "You really should tell Ellie," he reiterated sternly.

Eleanor frowned. "Not happening."

He had figured as much.

The diminutive woman looked up at him. "What about the push present? Did you find one? Is that why you stayed in San Antonio so long?"

Joe exhaled. "I don't have one yet…but I'll get one. I was away on army business."

"Well, you should have been here on *Ellie business*," Gran scolded.

Joe wasn't sure what to say to that. Part of him agreed wholeheartedly, but the situation was complicated.

"You'll be gone in two more weeks," Eleanor reminded him.

For two months, while he completed his current tour of duty. After that, well, Joe sincerely hoped not.

"That was some finish to our party," Ellie remarked happily hours later, when they were on their way home.

"I know." Joe lifted a hand to mime the red-and-green fireworks that had filled the Texas sky. "Joe and Ellie Forever!"

"Plus, the song the band played and everyone sang at the end."

Joe hummed "Feliz Navidad," picking up where the lyrics had changed to fit their special occasion. "We want to wish you a happy marriage from the bottom of our hearts…"

Ellie's eyes misted over. Again. "It was all so sentimental," she said thickly, still unbearably touched by all the affection their friends and family had shown them.

"And full of love," Joe agreed.

Ellie rested her hand on her belly. "And just think…our baby is going to enjoy all of this, too."

"No question about it," Joe said. "Laramie is a great place for kids to grow up."

Just not for him to live permanently, Ellie thought, before she could stop herself. Resolved not to go there, she changed the subject "So. What were you and Zane Lockhart talking about tonight? Gran told your mother and me you were going to visit his business?" Out of some sort of duty, Ellie imagined, since her gran had been pushing the idea of Joe working there every time they saw her. No matter how many times Ellie asked her not to.

Nodding, Joe braked to let a deer and her fawn cross the dark country road. "Yeah. Zane offered to show me Lockhart Search and Rescue."

Ellie felt a brief burst of excitement. "Are you thinking about taking a job there?" For an adrenaline junkie with his skills, it would be a perfect fit.

Seeing the road was clear, he drove on, his large hands capably circling the wheel. "The question of employment didn't come up. I think it's more of a tour, one ex-military guy showing another what he built kind of thing."

"Oh. Right."

Joe glanced over at her, his regard sharp.

Ellie's private hope—that he might find something to do here that really interested and challenged him—faded. With effort, she shoved the notion aside.

Joe had never expressed any desire to quit the military and move back home, even after he found out she was pregnant. Things were still so precarious with them; it would be wrong to push him now or put in her two cents about what he should or should not do.

"Are you saying you *want* me to do something like that?" Joe asked. "Here in Laramie?"

Yes, Ellie thought. *Absolutely, positively yes!*

But returning to a more traditional way of life here in rural Texas might not be what *he* wanted, so she pushed her secret longing away. She had signed up for this when she fell in love with him. She would not wimp out now.

So to honor the promises they had made to each other, she went the other way, dutifully saying the opposite of what she privately yearned to have. "We had a deal, Joe. To love each other and do everything we each wanted at the same time." She inhaled deeply. "Baby or no, that hasn't changed. But." Ellie reached across the console to cover his hand with hers. "Your mom was absolutely right about one thing tonight. We haven't celebrated where we are *right now.* Not nearly enough." She brought his hand up to her lips and kissed the back of it. "And it's high time we started."

Joe wasn't surprised Ellie wanted to make love the moment they got back to the apartment. He wanted to savor their time together as much as possible, too.

Afterward, while Ellie clung to him, slipping immediately into sleep, Joe remained awake. As he held her close, breathing in the sweet, familiar scent of her, he thought about what she had said, about wanting to retain their status quo. As always, she was not open to change, but just this once, he sure wished she would be. Regardless, he had to do what he knew in his gut was right for the two of them and their baby.

Even if initially she wouldn't be all that happy about it.

As soon as he got the rest of the details worked out, he would tell her what was on his mind. And let her know what their future was going to look like over the course of the next year.

"What do you think?" Joe asked Ellie late Saturday afternoon, in that sexy Texas drawl she loved.

Because she had the day off from work, they'd slept in, had a leisurely brunch and then driven to San Angelo to shop.

Usually shopping wasn't his favorite thing, but today, to her increasing delight, he really seemed to be enjoying himself.

He relaxed his muscular body, tilting his head back on the pillow and turned his gaze up toward the store ceiling. She did the same, snuggling down against the quilted bed top. He nudged her sock-clad foot with his. "Too firm? Not firm enough? Or just right?"

They were lying on the last of twenty different mattress sets in the shop. "Not sure," Ellie said.

It was crazy how much she liked doing domestic stuff like this with him. Never mind how good it felt to be nesting. She turned to look at him, taking in his handsome visage. A tiny thrill went through her. Envisioning making love with him on the roomy king-size mattress, she asked, "What do you think?"

The corners of his lower lip curled up in the way that always made her want to kiss him. His eyes twinkled. "I prefer the extra firm," he answered candidly. "I think it offers the most support."

So did Ellie actually. "Then the extra firm it is." Relieved to have the decision made, she sat up next to him.

Joe rose to a seated position, too. "You sure?"

"Yep." She clasped his hand, loving his abundance of warmth and strength. Then returning his quizzical smile, replied, "It really is what I liked the most, too, but you're a lot bigger than I am, and I wanted to make sure you were comfortable."

Joe waved at the salesperson. She came toward them, clipboard in hand.

Three hours later, they had purchased a king-size bed, linens and pillows for the house. They'd also bought a crib, changing table and rocker-glider for the nursery, too.

"You sure you want to wait on outfitting the apartment

for the little one?" Joe asked as they headed for his truck. He tossed the packages in the cargo area behind the bench seat, then, grasping her hand, helped her up into the cab.

"Yes, the apartment is so small, I want to start with a portable crib or maybe even a baby buggy for sleeping. I haven't decided."

"Let me know. I want to pay my half."

She went hands on hips. "Is it going to be a competition?" she quipped lightly.

Joe planted a hand on her spine and brought her close. "A coordinated, equitable effort." He bent down to kiss her soundly, sending yet another thrill through her. "And yes, darlin'." He kissed her one last time. "It is."

Sunday, Joe and Ellie had brunch with Gran. To Joe's relief, his grandmother-in-law looked much healthier than she had earlier in the week.

Afterward, he took Ellie to the hardware store to look over additional paint colors. This was usually the kind of decorating task that drove him crazy. But this time he didn't mind as Ellie mulled over each choice with quiet deliberation. She got samples of her four top choices, and they went back to the house to put them all up on white poster board, taped to the nursery walls. He had expected to have to wait another few days for her to make a final decision, but as soon as the samples were up and dry, she knew. She wanted the soothing sage green that would work for either a girl or a boy.

"Do you think we have time to paint today?" she asked him.

Joe nodded. He knew what he still had to do to secure their future, so the more they could get done before his leave ended, the better. He went back to the store to get the child-safe paint for the nursery while she taped it off.

"Good thing we got the paint that had the primer in it. Otherwise, I don't think this would have covered all that purple," Ellie remarked once he returned. She knelt near the baseboard, using a trim brush to cover the wall closest to the baseboard and the edges near the bedroom window.

Joe used a roller to spread paint on big expanses of wall. He smiled over at his wife, surprised at how *married* they felt now. Like they were a team. The kind that could last.

Ellie seemed to be feeling it, too.

And though he knew, technically, she still had one foot out the proverbial door, he also hoped that if they continued on the path they were on, they just might be able to make this work, long-term.

He was still mulling that possibility over the next day; Ellie went back to work at the bakery, and he drove out to Zane Lockhart's ranch to see the search and rescue organization.

A big lodge served as a coordination center and was equipped with a commercial kitchen big enough to serve hungry searchers. Another room held bunks for on-duty rescuers needing sleep. As far as he could tell, the training facilities were excellent. All the equipment they used was very well-maintained and state-of-the-art. Most of the employees Joe met were either ex-military or ex-fire department.

"Impressive," he said.

Zane nodded. "Eleanor told me your enlistment is up in a couple of months. That you might be looking for work here…"

Leave it to Gran to jump the gun.

"…I can offer you work as a sub, but otherwise I'm fully staffed."

That did not surprise Joe. "I appreciate the offer. And certainly I'd be glad to help out in an emergency," Joe told the man frankly. "But I'm not looking to work for anyone else."

"I can understand that. It's why I started my own business." Zane's pager went off. He looked at it. "Speaking of emergencies." He grimaced. "Some kids are stuck on the cliffs overlooking Lake Laramie."

Joe felt a burst of adrenaline. "Anyone hurt?"

Zane continued reading. "Apparently, there is a girl on a ledge with a cut leg. They've stopped the bleeding, but they can't get her down on their own."

The need to be of service rushing through his veins, Joe asked, "Want some help?"

Zane was already dialing the local paramedics. "Hell, yes."

That evening, Ellie had just taken the first of two pies out of the oven when Joe walked through the door. His clothes were smudged with dirt, and he had a scrape on one arm that looked as if it had already been tended to.

"Hey," she said, smiling. When he'd told her he was pitching in on a mission with Lockhart Search and Rescue, she hadn't been worried the way she usually would have. "Thanks for letting me know what was going on and when you'd be home tonight."

He walked over to take her in his arms. Pressing a kiss on the top of her head, he said, "I'm trying to do better with the communication."

She reached up to kiss him back. "Well, you did."

When their embrace ended, she went back to making dinner. "So what happened today?"

Joe tugged his cotton T-shirt over his head, grabbed a clean one from the bedroom, then ambled back into the living area. "A group of high school kids decided a little adventure was in order. They all went out to the cliff on the lake."

Ellie splayed her hand over her heart in distress. "Not that huge sixty-foot one? The one that hangs out over the lake at the top and goes down to the beach at the bottom? All the kids get hurt on it...even when we were in school."

He stepped to the kitchen sink and washed his hands. "That would be the one, yep."

Ellie put the spaghetti in to boil. "So what happened?"

Joe lounged against the counter, brawny arms folded in front of him. "Half of them decided to use ropes to belay down from top. The other half were going to free-climb up from the bottom. They were going to meet midway, get a bunch of shots of all of them to put on Instagram, and then the rope climbers would piggyback the free-climbers down to the bottom, sort of like you see happen in rescues."

She winced just thinking about it. "Sounds even more dangerous than some of the stuff you used to do when you were a kid, messing around out there."

Joe agreed soberly, "It was. Anyway, one of the girls ripped open her knee on a rough piece of rock and started bleeding. Everyone freaked out. Somehow, she managed to get herself up to the ledge that goes across midway, and a couple other climbers made their way to her and put together a makeshift bandage with their clothes to halt the blood flow. But they didn't think they could get her safely down without the bleeding starting again, so one of them called Zane directly. He answered, and we gathered the crew that was at LS&R, called the paramedics and headed on out."

"I'm assuming the rescue went well?"

"It was flawless, really. Zane's guys and gals are all either ex-military or ex-firefighters, so they know their stuff, and the kids were scared enough to follow every single instruction we gave them, no problem."

Ellie got the salad out of the fridge and shut the door with her hip, an action that elicited a sexy grin from Joe. Tingles of awareness shifting through her, she asked, "Did they explain why they did such a harebrained thing in the first place?"

"Well, like I said, they were all feeling a little restless and wanted some adventure. And they're all into climbing, either rope or bouldering or both. But the Texas climbing gyms are all in the big cities like Houston, Dallas and Austin. So, as they explained to Zane and the rep from the sheriff's department, unless they can organize a road trip, they make do with whatever climbing opportunities they can find here."

She got out the butter and put it on the center of the table next to a basket of crusty bread. "Like the back of the old warehouse."

Joe angled his head in surprise. "You know about that?"

"Oh, everyone does." Ellie drained the pasta, put it on a serving platter and covered it with meatballs in tomato sauce. "For a while some crazy kids tried to do something similar off the back of the historic district buildings in town, too, but the sheriff's department patrols the town at night now, and that swiftly put an end to that. At least I hope it did."

"Me, too," he concurred with a frown.

Admiring her husband's heroic nature, Ellie got out the block of Parmesan cheese. "Did you like working with the LS&R team?"

Joe smiled. "I did. And I agreed to sub for Zane in emergencies." He caught the sudden hope in her expression. As always, he seemed to intuit where her thoughts were going next. "But he's fully staffed with a list of people waiting for spots. So there is no possibility of full-time employment there, even if I did want it, which I...don't."

Once again, Ellie worked to quash her disappointment over that.

Joe watched her remove both golden brown pies from the

oven and place them on a wooden board to cool. "Smells like apple," he said admiringly.

"One definitely is. The other has filling that's made primarily of crackers."

"Test run of the pies for the Townsends?"

"I have to know what I'm sending out." After handing him the platter of pasta, she carried the salad to the table, and they sat down together.

Joe was famished, so she was glad she had made a little extra.

Finished, he leaned back in his chair, content, and praised softly, "That was incredible."

Ellie smiled back. "Thanks." She sighed. She was going to miss this so much—seeing each other every morning first thing and having dinner together after their long workdays. Or rather, *her* long days. She wasn't actually sure what Joe was doing most of the time. Just that he seemed busy and a bit distracted. Which was probably par for the course, given that he would be going back to active duty soon.

She had to keep reminding herself of that.

And yeah, it would be hard—maybe even feel unbearable at times—but she also had to remember she really was strong enough to let him go.

She and the baby would be okay.

And so would Joe. No matter where he was or what he was doing. Fitzgerald family curse or no.

Determined to enjoy every moment right now and worry about the future after he had gone, Ellie batted her lashes at him flirtatiously. "Ready to sample the desserts?"

Joe smiled. "For you, darlin'? Always."

Chapter Seventeen

"I got Joe's opinion last night," Ellie told Gran after lunch the next day. She set out two pieces of pie before settling back in her seat. "Now I need yours."

After tasting the offerings, Gran immediately recognized the difference in the two. "They are both absolutely delicious, Ellie, but only one has real apples. In the other, you can taste the butter crackers in the filling."

Ellie shook her head in consternation. "That's what Joe and I thought, too. I don't understand why anyone ever came up with this recipe."

"Apples were hard to come by during the Great Depression, as well as World War II, so crackers were used as a substitute. And a lot of people really liked it, although some were put off by the rather gelatinous texture of the filling."

"Yeah, I know what you mean. It's kind of like pecan pie filling with a lot of cinnamon and lemon instead of pecans."

"Mmm-hmm. In any case, you did a good job on the test run. Looking at the pies, prior to cutting into them, no one would know they were not identical. And you will have a real, beautiful apple pie for Vivian to serve at the luncheon, as well as a ton of other desserts on the buffet table, so it is possible no one will know about the switcheroo."

Ellie smiled. It always helped her so much to confide in her grandmother. "Oh, Gran, I hope that is what happens."

"Either way, you can't stop the reckoning that's coming between Monica and Vivian. All you can do is get out of the way and try not to make it any worse than it's going to be when it does happen."

Hormone-fueled emotion rose inside Ellie like a whirlwind. "I just feel bad to be forced into this. So the bakery wouldn't get sued."

Taking another bite of pie, Gran nodded in understanding. Then went on, "Do you remember the time about seven or eight years ago, when we were in the midst of prepping for the Sullivan-Garcia wedding? The groom's family wanted a chocolate caramel wedding cake, the bride's family insisted on apricot vanilla cream. We suggested a way to include both, with plain vanilla tiers in between, but they said no."

"Yeah. They argued incessantly all the way up to the week of the wedding," Ellie remembered.

"Until finally the bride's family agreed to let the groom's family's selection be served as a groom's cake. But only at the rehearsal dinner."

Ellie grinned, recalling the over-the-top familial drama. "The groom held firm. He wanted his family's favorite cake at the wedding, too. So they agreed to put it out, and then when the dust settled, the bride's family moved it to a place where almost no one would see it. The groom's family got wind of what had happened and why."

"And a brawl ensued, right there in the middle of the Sullivan-Garcia reception!" Ellie sighed. It was conflicts like this that had always made her want to avoid a big wedding herself. "People are still talking about it as sort of a cautionary tale, when pre-wedding tensions start to get out of hand."

"As they should." Gran put her plate aside. "The point is, these kinds of family conflicts have happened before. They will happen again." She held out her arms. "All you can do, darling, is your very best."

Ellie leaned over and hugged her. Breathing in the comforting warmth, she said, "I am doing that, Gran."

"I know, sweetheart. You've got this. It's all part of owning and running a business. And come Thursday, when the luncheon is over—no matter what happens—it will all be behind us."

She nodded, hoping in her heart her gran was right.

"In the meantime, how are things with you and Joe? Has any of the furniture you bought last weekend been delivered?"

Ellie took a deep breath, beginning to feel overwhelmed again. She knew the change was all for the good, but it still seemed like so much was happening, so fast. "That's not coming until later in the week, but that's okay because Joe decided he wants to go ahead and paint as much of the upstairs as he can beforehand." Ellie got out her phone and showed her gran the ivory hue they had chosen for all but the nursery.

Gran tilted her head. "You're not helping?"

"I wanted to at least do the master bedroom. But even though I took frequent breaks and we opened the windows to ensure good ventilation and used the new zero-VOC, fume-free paint, he saw how tired I got the day we did the nursery. He thinks it's too much for a pregnant woman on top of working at the bakery." Ellie shrugged. "So he talked his brother Alex into helping him, and I've been banned from wielding any more paintbrushes or rollers at the moment. He doesn't even want me to come by the house until it's finished. He knows how hard it is for me to simply sit around while others toil away."

Gran grinned and put a palm to her heart. "I love that new husband of yours."

"Me, too." So much.

A contented silence fell. "Well, I've got to get back to the bakery and finish up there," Ellie said at last, "and then Joe and I have birthing class tonight, so I better be on my way."

Gran stood and gave Ellie a fierce, loving hug. "I'll see you Thursday?"

She nodded. Happy that even though she and her grand-mother weren't working together every day now, they still were as close as ever. That was something that wasn't going to change! Smiling, Ellie promised, "I'll pick you up before the luncheon."

Joe was sitting in the apartment, his laptop open in front of him, Scout curled contentedly at his feet. The construc-tion bids for his business had come in. The overall cost was about what he had figured it would be and could probably be managed if he sectioned off the building and did it in stages. The timing for completion, though, was a lot longer than what he had hoped. That could be problematic from a cash flow standpoint. On the other hand, if he were to *open* in stages instead of all at once, then maybe—

"Joe? *Joe!*"

Jerked out of his reverie, he looked up to find Ellie stand-ing over him, a perplexed look on her face.

Not wanting her to see what he'd been looking at, he shut his laptop. "Sorry." He rose to give her a hug. "I didn't hear you come in."

She hugged him back, then knelt down to greet a furi-ously wagging Scout. "Obviously." The Westie stood on her hind legs and licked Ellie beneath the chin. She stood again. "What were you looking at?"

"Work stuff." Which was true, as far as it went.

She lifted a brow, waiting for him to go on.

There would be time to tell her what he planned to do, but not until he had all his ducks in a row. Not when he still only had 75 percent of his new venture worked out. He shrugged and, not wanting to lie to her, said nothing more.

"I know." She turned away, unhappy. "You can't talk about army stuff." She strode into the kitchen, all easy grace once again.

Trailing behind her, his body reacted to the fantastic view of her long, sexy legs and curvy backside.

She swung back to face him, her honey-blond hair swirling about her shoulders. That quickly, he saw the inner force field go up around her heart. She released a quavering breath. "Just please tell me you don't have to leave early?"

Even as he admired her inner toughness and tenacity, he wished she would lean on him a little more. Gruffly, he told her, "I do not have orders to report back to base until a week from Friday."

Ellie sighed.

Closing the distance between them, he wrapped his arms around her, and she relaxed into him. Loving the way she felt, so soft and warm and womanly, he pressed a kiss to the top of her head.

After a moment, Ellie drew back. An unhappy glint still appeared in her green eyes. "You forgot, didn't you?"

Apparently, he had. Worse, he still couldn't recall. "What?" He swore inwardly.

Ellie threw up her hands in frustration. "We have birthing class tonight! And a meeting with the mural artist in the hospital bistro directly afterward."

He swore again mentally. There was going to be no pretending. "Yeah, sorry. All the painting…and hanging out with Alex…talking to him about his ranch…" He frowned again, admitting, "Both things slipped my mind."

"Well, we have forty-five minutes until we have to be there. And the baby and I need something to eat before we go, so…"

Finally, something he could fix. Pronto. "I'm on it!"

The birthing class went well. Ellie and Joe both learned a lot about the stages of labor and how to best manage each. As much as she loved having her husband with her, Ellie couldn't help but think this was the second class they would attend together. There would be one more, and then his sister Sadie would take his place.

She knew this was just the way it had to be. Lots of military wives didn't have their husbands there with them for even one class, much less the birth of their babies. She should buck up.

Yet she couldn't shake her private disappointment. It was still with her when they met Adele Harper in the hospital bistro.

The ebullient twentysomething was an art teacher at the local high school who did murals on the side. She'd brought a folder containing photos of her previous work. All were stunning. And different as could be.

"As you can see, there is no limit as to what you can put in a nursery these days," Adele said. "A lot of my clients choose a favorite childhood story or movie as inspiration. Others want a themed wall centering around spaceships or ballerinas. Athletes. I've even done Western landscapes, with cowboys and horses."

"Wow," Joe said, seeming drawn to the boldly colored, action-oriented art.

Ellie liked the soothing pastel designs. "It's kind of hard to choose since we don't yet know if we're having a boy or a girl," she said finally.

"Are you planning to find out the sex?" Adele asked.

Ellie looked at Joe, remembering their discussion about this. "We'd rather know now," she said. *When Joe is able to be here with me when we find out.* Because this was definitely something they could share!

"When is your ultrasound?" Adele asked.

"Next Tuesday morning," Ellie said. And then Joe would leave early Friday… Which meant they had ten days left. Her heart sank. Where had the time gone?

Suddenly, it felt a little less like Christmas in July… And more like plain old early August…

"Well, how about you think about it and come up with ideas, and then we can brainstorm the theme of the mural once you know if you're having a boy or a girl?" Adele asked.

"Good plan," Joe said.

They thanked her and headed out.

By the time they got home at nine thirty, Ellie was so tired she could barely manage the stairs to the apartment. She got into her pj's while Joe took Scout out.

When he returned, she had tall glasses of cold milk and gingersnaps from the bakery waiting for them.

"Yum." He washed his hands and joined her on the sofa. "I am really going to miss these," he murmured, savoring the sweet and spicy treat.

Ellie snuggled next to him. "I can ship you some."

"I know." He took another bite. "So what did you think about Adele Harper?"

Ellie sipped her milk, then grimaced as she took her nightly prenatal vitamin and iron. She followed that with a bite of cookie to get rid of the medicine taste. "I liked her." Another sip of milk, another bite of cookie. "Didn't you?"

"Very much," Joe admitted.

"Then?" What was the reason behind his seeming reservation now, she wondered.

Intuiting where she was going with this, Joe laced an arm around her shoulders and drew her into the curve of his body. "At the end of our meeting, you seemed a little down or something."

Observant as ever. She rested her cheek in the crook of his neck, figuring there was no harm in admitting it. "I was just feeling overwhelmed. There is still so much left to get done." And she had liked doing everything together.

Joe regarded her affectionately, probably mistakenly thinking it was all a timing issue. "And four and a half months in which to accomplish everything."

"But you won't be here." The plaintive words were out before Ellie could stop them.

He started to say something but then halted without uttering a word. The conflicted expression on his face faded as he, too, worked to get his feelings under control. Finally, he said, "I'm going to be calling and emailing you every chance I get."

"I know you will." Suddenly, Ellie felt near tears and needed a moment to collect herself. Swallowing, she managed, "Communications are still spotty at best, though, and…" *Damn it, Joe, I'm going to miss you so...so much!*

Joe drew her all the way onto his lap. Sifting his hand through her hair, he tilted her face up to his. All the love and tenderness she had ever wanted was on his face. "Time is going to fly by," he promised her softly. "You'll see."

Which was, Ellie thought, exactly what she was afraid of.

Chapter Eighteen

At five o'clock the next morning, Sadie abruptly stopped measuring batter into the buttered and floured cake pans. She moved quickly to Ellie's side and half led, half pushed her onto a nearby stool. Hovering close, she finally said, "You do not look good."

A new wave of fatigue swept through Ellie. She gave her best friend the evil eye. Bad enough she still didn't have a pink chef coat that didn't need the last three buttons left undone, but now her persistent morning nausea left her with a pale demeanor rather than that healthy glow all pregnant women were supposed to have. "Thanks," she grumbled. "I needed that."

"I'm serious." Sadie pulled up another stool to sit knee to knee with her and blurted, "I've never seen you look this exhausted."

That's because, Ellie thought wearily, she had never *been* this tired. She felt it in every one of her muscles and bones. "Joe and I were out late last night."

"You mean past seven thirty?" Her employee got up and returned with an individual bottle of orange juice. She uncapped it and handed it to Ellie.

Ellie sipped slowly, careful not to trigger the morning sickness she often felt this time of day. Never more so than when she was tired. "Ha-ha. And yeah, I'm sure it was still early by your standards, since you're one of those people who can get by on six hours of sleep a night." Ellie needed eight hours, or six plus a nap, to feel human. And that was when she wasn't carrying a tiny, growing human inside her.

Sadie went back to measuring batter into pans. "What time did you two get to bed?"

"Ten." Although sleep had been a ways off. Ellie smiled, reflecting on the passionate lovemaking of the night before. How Joe could always make her feel so much better, just by taking her in his arms and holding her close.

Sadie lifted a halting hand that reminded Ellie that Joe was her brother. "Don't tell me any more..."

Ellie chuckled. "Not planning to."

Sadie slid the filled pans into the preheated oven and returned with a new cup of coffee for herself. She settled next to Ellie. "Seriously, it is becoming increasingly clear that you need more sleep now that you're pregnant. Maybe it's time to stop coming in to work predawn. And instead start around six or seven."

"I understand if you don't want to come in anymore at 4:00 a.m.," Ellie said.

Sadie waved off the comment. "I'm fine with the hours, whatever they may be. I like working here, and as I've mentioned, I need as much money as I can earn to get my lavender farm underway."

Ellie nodded. She knew from their long discussions that Sadie was planning to use all the cash from her trust fund to purchase the land and make the house at least livable on the rundown property she had her eye on. But her best friend still needed cash to erect a greenhouse for growing seedlings, get a tractor and get the fields planted, which was where her full-time work at the bakery came in. Ellie studied her. "So you really don't mind coming in so early?"

"No." Sadie began buttering and flouring a new set of pans. "Because then I'm completely done here by noon."

"Then?" Ellie got up off the stool and followed suit.

The two of them worked silently side by side for a few minutes. "If you want my honest opinion—" Sadie measured out more butter "—I don't think it's necessary for any of us to be here that early. Not since the third and fourth commercial ovens were put in a couple of years ago. Two people could start at seven, two more could show up at eight, and we would still have plenty of product in the case by the time we opened at nine. The cakes we're doing now could be done throughout the day while just one person mans the front of the store."

Part of Ellie wanted to make a change like that, too. The truth was, she was also over getting up at four six days a week to bake. And she was so tired. And getting more pregnant by the day.

"I'll think about it," Ellie said finally. It would be hard for her to make such a big change, right now, when her world already felt like it was in upheaval. On the other hand, with Joe leaving shortly, what would happen if she didn't start making accommodations for the new life growing inside her?

Sadie lifted a brow. "You're serious?"

Ellie realized she was. "Yes."

"Then you should really think about convening a meeting with the entire staff to hear some more ideas about how we could improve things around here."

So she had been right in her assessment—there was a minor mutiny brewing now that Gran was no longer in charge. In the midst of stirring the batter, Ellie realized she needed a new bottle of Madagascar vanilla. "I can't do it this week. My schedule is already jam-packed."

Sadie watched her get one off the supply shelf. "How about next?"

Ellie tore off the seal. When she twisted off the lid, the scent of bourbon and vanilla filled her senses, helping to push away the last of the nausea she had felt earlier. "That's Joe's last week here. But I will get to it, I promise."

Sadie huffed. "The sooner you do, the sooner you will get some relief," she said. "In the meantime, has Joe reenlisted for another tour yet?"

"I don't think so." But he had been having communication with the army and his CO.

Sadie slid more pans into the oven and set the timer. She turned back to Ellie with a commiserating shake of her head. "You know, I love my brother, but I don't understand him. The two of you are married now. He's having a baby with you. He should be doing everything he can to try and be with you."

"I know but—"

Her bestie held up a staying hand. "There is no rush for him to decide what he's going to do once he leaves the military since he has a trust fund, just like the rest of us," she continued. "He could draw from that, while he's trying to decide. Or just take time off if he wanted. And just enjoy being with you while you gestate your little one."

Lovely as it sounded, in theory anyway, Ellie knew Joe would never be content to be idle for long. He was practically going stir-crazy now.

Finding her knees a little wobbly again with fatigue, Ellie perched back on the stool. She sipped more OJ, letting the tart beverage linger pleasurably in her mouth. "I don't think Joe wants to do that. He's always preferred to make his own way."

Sadie retrieved her coffee. "And yet it looks like that fierce independence of his is sending him straight back to the military, a decision that's going to be very hard on you. Always wondering if the father of your baby and your husband is okay. Unless—" Sadie paused "—you actually prefer things this way, too?"

Her friend waited. From the expression on her face, Ellie sensed Sadie knew she was holding on to a whole lot more. Things she couldn't tell Gran or even her husband. Finally, she admitted, "The last few weeks have kind of changed my view on what it might be like to be married to Joe."

"Are you trying to tell me you *like* being hitched?" Sadie teased.

Maybe a little too much at times, Ellie thought uncomfortably. "So far it's been kind of cozy." Although there were still times when Joe kept her at arm's length. Not telling her everything that was going on with him and his work. Like last night, when she had come into the apartment and found him immersed in whatever work-related stuff it was he had been reading on his computer.

"How do you think you're going to react when Joe leaves to go back to Fort Carson next week?"

More scared, Ellie thought, than she wanted to admit.

"Those first few days and weeks are always hard, but then I get used to it. So I suppose I will this time, too." If only because she had no choice. Ellie smiled, glad she had such a good friend. "Meanwhile, what else is new with you…?"

Talk soon turned to the property Sadie had her eye on and all the things she wanted to do to get her lavender ranch up and running as quickly as possible. The next few hours passed quickly as Ellie and Sadie put a four-tier wedding cake together.

At quarter till nine, the other five employees came in one

by one. "I just saw Joe," Sherri said, hanging up her bag in a locker.

As if that were somehow unusual. He was still living with her in the apartment on the second floor, after all. "Walking Scout?" Ellie asked.

Sherri shook her head. "He was in workout clothes—looking kind of sweaty, like he'd been out running at some point—when I spotted him looking around the old warehouse. His brother Gabe was with him."

The old warehouse? That was on the very edge of town.

"Was Gabe running, too?" Ellie asked, perplexed. Joe hadn't mentioned going for a run with his brother this morning.

"No. Gabe was dressed like the attorney he is."

Which in Laramie meant either business casual or a suit.

Sherri continued, "They were standing near the front of the building, talking all businesslike, next to their pickup trucks."

That was weird, Ellie thought. What were the two of them doing together down there? Unless Joe and Gabe had just bumped into each other by accident. That clearly wasn't what Sherri was thinking, though. "And no one else was with them?" Ellie asked. "No teenagers messing around, trying to climb up the side of the building or anything?"

Sherri shrugged. "Didn't appear so."

"Yeah, I saw him there, too, last week with Skip Carlton, the commercial realtor," Ingrid chimed in, pinning up her hair. She stepped over to the sink to wash her hands. "Neither of them were out for a run, though. Both of them were in business casual. There was a crew there with them, too, like they were surveying the property."

Surveying the property!

"Is his dad's business buying the building to put in some new manufacturing there?" Terri asked.

"Yeah, it would be great if it were no longer empty," Lynette agreed.

Everyone looked at Joe's sister. Sadie seemed as stunned as Ellie felt. She shrugged. "Dad hasn't said anything to me about buying the place, although it's going to become an eyesore and a hazard if it sits empty too much longer."

"Ellie?" Lynette asked, her curiosity growing as much as everyone else's. "Do you know what's up?"

She shook her head, sad to admit, "I have no clue."

Was this part of what had been keeping Joe so busy? And if so, why hadn't he said anything to her about it? She had thought they shared everything.

Except their private fears. If this were just some sort of routine business deal going on for his family, he'd have no reason not to mention it, would he? Especially since they had just talked about the warehouse and how reckless teens used to hang out there.

Hours later, Ellie was in the apartment making the two pies for the following day's luncheon when Joe walked in, his backpack slung over one shoulder.

Still perplexed and a little hurt by his clandestine behavior, she surveyed him. He was dressed in freshly pressed gray slacks and a pale blue button-down shirt. Dress boots. Not the workout clothes he had apparently been wearing earlier in the day. Which begged the question, what had he been doing since? And the other times he'd been spotted at the old warehouse?

His brow lifting in surprise to see her at the apartment at this time of day, he strolled over to give her a brief hug and kiss, being careful not to get in her way. Despite her pique, she luxuriated in the intoxicating scent of him, the sensual feel of his lips.

"You're off already?" he asked.

He had a point. It was only 4:00 p.m.—usually, she worked till six. Which would have given him plenty of time to change into his usual jeans and T-shirt, with her none the wiser about whatever he had been doing.

Noting he seemed more stymied than happy to see her already home, she pointed to the pies in progress. "I needed to make these for the Townsends, and I didn't want to do it in the bakery kitchen, since no one there knows what the ingredients of the second pie filling are going to be."

"Ah." He went to the fridge and brought out a beer.

The last thing she wanted was to start a fight, but it just might happen anyway, given how upset she was. Ellie watched him take a lazy swallow of the golden brew. Damn, he was handsome no matter what he wore. The color of his shirt brought out the deep McCabe blue of his eyes. She struggled not to succumb to the thrill soaring through her and instead worked to satisfy her curiosity about all he apparently had not been sharing with her.

Trying not to jump to conclusions like some jealous spouse, she forced a pleasant smile. "So. How was your day?"

Joe knelt to pet Scout. Her pup rolled over onto her back, luxuriating in the affectionate tummy rub. "Long."

Which told her precisely nothing. She nodded at his clothes. "Were you helping your dad with something at McCabe Industries?" Like the purchase or lease of the old warehouse?

After giving Scout a final pat, he stood and strolled closer. He lounged against the counter in the apartment's tiny kitchen, beer still in hand, feet crossed at the ankle. "What makes you think that?" he asked casually.

"Sherri saw you and Gabe at the old warehouse this morning. And Ingrid mentioned she spotted you and Skip Carlton there last week while some sort of survey was going on. So I just wondered if maybe your dad is going to buy the place and put in some sort of environmentally friendly manufacturing there."

Joe shook his head. "No. The building is four stories high. Perfect for the long-term storage facility it used to be, but not suitable for any kind of manufacturing without having a lot of wasted space."

To her frustration, he seemed content to leave it at that. She was not. "So…why were you there last week? And today as well?"

"Skip's an old friend. We were talking about the potential for investment property here in Laramie County."

"And he wanted you to buy the old warehouse?" She couldn't help the incredulous note in her voice.

Joe lifted his broad shoulders in a noncommittal shrug. "He showed it to me."

"But you told him you—and your dad—weren't interested."

He clenched his jaw, clearly not appreciating the third degree. And the part of her that had always trusted him could hardly blame him. "I told you," he said curtly. "I'm not going into business with my dad, or working for him. When I depart the military, I'll be doing my own thing."

That at least sounded more like the Joe she knew. Independent to a fault. "So then why were you and Gabe there this morning?"

"Because my brother had a meeting there at seven this morning."

Gabe.

Not him.

"So *someone* is buying the property?" This was news. Big news in Laramie County, as a matter of fact.

Joe's lips compressed. He returned her annoyed glance. "Looks like. Although nothing is set in stone just yet, and that is *all* I am prepared to say on the subject of the old warehouse right now."

Whoa there, soldier, Ellie thought, tensing. It looked like she had just crossed some sort of line with him. He definitely sounded irritated. Probably because this was someone's private business. And technically none of hers, though she *was* his wife.

Shouldn't they be able to share confidences? Apparently not. At least not when it came to this.

Well, she could be just as difficult. "So why were you there?" she persisted stubbornly, wishing this once he could let down his guard and be completely forthcoming with her.

Joe took another drink of beer. He studied her over the rim of his bottle, then continued impatiently, "Because Gabe was due in court. And he didn't have time to go over to his office to talk about what I needed him to do for me. Us."

Ellie blinked in surprise. "What do you mean?"

"I was given time off and sent back to Texas to get all my affairs in order. Now that I'm married with a baby on the way, that includes some changes to my estate. And some stuff with my trust, too." He raked a hand through his hair and sighed. "So yeah, I've been quietly working on all that for the last couple of weeks. I didn't mention it, because you don't usually like to talk about the money my parents gifted me with when I turned twenty-five. Or," he added even more stoically, "the details of my last will and testament."

No, she certainly didn't. It was too grim. Too close to the Fitzgerald family curse she was pretty certain she no longer believed in. "Oh." Ellie released a tortured breath, and guilt swept her anew.

"But if you want," he said, pushing away from the counter and coming toward her, "we could talk about it all now."

Chapter Nineteen

"In fact," Joe continued, aware he could really use Ellie's customary optimism and support right now, "it's probably a good time for us to talk about it all."

"No," Ellie said quickly, crushing his hope that they could finally be completely and fearlessly honest with each other. She lifted a staying hand and moved away, before he could get any closer. "You know how I've always felt about that." She looked him in the eye. "The incredible amount of money your mom and dad gifted you with has always been, and will always be, yours and yours alone. They wanted it to be your nest egg. And I agree."

"We co-own the house your *grandmother* gifted us with."

She lifted her chin and speared him with a testy gaze. "And that's fine because that was her wish, as well as a matchmaking ploy to get us to make a legal commitment to each other."

Which they had, when they'd gotten married. Or at least he *thought* they had. Even though Ellie had expected them to be formally hitched for just a year or two.

He had figured they would like being married, and eventually just opt to stay that way. Since they both knew how she felt about change.

"But you and I both know," Ellie went on emotionally, "that we did not need to co-own a house to love each other."

Also true, Joe thought. He had loved Ellie from the first, just as she had loved him. His heart went out to his wife; she was looking so stressed. Which he knew was what happened every time they had to get ready for him to leave again.

Ellie went back to precisely mixing water, granulated sugar and cream of tartar in a saucepan. She bent her knees as she checked the gas burner and turned up the flame. Satisfied all was well, she whirled back to him, a feisty expression on her lovely face. "In the meantime, you have your work in the military, and I have mine at the bakery. I'm also sole proprietress of the bakery and the apartment above. So we're both set financially."

"And your point is?" he prodded.

"That you can invest the money from your trust however you want without first discussing it with me." She paused before going on firmly, "We won't ever have to be fighting about money because we each have our own."

Joe figured that was true, to a degree. He watched as Ellie added butter crackers to the sweet, simmering mixture. She was right, he conceded reluctantly to himself. They really shouldn't be talking about any of this. Not just yet. He had to have everything worked out and finalized before he told her. So there was no second-guessing from either of them and no going back. Only forward with the life he knew they both wanted, even if she wouldn't come right out and admit it yet.

Nodding his understanding, he changed the subject. "By the way, I got a call from the furniture store earlier this afternoon. They will be delivering the new bedroom furniture and mattress set to the house tomorrow afternoon. The baby furniture is being delivered then, too."

"That's Thursday!" Ellie paused in the midst of adding brown sugar, crushed crackers, cinnamon and melted butter to a bowl. "I've got the luncheon for Vivian Townsend."

"I know." As he stepped back to give her room to work, he let his gaze sift over, aware again how pretty she always looked. Even now, in her distressed state. "Not to worry," he said soothingly. "I'll take Scout over and be there all day."

She turned away and drew another breath before pouring the syrupy cracker mixture into the pie shell and topping it with lemon juice and cinnamon. He lounged opposite her while she added the crumb topping, spreading it into an even layer. "Do you know how you want the master bedroom set up?"

"Unless we want to put the headboard in front of the bay windows and block the light," she answered wearily, reaching into the cupboard for a clean glass and filling it with water from the fridge, "there is only the one wall where the bed can go. The nightstands should go on either side of that."

"And the bureau?" he asked, wanting to make sure he got it right, so she wouldn't be tempted to try and rearrange it later.

Her green eyes clouding over, she took a sip of water, then set the glass down on the counter. "Wherever you think it will fit would be fine."

There were times, like now, when he knew she was trying to wedge distance between them in preparation for his departure. It made it very difficult to be there for her. Which was all he ever really wanted to do.

Gently, he asked, "Do you want me to make up the bed? Cause that's one thing I have learned to do in the army really well."

She chuckled, as he hoped she would. Relaxed by his teasing, she returned much more affably, "I can help with that. Same with the crib in the nursery. Because," she continued, reflecting, "that's the only thing that has to be assembled in there."

She had such a tender look on her face as she talked about

getting ready for their baby's debut in the world. A rush of excitement running through him, Joe took her into his arms, breathing in the fresh sweet scent of her. "Hard to believe we're doing all this," he murmured against the top of her head.

"I know." Ellie cuddled close. She moved one of his palms to her gently rounded belly. "Our little one never lets me forget for long."

Joe felt movement. Tentative at first, then stronger and more deliberate. "Is that him or her kicking?" he asked, the joy inside him increasing by leaps and bounds.

Ellie managed to simultaneously snuggle and hold very still. "Or waving at us. Yes... I think so." She tipped her face up to his, her eyes filled with the happiness he felt.

Joe sifted a hand through her hair and bent his head to kiss his wife. "I can't wait to meet our baby."

"Me, either, Joe," Ellie whispered, kissing him back. "Me, either."

Monica Townsend had asked Ellie to bake the mock apple pie in a plain glass pie dish. To further the impression she had baked the prank confection herself, she had also brought a domed plastic carrier instead of the trademark Sugar Love cardboard bakery box. As previously arranged, she arrived at 8:30 a.m. to pick up her order. It meant opening half an hour earlier than usual, but Ellie had figured she just needed to get the secret pickup over with.

Monica breezed in smugly. She had a twenty-dollar bill in her hand. "Is this it?"

Ellie nodded.

Monica inspected the pie critically. "Actually," she said, crumbling the crimped edges a little here and there, "it's a little too perfect for anything I made." She stepped back to admire the broken edges of crust. "Yeah. Much more believable. This is going to be such a hit at the luncheon. Everyone will remember today," she predicted.

Exactly what Ellie feared. "I'm taking my grandmother," she told Monica. Under the other woman's watchful eye, she slid the mock pie into the plastic carrier, glass dish and all. "So Eleanor and I will see you there."

As soon as Monica left, Ellie went to fetch the real apple pie she had made for Vivian. She crumbled the crust here and there, so it would appear identical, then put it in a bakery box to transport it to the luncheon. She added that to the trays of cupcakes the bakery was donating to the event, ready to be stowed in her delivery van. With Sadie's help, she moved everything out to the van, then drove to Laramie Gardens to pick up her grandmother.

They arrived a little early. A longtime member of the women's club, Eleanor went in to help with the table setup while Ellie carried the boxed bakery sweets into the kitchen adjacent to the dining room. Vivian, the luncheon's honoree, was waiting for her. "Is that for me?" she asked, pointing to the pie box.

Ellie nodded. "Some of the edges got a little messed up, but to be identical…"

"Got it." Vivian disappeared with the pastry box.

Ellie didn't know where she put it. She didn't *want* to know. Bad enough she had been forced into this. But on the other hand, all she had done was fill two orders. One against her will. The other…? To even the playing field, she guessed. And try to keep a wonderful woman from being purposefully humiliated by a vindictive in-law.

As members came in, the desserts they brought were collected in the kitchen. This eventually included Monica's special order pie in its plastic carrier.

After that, things got lively. The most community-minded

women in Laramie joined together to celebrate Vivian and her years of work. A delightful lunch was served by the caterers, speeches were made, and then all the desserts were brought out and put on the buffet tables.

Tradition said Vivian should lead the line.

And that was of course when Monica stepped in. "I don't know how many of you know this, but apple pie has always been Vivian's favorite dessert. So I made her a very special one to commemorate today."

Vivian kept her poker face while splaying a hand across her chest. "Why, thank you."

"I'll cut you a piece!" Her daughter-in-law served up a generous slice and handed the plate and fork to Vivian. And waited.

Acting like the good sport she was, Vivian took a bite. Smiled. "Delicious!"

Monica's look of triumph faded. Clearly, Ellie thought, this was *not* the reaction the woman expected. She stared at Vivian. "You don't think it's off in the slightest?"

"No," the guest of honor said. "It's perfect."

For once, Monica seemed at a loss.

Vivian's best friend, Sally, stepped in. "I love apple pie." She helped herself to a slice and proclaimed, "Honestly, I think this is the best one I've ever had." Somehow, she managed not to look at Ellie. "Congratulations, Monica! For a job very well done!"

A third person tried the confection. Then a fourth. And a fifth. Everyone raved.

Monica grabbed a slice for herself. Took a bite. Then stopped, clearly infuriated. "This does not taste like butter crackers!" she said.

"Why would it?" Sally asked deliberately then waited for Monica's reaction.

"Because—!" Monica whirled on Ellie.

Another of Vivian's friends came up, the switched-out pie in hand.

Vivian took it and said, very calmly to one and all, "This is the pie my daughter-in-law made for me. I was never clear on what exactly the planned prank was. Just that Monica was threatening to sue Sugar Love if they didn't make it to specification for her. So I commissioned Ellie to make a delicious apple pie, and then I switched them out, so no one else would be subjected to the hot sauce or whatever it was Monica wanted in the pie."

"It wasn't hot sauce! It was butter crackers instead of apple slices. For a mock apple pie, the kind made years ago when fruit was scarce. And it was all in good fun!" Monica declared, her cheeks flaming.

Except, Ellie noted, no one was laughing or smiling or in any way amused.

Monica glared at everyone. Started to speak. Then changed her mind and stomped out, saying, "Honestly, I don't know why I waste my time! The people in this town are *hopeless*!"

Well, that was one way to put it, Ellie thought wryly.

"So how did it go?" Joe asked her later, after she had dropped an exhausted Gran back at Laramie Gardens and gone to meet him at Gran's old house.

Ellie joined him in the living room and told him how it had all gone down, concluding, "So in the end, Monica was humiliated by the attempted prank, not Vivian."

Joe shook his head. He took her hand and pulled her down next to him on the sofa. "Mean girl stuff," he said. "I never understood it."

"Well, fortunately, there's not a lot of that kind of behavior around here," she murmured. From a very young age, most everyone she knew had been taught to be kind and respectful of their neighbors, to live life by the Golden Rule.

Joe grinned. "You're right about that, darlin'. When there is unpleasantness, it's usually the outsiders bringing it in."

Ellie rested her head on his shoulder, amazed by how good she could feel simply by spending time with him. "The ones who don't know the Laramie way."

He planted a kiss on the top of her head. Tingles of awareness swept through her. "Neighbor helping neighbor. Not *fighting* neighbor."

"Right." Ellie cuddled against him a moment longer, then noticed the boxes of toys next to the coffee table. The bulletin board and other keepsakes she had once had in her room. All had previously been stored neatly in the garage. "What's all this?" Why was this all suddenly back in the house?

"Remember when we were teasing each other about putting Barbie and G.I. Joe in the mural? Well, I had an idea how to actually make that happen," he said.

As Ellie listened to his proposal, she began to smile. "Your idea sounds every bit as perfect as you," she said.

Joe was pleased Ellie liked his idea. An hour later, they had the artist on the phone for an impromptu video call to show her what they had in mind.

"So you'd like a collage of all your favorite toys, from infancy to preteen years," she concluded. "And some nod to Christmas in July, and holiday fireworks, too."

"If you think you can make it work," Ellie said.

"Of course I can!" Adele enthused. "I'm going to need photos of all the toys, though, so I can work up a collection that's beautiful and thought-provoking. Kind of a trip down memory lane and a road map for the future for you and your baby. It'll be extra eye-catching because we'll be able to use all sorts of colors on the wall."

"Sounds good," Joe said.

They promised to get Adele what she needed by the weekend, then hung up. Joe turned to his wife. "So. Are you ready for your next surprise?"

"What?"

"Come and see."

He took her by the hand, and they mounted the stairs. The first stop was the nursery. The crib was still in the carton, a toolbox beside it. But the changing table and drawers, rocker-glider and matching footstool were already set up.

"Wow." Ellie walked in, a dazed and happy look on her face. "This is all getting so real."

And it was going to get even more real when he told her his plans next week before he left.

"Good real?" His heart full of hope, Joe splayed his palm across her back and brought her close for a long, tender kiss.

Ellie smiled and returned his embrace with all the enthusiasm he desired. "Very good," she whispered.

"Now for the even bigger change." He led her down the hall to the master suite. The king-size bed took up the center of the room. "We forgot to buy matching lamps for the nightstands," he said, a little embarrassed about that, "but—" He stopped short at the tears suddenly shimmering in her eyes. "Ellie? What is it?"

"It's just—" she inhaled deeply and shook her head in consternation "—so different. I knew when we took Gran's old furniture out and donated it like she asked that it was going to be altered irrevocably, but..."

"What?"

"It just means..." Ellie burst into tears. She buried her face in her hands, her shoulders shaking with sobs. "She's never coming back here to live."

Joe had known Ellie was quietly devastated by her gran's decision to move into Laramie Gardens just days after retiring. But in the mold of all Fitzgerald women, she had worked hard to keep her chin up, her attitude deliberately cheerful and as supportive as she would have wanted her grandmother to be if their roles were reversed.

Joe wrapped his arms around her, wishing he could ease her pain. "I know that makes you sad, sweetheart," he whispered. It made him melancholy, too, to see his wife feeling so alone...and prematurely abandoned.

Ellie lifted a delicate hand. Struggling hard to pull herself together, she wiped away her tears. "It's just not how I thought the rest of her life...*our life*...was going to go."

"Do you want to ask her to come and live with us?" Because that was an option.

"Yes. No. I don't know." Ellie drew away long enough to retrieve a tissue. "I don't think she would agree even if we asked."

Joe knew Eleanor wouldn't. With her heart condition, she had to feel a lot more secure in a senior living facility with a skilled nursing staff right there. Not to mention that it had a lot to offer her socially. At Laramie Gardens, Eleanor would always be safe and happy. At home, alone during the days, she wouldn't be.

Ellie blew her nose. "It's just been a lot this last month or two."

"I know," Joe sympathized. "Marriage. A baby."

"A baby, *then* marriage," she corrected with a sigh.

Did she really think that was the only reason he had married her? That stung.

One thing was for sure...they had even more changes on the way. Even bigger ones than her gran moving into senior living. And Ellie was going to have to buck up to weather them.

They both were.

Chapter Twenty

Ellie and Joe's last weekend together passed all too quickly. And though they still had a solid three and a half days to spend together, she was definitely feeling their pending separation Monday evening when she and the other employees of Sugar Love gathered in the back of the bakery for the much anticipated work meeting.

"I don't think any of us should be working more than five days a week," Ingrid said.

"Especially you, Ellie, since you're pregnant," Lynette agreed.

"And no one should be here before six in the morning," Sadie reiterated her earlier thoughts to Ellie.

Sherri brought out a really nice bakery-pink T-shirt. Her twin Terri held up a white apron with the Sugar Love logo. "This is the new uniform we're proposing, instead of the pink chef coats," Terri said.

Ellie had to admit they looked nice and would also pair well with the jeans and sneakers everyone wore to work. "We won't have any trouble getting them in from the online retailer, and they're sized in maternity, too," Sherri added.

"These are all good suggestions," Ellie said, looking down at the list she had been making.

"But are you going to implement any of them? That's what we want to know," Ingrid said.

Ellie looked at the earnest expressions of the women gathered all around her. All had worked at the bakery for years, and given it their all.

The previous management system had been an autocracy. Whatever her grandmother had said had been the law. The same when her mother was alive. There had been no room for suggestion or change.

Ellie realized she, too, was ready for improvements that would take them into a happier, more productive future. "I think we should implement it all," she said.

Everyone grinned. A cheer went up.

"Do you have any wishes, too?" Sadie asked.

Ellie realized she did. "Yes," she said, gathering her courage and becoming the boss her grandmother had always wanted her to be. "I actually have several things I'd like us to do. First, I want us to work together on new offerings for Christmas this year. Things like peppermint bark and white chocolate fudge and edible gingerbread houses. And I want you all to make suggestions and help develop the new recipes."

As the meeting went on, the excitement grew. In fact, Ellie's ideas were received so well, she was still grinning when she went back to the house to see Joe.

They had been sleeping there instead of the apartment since the new bed had been delivered. But Ellie had only moved the bare minimum of her stuff, since she planned to return to the cozier apartment as soon as he left for Colorado again.

Joe was out back. He was grilling chicken, while Scout sat nearby, watching attentively.

"Hey, darlin'." He flashed her a sexy grin. "How did the meeting go?"

"Great." Ellie summed up the modifications in their business operations, ending with her idea. "And we're going to start creating holiday items, plus a new cookie and cupcake of the month, and add to the specialty cake options. People will not only be able to enjoy our tried and true treats, but sample something new and exciting, too."

Joe closed the lid on the grill. "Well, you know what they say. Life can never be too sweet." He pulled her into his arms and kissed her.

"Yeah, got to get your sugar where you can." Feeling like she just might be able to run the bakery on her own, after all, Ellie kissed him back.

"You ready for the ultrasound tomorrow morning?" he asked, holding her even closer. "And our last birth class together tomorrow night?"

Loving the strong, masculine feel of him pressed against her, Ellie tipped her head up. "I'm a little nervous for the ultrasound. Is that weird?"

His warmth engulfed her as he tucked a strand of hair behind her ear. "Nervous slash scared?" He searched her face tenderly. "Or nervous, as in happy anticipation?"

Joy bubbled up inside her. "Both."

"It's going to be fine," he assured her, kissing her again slowly and deliberately.

When they started the procedure the next day, at the doctor's office, it did seem extremely routine. Maybe Joe was right, and she'd been worrying needlessly after all, Ellie told herself as she got into a gown, climbed onto the examining table and lay back, a sheet drawn across her bare midriff.

Joe stood beside her, holding her hand. Dr. Banks, the obstetrician, came in. Spreading gel across her abdomen, he moved the wand over it. On the monitor, they could see the shifting white waves and blurry images.

"You wanted to know the sex of the baby?" Dr. Banks asked.

"Yes!" Ellie and Joe said in unison.

The physician zeroed in on an image. "Looks like you've got a baby girl."

Ellie and Joe teared up simultaneously. Joe squeezed her hand.

But Dr. Banks was still squinting at the screen. He moved the wand again, and again. And again. Finally, he told them, "Looks like you've got a second baby here, folks. A boy."

"Twins?" Ellie echoed joyously. Joe's eyes widened happily, too.

"No…" the doctor said slowly. He went from one image to the other and back again. "Unbelievable," he said finally. "The odds are so impossible. I never thought I would see it in my lifetime…"

See what? "Uh…you're kind of scaring us," Ellie said, gripping Joe's hand all the harder.

"Sorry." Dr. Banks shook off his awe. "It's a rare phenomenon called superfetation." He turned away from the monitor to explain. "There are two babies in Ellie's uterus, conceived at two different times, during two different menstrual cycles, about a week apart. And—" he used the wand again, to show them the differing images on the monitor "—according to the infants' size and development, your little boy was conceived first. Your little girl second."

Ellie and Joe took a moment to absorb that.

"Well, if our babies are a week apart in development, what happens when it comes time to give birth?" Joe asked.

Good question.

"We will wait as long as possible, but then schedule them to be born at the same time."

"Via vaginal birth?" Ellie asked.

Dr. Banks nodded. "Hopefully, yes. But a cesarean section is always possible, if needed. Either way, both babies should be just fine."

Thank god, Ellie thought in relief.

Later, as they left the obstetrician's office hand in hand, she said, "I'm not sure if I'm walking on cloud nine or just… in a daze."

Joe escorted her across the parking lot to his truck. His ruggedly handsome face was etched with the determination he had whenever he was undertaking any kind of mission. "Gotta admit, I'm a little stunned, too."

"Really? This threw you?" Ellie teased playfully.

"*You* throw me." Grinning broadly, he gathered her in his arms for a sweet and tender kiss. "But yeah, two babies, who are going to be born at the same time who aren't exactly twins. I think we're going to be explaining the rare phenomenon known as superfetation a lot."

"You're probably right."

He danced her around the parking lot, sans music. "So what next?" He stopped to give her a spin. "Do you want to have lunch before you go back to work?" Slowly, he righted her, looking like he wanted to make love with her then and there. "Or…?"

Ellie wanted to continue dancing the day away. Unfortunately, she couldn't. "Actually," she told him reluctantly, "I really have to go back to work." She had already missed almost half the day. She took Joe's hand and squeezed it fiercely. "But first, I want to tell Gran in person, and I want to tell your folks, too."

"I think we're going to have to turn our cell phones off during birth class," Joe said hours later, winding an arm about her waist.

Ellie walked with him into the hospital annex where the classes were held. "I know." She leaned into his protective touch. "My cell hasn't stopped ringing since word got out."

Crinkles appeared at the corners of his blue eyes. "Mine, either."

"Everyone is really happy for us, though."

"As they should be." He stopped to sweep her into his arms, dip her back and press a kiss to her lips. "I can't get over it. A girl and a boy. Conceived almost but not quite simultaneously."

Ellie laughed, aware she hadn't felt this giddy since that destination wedding in Hawaii. "It really is Christmas in July! Even though it's now... August!"

Joe chuckled. "You bet it is. And it will be Christmas in December, too..."

Christmas all the way til then...!

"Since that's when our *two* babies will be born!" Ellie hugged him close while they let it all sink in. "Now all we have to do is tell the instructor and birth class."

"And be prepared to answer about a zillion questions." Joe winked, his celebratory mood increasing.

"Yeah, good thing we both spent time researching the subject online this afternoon."

As expected, their happy prediction proved true. By the time they left class, both of them were all talked out.

Joe drove them quietly back to the house, where Scout was waiting. They took the Westie out into the fenced backyard and sat, watching the little white dog race around. Joe left briefly, returning with two tall glasses of sparkling water with lime, and sat down next to her on the cushioned swing. Moonlight shining down upon them, they watched Scout enjoy the freedom of being off leash and still safe.

"I'm going to have to move into the house," Ellie said,

knowing that her pet's happiness was going to be just one of the many benefits. "And I probably should do it before you leave. Just use the apartment for resting."

Joe squinted at the sprinkling of stars overhead, in the velvety black night sky. "Or nesting. On the bright side—" he turned back to her, planning ahead as always "—if you're not living there with all your stuff, then you should be able to put two full cribs there for when you're at work and you want the babies and their sitter nearby. Of course, we need two cribs in the nursery here, too."

"That's a total of *four* cribs." Ellie started feeling overwhelmed again.

"I have a lot of money in savings, Ellie, aside from the funds in my trust," Joe told her. "We can afford it."

But could she manage two babies and a business, not to mention a house and a dog, on her own? When she had just cut the work hours for her entire staff at their request? That was the question.

And Joe was going to be so very far away, often not even able to be contacted.

Joe knew by the way Ellie had gone silent that she was worrying again. He couldn't blame her. He was worrying, too. Not about the long-term future, but about the next two months while he served out his current enlistment.

Figuring she needed a boost, he went back into the house again, returning with a folder containing a sales brochure and a velvet box.

She wrinkled her nose. "What are those?"

He settled next to her on the swing. "Early push presents."

Blinking in surprise, she asked, "You got me two?"

"Well, just one is an official push present," Joe hastened to correct, hoping he wasn't making the worst mistake a new husband could make gifting her the wrong thing. "The other is a just a present."

She went still. "For?" Her eyes were lit with wariness.

"Being you. Doing all that you do. And because I want you to have everything you need. Always and forever."

She shifted to face him, her bent knee brushing up against his thigh. "Joe! I do have everything I need." She curved her soft hand around his biceps beseechingly. "I have you, and our babies."

But he wasn't going to be here for the next couple of months while he served out the rest of his enlistment. There wasn't anything he could do about that, so he wanted to make up for it. Joe pressed on. "Which do you want to open first?"

She eyed the velvet jewelry box, then the folder. "How about that?" She pointed to the latter.

He handed it over, still hoping this idea wasn't a mistake.

She opened it. Blinked at the color brochures of six-burner Viking and Wolf gas stoves with double ovens. "I don't get it."

"This house has all new appliances except for the stove, which we both know is likely on its last legs. You love to cook, and you deserve something like that to whip up your amazing meals. Especially now that you're going to have a family." He flashed her a lopsided smile. "And I wanted to gift you one, but then I realized that you would definitely want to pick out exactly what you wanted. So... I'm asking you to review all the options and colors and so on and let me know what you want. And then I will get it for you ASAP."

Looking a little stunned, Ellie sucked in a breath. But then to his relief, happy tears glistened in her eyes. "You know," she teased, splaying her hands across his chest, "giving your wife an appliance for a sentimental occasion..."

"Is typically the kiss of death. But you and I aren't the normal couple, Ellie, are we?"

"Nope," she agreed proudly. "We definitely are not. And the superfetation proves it."

True. So true. "So promise me you'll study the brochures and do any additional research you want and let me know."

"I will." She kissed him lightly on the lips. "And thank you."

"You're very welcome. And you've got one more. And this one *is* a push present."

Her blond brow quirked. "I haven't delivered either baby yet."

All Joe knew was that he wanted to be here when she opened it. He felt imperative it be now. "Then consider it an early push present. Or an ultrasound present. Or whatever. Just open it."

With a shy look and shaking hands, Ellie opened the box.

Inside was a gold, double heart locket necklace. There was room for four photos—two for the babies they were going to have, even though he had only known about one of them when he bought the necklace. He had just hoped to have another child with her.

He'd already filled both lockets. The first contained photos of the two of them as kids. And, as placeholders until their kids were actually born, in the other heart locket were her favorite Barbie and his G.I. Joe. "Because," he said, "we always knew, even way back when we were still really just kids and tried to elope, that we were destined to be together."

And now, finally, they were.

Ellie had just gone upstairs to get ready for bed when Joe got a call from his commanding officer. He stepped outside to take it.

"Got your letter this afternoon," Major Wilson said. "About your decision not to reenlist. Are you sure about this?"

Joe had been certain for a while now. He just hadn't wanted to tell anyone his plans until everything was official. "Yes, sir." He reiterated what he had said in his resignation letter. "We just found out today that Ellie is having two babies instead of one. Her grandmother is the only family she has and is now starting to have heart problems. I can't leave this all on Ellie to handle alone."

"Understood. Just remember, for this to work, this needs to be about what you really want and need, too. Not just something you feel forced into," his CO said. "In any case, the opportunities and promotion we talked about are still in the offing, should you change your mind once the shock and excitement wears off and you get back on base."

Joe thanked the major, and they ended the call.

He walked upstairs.

Ellie was wearing a sexy satin nightshirt that stopped at mid-thigh. She'd let her hair down, and her scent was as intoxicating as her silky skin.

"Are people still calling about the superfetation news?" she said.

He nodded. "Not to worry. I turned my phone off and left it on the charger downstairs."

Nothing was going to interfere with his last couple of nights with his wife. He reached for her, his heart full of love. She melted into him just as ardently. And they began to make love as sweetly and passionately as they had in Hawaii, when both their babies had been conceived.

Chapter Twenty-One

Ellie was in the kitchen the next morning when Joe came in from walking Scout. He looked more surprised than happy to see her still in her pajamas, cooking breakfast for them. He leaned down to kiss her temple. "Aren't you going to work this morning?"

Ellie grinned, delighted about the decision she'd made. "I'm taking Wednesday and Thursday off, so we can spend time together before you leave early Friday."

Joe shoved a hand through the rumpled layers of his hair. "I wish you'd told me."

Uh-oh. Ellie layered bacon on a paper towel-lined plate to drain. "You have plans?"

He nodded, confessing reluctantly, "I have to be at Gabe's office by eight this morning. We're going to get all my documents I told you about signed. Because they have to be witnessed and notarized, it all has to be set up in advance."

The whole process would likely take several hours. "And it all has to be done before you leave again?" Ellie guessed.

Joe snagged a strip of crispy bacon. "Yep."

Too late, she realized she shouldn't have taken it for granted that they'd able to spend all their time together before he left.

Joe, however, was undeterred. He lounged beside her, his

back to the counter, while she continued to man the stove. "You could come with me, if you want." His voice dropped a persuasive notch. "You need to know what's in those documents anyway, and I was planning to go over them with you later."

The last thing Ellie wanted to do with her last two full days with him was go over the terms of his last will and testament, medical power of attorney, and never mind the details of the trust given to him by his parents.

"We could go to lunch afterward," he offered, "just the two of us."

Ellie smiled. "Lunch sounds good." Romantic even.

"But you don't want to go with me to Gabe's office?"

Ellie shook her head. She knew it was superstitious and silly, but she couldn't bear the thought of anything happening to Joe, never mind preparing for just that eventuality. "I really need to go see Gran and tell her about the changes the staff and I agreed to make at the bakery. I don't want her to hear about them from anyone else first."

Disappointment etched his handsome face. "I understand," he told her softly, kissing the back of her hand. "Where do you want to meet?"

Ellie broke some eggs into the skillet. "How about here? We can decide where we want to go to lunch then."

"Sounds good. I should be back around noon."

"I'll be here," she promised.

Ellie tried to hide her own disappointment over her botched plans as they both ate and then got ready for their separate outings. Joe left first, dressed in business casual again. Ellie put on a pretty maternity dress and headed for Laramie Gardens.

The receptionist at the front desk smiled as she walked in. "Hi, Ellie."

"Hi, Diane. Is my gran still at breakfast?" If so, Ellie could intercept her in the dining hall.

"No. She signed up for the eight o'clock senior yoga class this morning."

"Instead of her usual 9:00 a.m.?"

Diane checked her computer screen and nodded, stating, "Eleanor said she wanted to see if working out earlier made a difference."

"In what?" Ellie asked curiously.

"She didn't elaborate, so I don't know. She should be done in another forty-five minutes. You can wait in her suite if you'd like."

"Thanks." Ellie was barely out of the reception area when she saw her grandmother coming down the hall.

Gran's shoulders were slumped as if in defeat. Her right hand was resting on her left collarbone. She seemed to be rubbing it lightly, as if it were bothering her.

Ellie cut her off at the intersection of hallways and fell into step beside her. "Gran! Are you feeling okay?"

Eleanor looked up in surprise. "Of course, darling!" She straightened perkily. "Why do you ask?"

Ellie hooked her arm through her grandmother's while they continued down the hall. "Well, I didn't think you were going to be done with your yoga session for a while."

"Oh." Gran waved an airy hand as they headed into her suite. "I wasn't feeling it."

"So you just left?" Ellie ascertained.

"Yep." Moving away, Gran pulled a small bottle of water from her mini-fridge. Offered one to Ellie, too.

Still thinking something was really off, Ellie accepted it. "Thanks." She went over to sit on the settee by the bay window. On top of a stack on the side table was a book titled *Stress Management for Seniors*. It looked like a textbook for a class. On top of it was a journaling workbook that went with it.

"Gran? Why are you taking a class in stress management?"

"So I can live a less stressful life." Gran's voice was rich with irony.

Ellie paused, intuiting there was more to this than met the eye. She uncapped her bottle, took a gulp of water. "Retirement is stressful?"

Gran nodded, abruptly looking a little depressed. "In certain ways, yes."

And suddenly it all became clear to Ellie. "I *knew* you weren't going to be happy here." She leaped to her feet and began to pace. "Not for more than a month or two!" She spun around to face her gran, noting she was starting to look a little pale. "You regret giving us your house, don't you? And now you don't know what to do about it because you had us painting rooms and giving away furniture, and it's all such a mess!"

Gran went back to rubbing her left shoulder and the region above her heart. Color swept her cheeks. "It's not a mess. And I don't want to go back to my house. Nor do I regret giving the property to you and Joe, especially now that you're having two babies!"

None of this made sense. "Then why did you leave your yoga class early? And look so miserable in the hall just now? Why are you suddenly having to take a class to figure out how to handle stress?" Her gran had always been the most capable woman Ellie knew!

Gran removed a small heart-shaped tin from her bra, opened it up, took out a small pill and put it under her tongue.

More medicine? "And what is that?" Ellie asked, feeling even more upset. Afraid if it was what she had seen on television, she already knew.

"Nitroglycerin. It's for my angina."

"Angina!" Ellie's knees wobbled.

Gran put a hand on her shoulder and pushed her to sit down, then settled beside her, taking her hand. "Yes, darling. I have a heart condition. A slight arrhythmia that, while not life-threatening, sometimes leads to chest pain. I didn't want to tell you because I didn't want to upset you or have you worry."

Well, she was plenty worried now. Trying not to cry, Ellie asked, "Have you seen a cardiologist?"

"Yes, Claire Lowell. She's taken all the necessary precautions with my heart."

"By prescribing you blood thinner and nitroglycerin?"

Eleanor nodded. "As well as a mild beta-blocker and blood pressure medication. And a class to help me manage the stress of being diagnosed with an illness. Dr. Lowell also wants me to exercise regularly but only as much as is *physically comfortable*, which is what I'm still trying to figure out. That's why I left class early, because I didn't want to overdo it."

"Are you in pain now?"

"No, a very small dose of nitroglycerin takes care of that," Gran assured her.

"How serious is this heart condition?"

"Dr. Lowell expects me to easily live another ten or fifteen years. Maybe even longer if I take good care of myself."

Relief poured through Ellie, mixing with the guilt that came from not having been there for her grandmother the way she should have, had she only known. "Oh, Gran…"

The elderly woman rubbed Ellie's shoulders affectionately. "I'm all right, darling. But you can see now why it's better that I am here, in a facility that has twenty-four-seven skilled nursing, plus everything I could ever want or need."

Ellie talked to Gran some more, then went back to the house to wait for Joe.

He arrived shortly before noon, backpack slung over one broad shoulder. Unlike her, he seemed incredibly happy and relieved. He paused, taking her in, knowing her well enough to ask. "What's up?"

Ellie was still so upset, it was all she could do not to burst into tears. "My grandmother has a heart condition."

An inscrutable look on his face, Joe set his bag down. "She told you?"

Clearly, he was not surprised by the news. Not at all. She swallowed around the tightness in her throat. "You knew?"

Joe exhaled roughly, looking as if caught in a trap of his own making. With a frown, he nodded. "She had an angina attack when I visited her a couple of weeks ago and couldn't find her pills."

"Why didn't you tell me?"

Joe moved to sit beside Ellie on the sofa. "Because she swore me to secrecy."

"What about your obligation to *me*?"

He took her hand in his and clasped it warmly, admitting reluctantly, "It was Gran's news to tell. Not mine. I encouraged her to be open with you, but that was all I could do."

Ellie stared at him numbly, her sense of betrayal deepening. "So you left me in the dark?" she countered, in a soft, strangled voice.

A muscle in Joe's jaw clenched. "Not willingly, but yeah, I guess you could say that." The tough soldier, the one who apologized for nothing—who *explained nothing*—was back.

And it was so unfair, Ellie thought, as anger roiled in her veins. For her gran to deliberately cut her out and Joe to go along with it! Instead of realizing that his first loyalty should have always been to her.

"Is there anything else I should know?" she demanded. Expecting him to say, *No, of course not!* "Are you keeping anything else from me?"

Joe stared at her. He started to speak but then stopped. He squared his broad shoulders and inhaled deeply. "As a matter of fact, yes," he said. "There is a lot more you should know."

This wasn't how Joe had hoped to tell Ellie about his plans for their future, but now that his new business venture was all set, he also knew it was time that they got everything out in the open.

"I wasn't just signing a will and testament today," he admitted. "I was starting a business here in Laramie."

Staring at him, she lifted her chin. "What kind of business?" Her low tone was as taut as the string on a guitar.

Trying not to read too much into her stiff posture, he replied, "A climbing gym for kids. Families. Athletes and soldiers who want to train."

She stared at him in disbelief, the way he had always half expected she would. "The old warehouse..."

"Yes."

She shook her head, still looking completely shell-shocked. And something else he couldn't identify.

Trying to squash his uneasiness, Joe massaged the tense muscles of her shoulders. He knew she would understand all he wanted to do, for them and their community, if she would just give him a chance. "I used funds from my trust to buy it and secure a construction loan."

She placed both her hands on his chest and, still mired in confusion, asked, "How are you going to build all that and be a soldier, far away?"

"I'm not reenlisting. I turned in my resignation yesterday."

Her lips pursed. "And you didn't think to discuss all this with me?"

"You always said it was my decision to join or quit the army."

"This affects both of us, Joe," she reminded him.

Like he didn't realize that! Like everything he had been working tirelessly on for the last month hadn't been for all of them! Gut tightening, he stepped back. "So you're saying what exactly?" he countered, bitterness creeping into his low tone. "You don't want me to stick around and be your husband and a daddy to our kids? You'd rather I be some picture on the mantel? Or vague memory? The guy they see only once a year? Who's never there for Christmas? Or birthdays?"

She looked over at him, a world of hurt and disappointment in her eyes. "You remember when we were kids and you said the only thing you had ever wanted was to be a soldier?"

His aggravation mounted. Curtly, he reminded her, "And I've been that."

"I don't want you to blame me—or the kids—for robbing you of the lifetime career you always wanted."

But she would let her lack of faith in him—*in them*—keep him from pursuing a new career? "Dreams change," he told her in a level voice. "And even if they didn't...my duty is here."

Ellie looked like she wanted to deck him. "Your *duty*?" she echoed in distaste, looking even more betrayed.

Okay, maybe describing it as an obligation wasn't the best way to frame it. He tried again, sticking to the practical. "Be realistic, Ellie. This birth could be complicated."

She drew a deep breath. "I'm not arguing that, Joe."

Good. Because he intended to be present for their delivery. And every day after that. "And once our son and daughter are here, there's no way you can handle two babies and run the bakery and take care of Gran all on your own." Leaning closer, he appealed to her emotion. "You need my help, Ellie, whether you want to admit it or not. And bonus! You won't have to worry about the Fitzgerald family curse anymore, because two months from now, I won't be in the military any longer, I'll be coming home for good this time."

So she could stop using that irrational superstition—and any other lame excuse—to put a limit on the time they were actually legally married. Again, he had figured this would be good news to her. Wonderful, life-changing news! Instead, she was glaring at him like he had given Scout away behind her back!

"I'm not some Special Forces team you are in charge of, Joe."

What the hell? He shook his head, hoping that would clear it. "I never said you were."

"Really?" Jumping up from the couch, she planted her hands on her hips and glared down at him. "'Cause you're acting like you think this isn't a marriage or a partnership, it's a dictatorship! *You* have decided our future all on your own!" she added indignantly. "Well, what about me, soldier? Don't I get a say? Shouldn't you have consulted me on *all* of this? And gotten me to agree before you went off and signed on the dotted line?"

He would have if he had thought she would be reasonable. Or not get too stressed out. Or just upset at the thought of change! "I tried to broach the subject with you several times…"

She glared at him in disbelief. "When?"

"The night you were asking me why I'd been at the old warehouse with Gabe and Skip."

Unable to dispute that, she said nothing.

He stepped closer, unable to completely tamp down his disappointment. Reminding, "Even this morning, I wanted you to go with me to Gabe's office, so we could go over everything with you before anything at all was signed. If you had been willing to do that, I would have told you about my business plans then. But you weren't, and you needed to talk to your gran about the bakery changes. So I told you we would talk when we both got back. Which is what we are doing now."

She stalked away, the skirt of her summer dress swirling around her legs. "Are we talking, Joe?" She swung back to face him. "Or are you just telling me the way it's going to be? No matter how I feel about any of it!"

Did she even know him at all? Did they know each other? He rose to his feet, needing them to be eye to eye when he faced off with her. "Answer me this, Ellie. Would you have agreed if I had confided my ideas and plans? To any of it? Especially when I was in the midst of still trying to get everything worked out?"

Now it was her turn to be caught off guard by a question. She paused a long moment. "Honestly? No." She ran her hands through her hair, looking like she was struggling to stay calm. Looking for some way out of this ugly reality. "Because if you want my honest opinion, I think it is all way too much too soon."

Of course she did. Aware it was his fears now coming to pass, he remained silent.

"Look, maybe it's not too late for you to reverse all this," she said. Her expression desperate, she stepped closer. "Isn't there some statute…or federal cooling-off rule that allows you to reverse a business decision or contract or even *real estate purchase* within three days without penalty if you change your mind?"

There was, actually. But that wasn't the point. "So what are you saying, Ellie? You want to pretend this never happened? That I never had such a wild and crazy idea as returning to Laramie a civilian and staying married to you for the rest of our lives?"

His scathing remarks seemed lost on her. She nodded, looking both hopeful and relieved. "As best we can, yes."

"So we can go back to living with one foot out the door and stay legally married only as long as we need to be, in order to protect our kids?"

Her expression turned as wary as her posture. She did not try to conceal her irritation. "Well, that was our agreement."

"Right," he muttered. "Of course." Wondering why he had ever bothered to try to get her to change her mind on anything, he grabbed his backpack. "The most important thing to you has always been your independence!"

"That's not true!"

"Isn't it?" He stared at her furiously. "Can you really stand there and tell me you haven't always had one foot out the door? From the very first moment we knew each other till right now!"

Her lower lip trembled. "I thought we were alike in that regard!" she said. "Or have you conveniently forgotten all the times you didn't want me to question you about your comings and goings? Like when you almost missed Gran's retirement party. Or the night you didn't come home from San Antonio as promised, and I didn't know why until you actually arrived, a day later, and even then, you only told me half of it."

That stung.

Mostly because it was true.

He had been doing his own thing.

Thinking she would be fine on her own till he got back.

Indignant color filled her cheeks. She stomped closer. "Whether you want to admit it or not, Joe, you are a guy who wants his freedom. Just like I want mine. We're alike in the regard that neither of us wants to be the other's ball and chain."

Was that really how she felt?

Like he was weighing her down now?

He sure as hell didn't feel that way.

"Actually, Ellie, we're not alike," he retorted grimly. "And we haven't been. Not for a while now. And especially not since we found out we were pregnant. I just played along with your need for freedom because it was the only way I thought I could ever have you in my life!" He forced them both to face the truth. "I always wanted more, Ellie. Always!"

Which just went to show what a damn fool he had been. To think he could ever get more, if he were just patient enough. To think she would ever want to stay married to him for the long haul as much as he wanted to stay married to her.

She had carefully told him how she wanted things to be, all along. Every single time the subject had been brought up.

He had been the one fantasizing about a more traditional love, and life together, as husband and wife. Once he got out of the military and finally came home to her and their babies for good.

He should have known better.

He should have known Ellie.

Who always—always—was ready to bolt at the slightest provocation.

Heart aching he turned away from her bitterly.

"Joe!" She followed him to the door. "Where are you going?"

He spun around, hand still on the knob. The hurt and anger he had been holding back exploded like a grenade in the center of his chest. "I've had it, Ellie. With all the excuses, the nonsense about the Fitzgerald family curse, your ever present need for independence, your insistence that I can't be happy anywhere but in the military. *Everything!* You know the real reason you can't commit fully to me heart and soul?"

Her whole body trembled. "And what would that be, Joe?"

"You don't really love me. And you never did."

And done with everything, he stormed out, not looking back.

Chapter Twenty-Two

"I thought I might find you here," Gran said early Thursday.

Ellie looked up from her laptop to see Gran standing in the open doorway of the house, keys in hand. She rose from the dining room table and went over to give her grandmother a hug hello. "You drove here?"

Nodding, Gran set her bag down. "I wanted to know why you weren't picking up and Joe seems to be spending the entire day at his brother's law office."

A pit settled in Ellie's gut. Her blowup with Joe was the last thing she wanted to discuss. "How do you know Joe is with Gabe?" And what was he doing with their lawyer? Except more stuff Ellie knew nothing about, she thought resentfully.

Gran took a chair at the table, where it had all began when she gifted them the house. "He told me when I phoned him asking if you were okay."

Ellie sat, too. "What else did he say?"

"That if I wanted to know more I'd have to talk to you myself, so here I am." Eleanor leaned toward her urgently, her eyes full of tender concern. "So what is going on, darling? Why are you here, and Joe there, and why is Scout looking like she lost both of her best friends?"

Her dog *was* sad. The poor thing had been moping around

the house for the last couple of days. Ellie swallowed around the rising lump in her throat. "It's a long story."

"That's the thing about being retired. You've got tons of time to just sit and talk. And speaking of time, why are you sitting here on your computer, when Joe is set to leave Texas again tomorrow?"

"I was doing payroll." Ellie maneuvered her laptop between the two of them to show her grandmother the new system.

Gran blinked at the end of the short demonstration. "You can run the whole thing in half an hour! Taxes, too. That's incredible!"

"I know. We have Joe to thank for it. Well, him and his dad and Tom Ryan, their payroll person."

"I'll be sending them all some baked goods, as a thank-you," Gran vowed.

Ellie smiled, glad to see her grandmother looking so strong and chipper again. "Sounds good." She pulled up another screen on the computer. Then proceeded to tell Eleanor about the meeting she'd had with the employees and the rest of the changes they were going to be implementing at the bakery. Including the new T-shirt and apron uniform tops.

"It's very attractive," Gran approved. "Looks more comfy, too."

"I think it will be," Ellie agreed. Happy to find her grandmother wasn't the least bit upset by all the changes she was making at the bakery, she closed the computer. As her thoughts returned to Joe, her mood crashed once again.

"So what is going on, darling?" Gran asked. "Did you and Joe quarrel?"

"And then some." Ellie sighed and spilled all.

"So." Gran paused. "Are you upset about the fact that your husband didn't clear things with you first? Or that he made changes that will affect all of you?"

Ellie stiffened. "Both, obviously."

"And you're uncomfortable with that—even though as you have just showed me, you've made some pretty big changes at the bakery since taking over. And you feel fine with those."

Ellie defended herself hotly. "Because they were reasonable, and a long time coming!"

"Did you go over them all with Joe first?"

Ellie scoffed. "No."

"Why not?"

"Because he doesn't have any part of my work life, except for helping me streamline the payroll issue, and that was a one-off!"

Gran squinted as if still trying to figure out why Ellie was so upset. "So you disapprove of his business plans because you think his idea won't work? And it's going to be a big mess?"

Ellie bit her lip. She hadn't thought about that. "I guess that's part of it," she admitted slowly, "although I've never known Joe to actually fail at anything."

"Then?"

"He never told me he wanted to do anything but be in the military, so if it turns out he is moving way too fast out of guilt or obligation, and then is unhappy with the new life he's swiftly building, it's all going fall back on me and the babies."

Gran nodded solemnly. "That could happen. Or he could find what I suspect that he will..."

"Which is?"

"That after spending so much time with you the last month that he will realize he has indeed fulfilled his service to our country, just as he always wanted, and that a settled married life with you and the babies is what he wants and needs now."

"Believe me, if I could just be sure that were the case,"

Ellie said miserably. Then it wouldn't matter to her what Joe did to earn a living.

"So what are you saying?" Gran met her eyes. "That you want some kind of glimpse into the future?"

If only there were a way to do that. "Yes!"

Gran clasped her hands and told her firmly, "Darling, there are no guarantees in life. Or love. You put your heart out there, and you take your chances."

Ellie's eyes welled.

So did Gran's.

"I was only married to your grandfather for a very short time, but I wouldn't trade that for anything in the world," Gran told her huskily. "Your mom felt the same way about your dad. When you find the love of your life, Ellie, you don't walk away. You hold on with everything you've got."

Gran reached out and took Ellie in her arms, holding her fiercely as tears of fear and regret and yearning spilled down Ellie's face.

"I thought you knew that," Gran whispered. "I thought that was why you and Joe have always been so inseparable."

"You want me to do *what*?" Gabe asked Joe when he had finally finished with his scheduled client and was able to join Joe in the conference room.

Joe swung away from the view of historic downtown Laramie. He wished like hell he wasn't here, asking for this. But he was. "I want you to draw up a legal separation agreement. Or maybe an annulment."

His brother looked at him like he was crazy. "No way."

Joe did a double take. "What do you mean, no? I'm the client here." And family, too!

Gabe leaned against the conference room wall, not bothering to even sit down. "And I'm your attorney, and as such, my duty is to look after your interests. And ditching Ellie would not be in your best interests. Not to mention the impact that would have on your legal rights as the children's father, which we've already discussed. So, no. I'm not doing that."

Joe huffed. Angry enough to threaten, "I could hire someone else."

"No one with any ethics."

Knowing time was short—he only had eighteen hours before he had to leave for Colorado—Joe tried again. "The truth is, Ellie only married me for legal reasons. She never intended to stay married to me. She was only planning to do so as long as it was necessary."

"Legal reasons?"

"To ensure my rights as the babies' daddy, yes," Joe confirmed.

Gabe regarded him with skeptical disbelief. "So you're going to forget the whole thing about the climbing gym, too? Sell the old warehouse to someone else? Go back to being a soldier for life and reenlist?"

Irritated that his brother thought him just as much a fool as Ellie did, Joe scoffed. "No, of course not. Whether I am married to Ellie or not, my kids are going to need me here, and I am going to be here for them."

That much Gabe respected. "Just not for Ellie."

The accusation stung. "She made it pretty clear—she does not want me as her husband any longer." Not that she ever really had. And that sucked. The idea he could have been so much of a fool, given so much of himself...everything he had to offer. He had believed in his heart that she loved him, too. Only to find out it was all...conditional to him not being there with her full time.

Gabe scowled, as if he could not believe how oblivious

Joe was. "So you're just going to let her go without a fight, after all these years."

Forcing himself to be realistic in a way he hadn't been before, Joe reminded him, "She's pregnant with two babies. I don't want her under any stress." He had seen the way she looked at him. Like he was the lowest scum on earth. "Sadly... I bring the stress."

"Are you sure she's not just ticked off about everything you've been doing on the down-low? Deservedly so, I might add?"

Joe winced at the description of his actions. If only Ellie weren't the kind of woman who always stuck to her plan. He exhaled. "It's more than that."

"The Fitzgerald family curse?"

He slid his brother a glance. "She has never liked change. Never liked it when I took charge of a situation and just simply got things done." Never liked...a lot of things. The move to the house, the changes to her gran's old bedroom, turning the master suite into a comfy lair for them... It had all been too much.

He'd been too much.

"I'm not sure I would like what you've done either if I were your woman," Gabe said, a smile in his voice.

Teasing now? Really? "Well, thank God you're not," Joe countered gruffly.

An aggravated silence fell.

Gabe pushed Joe into a seat and said, more kindly, "Do you know what I tell my clients the secret of marriage is?"

"First of all, you're not married," Joe shot back, watching his brother sit, too. "So how the hell would you know?"

Gabe braced his elbows on the table and leaned toward Joe. "I know, because as a practicing family and general law attorney, I see a lot of couples come in here ready to throw in the towel. At least they think they are. But the majority of them just need to cool off and calm down and think about what's really important in this life. And it's not being right. Or the one who calls the shots. Or even who did what wrong. It's about making a vow to stay together for better or worse. And keeping that vow. It's about putting your pride aside and risking it all because it's the right thing to do when you truly love someone." He pinned his brother with a hard stare. "And I don't care what you say, you do love Ellie, Joe. Always have. Always will."

Late afternoon, Ellie was just walking out the door when Joe turned his pickup into the driveway. He got out of his truck and walked toward her, his movements strong and purposeful. She felt her heart stutter in her chest.

He was the most welcome sight she had ever seen in her life. She hated that they had wasted even a moment of their precious time together arguing. Because really what had he done except try to move heaven and earth to be with her and their babies?

Realizing all over again what a stubborn fool she had been, she drew a deep, enervating breath.

He came closer, his eyes still level on hers.

Not afraid to reach out, she took his hands in hers. "I'm sorry I haven't been more supportive of all that you've been going through, Joe."

"Hey." He wrapped both his arms around her waist, looking every bit as ready to make up as she was. "It's been a challenging time for both of us," he said, his voice firm and strong.

She fought back a grin as her heart kicked against her ribs. "You're right about that."

One hand splayed over her spine, he drew her even closer.

His voice dropped to a husky timbre as he continued frankly, "But I could have made it a lot easier if I had confided in you all along, Ellie. I'm sorry that I didn't let you know what I was thinking, from the very beginning. I should have."

Tilting her face up to his, she spread her hands across his chest, feeling his heart beating as hard as her own.

Raw emotion glittered in his eyes. "Because if I had," he said in a low, gravelly voice, "then you would have known this idea of mine wasn't a whim. That I had known for years what I wanted to do when I eventually got out of the service. And that is to create the kind of place I needed when I was a kid that could provide the thrill and adventure, discipline and mountaineering skill, that rock climbing offers. And I wanted to make it accessible." He wove his fingers through her hair. "When the facility opens, the kids around here won't have to drive several hours or test themselves on the side of buildings or cliffs overlooking the lake. They'll be able to come in and learn in a safe environment. And I'll have the challenge of making it all happen."

Ellie was so proud of him! She rose on tiptoe and met his lips in a searing kiss. Wreathing her arms about his neck, she said with open admiration, "So you're not just a soldier after all, but an entrepreneur, just like your dad."

He pulled her even tighter against him. "Looks like."

She tucked her face into the crook of his neck, shivering at the delight she felt being with him again. She drank him in. His heat, his size, the woodsy masculine scent of him. Still needing to understand all that had gone wrong, she drew back to look deep into his eyes. It was time to let her defenses go. To dare to take risks the way he had. "Why didn't you tell me?"

He released a slow breath. "I hadn't ever done anything like this." His eyes crinkled at the corners as he confessed,

"I didn't want to embarrass you or my family." He inhaled. "You were already under so much stress, with the bakery and Gran moving out…and not feeling well because of the pregnancy. I didn't want to add to that emotional overload, by letting you in on plans that were only half-complete. Or put the health of you or the babies in any kind of jeopardy, with the addition of any extra stress, since my job as the baby daddy is to protect all of you."

"So you kept me in the dark…" Finally, Ellie understood why.

Joe nodded soberly. "I wanted everything worked out before I told anyone what I was doing."

Joy bloomed within her. She admired his courage so much. She grinned, a grin big as all Texas. "From what you showed me, you've done that, soldier."

They shared another conciliatory kiss, lingering and sweet.

He cupped her face in his big, gentle hands and rested his forehead on hers. He drew back, continuing gruffly, "The point is, I shouldn't have shut you out and kept my intended resignation from the military a secret from you." His eyes darkened. "We should have agreed upon it every step of the way. And we still can," he promised sincerely, "because nothing of what has been done is set in stone. Nothing will be until we are of one mind, one heart, one soul."

"Oh, Joe, we're already there." She released a shuddering breath, reveling in the closeness of their bodies. The melding of their hearts and hopes and dreams. "I know you've found the perfect career for yourself. It's going to be a welcome addition to the community. And the kids and I'll support you every step of the way from here on out," she vowed.

A wry smile started on his lips and lit his eyes. "That means the world to me, Ellie. *You* mean the world to me."

If she were honest, she had always known that. Even if she hadn't always been able to admit it. "But you're not the only one who has made mistakes here," she admitted.

He listened intently, all the love and commitment she had ever wanted to see reflected on his face.

"I owe you an apology, too. You were right. I never really believed in the Fitzgerald family curse or thought that history would repeat itself if we tied the knot while you were in the military."

He rubbed his thumb across her lower lip. "Then?"

She inhaled a shaky breath. "I was using it as an excuse to keep from putting my heart out there the way I did the night we tried to elope and were stopped."

He exhaled slowly, all the regret he felt evident. "That was a pretty tough night for all of us."

Ellie nodded, recalling her culpability for everything that had transpired since, too. "And a big part of what followed was my fault." Because he had tried to be serious. She was the one who wouldn't be.

"You see, Gran and my mom had always believed in me, believed I could do anything I set my mind to, but it was clear that they didn't believe I could be successfully married. Not at eighteen, or *ever* it seemed to me that night. And that shook me. I let the doubts creep in. But I told myself as long as I had the proverbial foot out the door that I could make an escape if I needed to. And that way we could be sure we wouldn't ever hurt each other. I know it sounds weird, but that lack of permanence made me feel safe in an odd way."

Joe nodded, accepting his own guilt. "I kind of felt the same way. It was like as long as we were together willingly and knew we could leave at any time, we were never going to be trapped or unhappy, the way some of the couples we knew eventually were." His voice dropped a notch. "Discovering we were pregnant changed all that."

She kept her gaze locked with his. "It sure did." She snuggled against his hard, strong body. "I no longer want to escape. I want it all with you."

The need she felt was reflected in his face. "I want it all with you, too," he echoed, delivering another long, soulful kiss.

Tenderness wafted through her, fueling an even deeper connection.

"So we're agreed then?" Joe rasped, cupping her jaw in his hand. "We're going to stay married from here on out?"

"And live happily ever after," Ellie concluded. Finally... finally...all their dreams were coming true. "And we'll have our very first Christmas together with our son and daughter, too!"

Epilogue

Four and a half months later

"Let me help you with that, sweetheart." Joe reached over Ellie's head and settled the glittery silver star ornament on the branch she was aiming for.

Ellie sighed and picked up another handmade ornament. She loved Joe's protectiveness. But these days it seemed like he wanted to help her do everything, practically even breathe, to prevent her from overextending herself.

She turned to him, admiring how masculine he looked in his dark green sweater and jeans. "I think I can add a few more decorations to our Christmas tree, handsome," she teased, brushing a light kiss across his jaw. "Even if I am nine months pregnant. Besides—" she turned back to select another glitter-encrusted globe "—it was so nice of Gran to make all these for us in her craft class. I want to get them up on our tree."

The only problem was they had decorated their Christmas tree a few weeks ago, right after Thanksgiving. And there wasn't a lot of room for more, although Ellie was determined to get them all up without taking anything else down.

"They are beautiful," Joe said solemnly, helping her place the ornament up high. His body brushed hers lovingly as they moved. "And very sparkly, too."

Tingling everywhere they touched and especially in all the places they hadn't, Ellie mugged at him comically. "That's because everyone knows how much I used to love glitter when I was a kid."

Joe chuckled. "And still do?"

Aware he knew the answer to that, when it came to nostalgic treasures anyway, Ellie merely smiled. "You laugh now, but you haven't seen what you're wearing to the annual ugly sweater competition at Laramie Gardens yet."

Intrigued, Joe asked, "Did Gran make that, too?"

"Mmm-hmm. She and her friends went all-in. For both of us. I've heard the sweaters are matching."

Joe laughed and shook his head. Like her, he was always ready to have a little fun. "Can't wait."

"Me, either."

They put another two decorations on the tree. "Think we're going to make it to that party?" Joe asked.

Ellie hedged, knowing she would be disappointed to miss it. But they had been warned in their birthing classes of the suddenness with which labor could come on. Plus she had been feeling a little off all day, although it was nothing she could put a name to…except maybe late-pregnancy fatigue, which seemed to be ever present.

Another reason Joe was hovering over her incessantly. His spidey senses were probably going off, too.

"The party is tomorrow," she said slowly.

Joe nodded. "And your due date is the day after."

"So we should probably…be able…uh…to…" Ellie stopped as a band tightened around her middle. Then tightened some more. Perspiration broke out on her brow.

"Ellie?" Joe's low voice radiated with concern.

Their eyes met. She was relieved to see that he at least

was completely calm. It had to be the soldier in him. Her emotions were all over the place.

"Is that a contraction?" he asked.

She could barely breathe. Much less get the words out. "I think…so…soldier."

As always, Joe did not hesitate when a task needed done. "I'll grab your hospital bag. And then we'll get you in the truck. We can call the hospital on the way there."

Abruptly, the pressure in her midriff began to ease. Ellie huffed, "You don't want to wait till this has passed and then see how long before I have another?"

"Nope." He cupped her belly fondly. "Not with two babies due at different times in there. We're going to the hospital now."

"You sure you're not being overly dramatic?" Ellie challenged as he gallantly helped her across the porch, down the steps, and onto the sidewalk.

He tightened his arm around her waist. "You sure you're not being overly casual?" he retorted.

Ellie was about to quip something back when she got hit by another contraction. This one was worse than the first. Enough to scare her with its ferocity, it happened only thirty seconds or so since her first had eased.

Luckily, she had her strong, commanding husband with her, and they were in the driveway by then. All Joe had to do was lift her up and put her in the truck while she started her first-stage breathing exercises.

He had the hospital on speed dial and called them to let them know they were on the way, right before they left. The medical staff was there to greet them at the ER entrance and whisked Ellie off to the obstetrics floor where delivery teams for each baby were already gathering.

Joe was with her every step of the way, guiding her through

every breath, every contraction, every moment of comingled pain and joy.

As expected, their son was born first.

Their daughter, second.

Both were incredibly healthy. With fine sets of lungs.

"Music to my ears," Joe said, laughing as their two children did their best to out-wail each other.

Ellie didn't blame either of them for being furious. To go from the snug comfort of her tummy to the outside world... Well, it was a change. And she understood better than most how one could be fearful of change. But as soon as the babies were cleaned up and wrapped in soft cotton blankets and caps and returned to their parents' loving arms, both of their babies settled down.

Joe sat beside her on the hospital bed, their son, Jaime, in his arms. Ellie held Jenni in hers.

"They are so gorgeous," she said, admiring their blue eyes and dark hair.

Joe snuggled close to her, looking just as thoroughly smitten as she was by their two newborns. He pressed a kiss to the top of her head. "Just as beautiful and feisty as their mom."

"And courageous as their dad," Ellie observed tenderly. Because now that they were being held and awake enough to take it all in, Jaime and Jenni didn't seem scared of the world after all.

"Just think, in another twelve days they'll celebrate their very first Christmas," Ellie whispered to Joe.

"Actually, I think it's already Christmas," Joe teased her lovingly. "And has been. And always will be. As long as we're together."

Ellie leaned closer to kiss his jaw. All the love she had ever longed for filled her heart. She was so glad they had